US 98: Destination Dade City

WORKBOOK PRESS LLC
187 E Warm Springs Rd,
Suite B285, Las Vegas, NV 89119, USA

Website: https://workbookpress.com/
Hotline: 1-888-818-4856
Email: admin@workbookpress.com

Ordering Information:
Quantity sales. Special discounts are available on quantity purchases by corporations, associations, and others. For details, contact the publisher at the address above.

ISBN-13:   978-1-961845-07-7 Paperback Version
                978-1-961845-08-4 Digital Version

PUB.DATE: 11/28/2023

"Since 1970, the Federal Witness Protection Program has relocated thousands of witnesses, some criminal, some not, to neighborhoods all across the country. Every one of those individuals shares a unique attribute, distinguishing them from the rest of the general population. And that is, somebody wants them dead."

U. S. Marshall Mary Shannon as portrayed by Mary McCormick in "In Plain Site" during season 5, episode 7, titled "Sacrificial Lam."

US 98: Destination Dade City

Prologue

What can be more wholesome, more captivating than a teenaged boy and his faithful dog living in a small town in Central Florida? A place of relative peace and safety, where neighbors watch out for each other; where the pace of life is a half-step slower. An hour from the theme parks and their hordes of visitors, each looking for an escape from reality. A town where pride and hard work are valued; modest homes are well kept with plenty of green grass to sooth the eye.

The boy is a high school student who likes school and understands it is a first step on the road to the rest of life. He is respectful of his single mom, authority figures, teachers, and fellow students. Life is never perfect but he will find his place.

And the dog, not a tiny canine with more hair than bite, but a working dog by classification. Loyal and extremely intelligent; always watching, always ready. Side by side with the human family in Dade City.

A reminder – looks can be deceiving.

Settle in: this is their story.

Chapter One

The weather was foul, and the clouds in the sky a foreboding mixture of grays and white while shifting with the west wind. Assistant Federal Prosecutor, Jack Butcher, pulled his 2008 Ford Explorer into the parking garage across State Road from the county jail in Philadelphia. How many times had he come into a dirty, smelly county jail for some vague promise of information from an inmate? Butcher did not dislike his job, but this kind of fishing expedition seemed to be more trouble than useful. This visit seemed to promise more of the same. Sit across the table from some low life, who would promise anything to get a reduced sentence or stay out of jail.

Just last month, a woman said she could tie her arrest to the Medellin drug cartel. She knew nothing worthwhile. She did not even know the last name of her supplier. *Tony, really, just Tony*! He remembered laughing as she pleaded to get a five-year sentence cut to two in a state institution. And the tears, she should have been an actress. *Waste of time, my time,* he thought. But, checking these leads out was part of his job.

As he walked in, Detective Randy Johnson was waiting. They had worked together in the past. "Johnson, good to see you." Johnson was a ten-year veteran of the Philadelphia City Police. Not a big man physically. With those clear brown eyes and mousy brown hair, he was a bulldog while investigating crime.

"We need to talk before you see this perp." Both men showed their credentials as they passed through security. Johnson had arranged for a small conference room for their short meeting.

Johnson asked, "Have you ever heard of Malik Adams before I called you?"

"I read the arrest report. But this is the first I've heard the name."

"I thought he was a nobody, too. Then a couple detectives mentioned his name to street contacts. Their reactions were, let's say, interesting. It was like his name threw the fear of God into their souls."

Butcher's eyebrows went up. "Is that all you have?"

"No, there's more. With the contacts reaction, the detectives pushed for information and got stonewalled. Then one of the guys said, '*I ain't telling you nothing about Adams. I want to be breathing tomorrow morning.*' There was pretty serious fear in that answer. So, we dug a little deeper. We talked to his landlord. He said Adams was a quiet man, didn't cause problems. Paid his rent on time, cash. Drove a used car, Acura. But the landlord said Adams first showed up about six months ago and the car he had had Jersey plates."

Johnson continued. "I had a hunch. I called a friend who's with vice in the New Jersey state police. I came right out and asked him if he ever heard of a Malik Adams? He asked for a physical description so I sent one along with the mugshot. He called me right back and said, '*he is Juan Malik Adams.*' Then he said, '*don't look him up. You won't find anything. We have been watching Adams for the past ten years. We think he is a top lieutenant with the Maguire family in New Jersey. But he has been like Teflon – smooth, and nothing sticks.*'"

Butcher said, "Holy crap, the Benjamin Maguire family?"

"Yep, that's the one. And Adams demanded I contact your office."

"Did he tell you why?"

"Said he would only talk to the feds."

"And he was arrested for DUI. This makes no sense."

Thirty minutes later, three men were seated in an interview room on the second floor of the Philadelphia County Jail with every word on tape. The room looked as inviting as a busted urinal, and smelled like one, too. Detective Johnson made the necessary introductions.

Adams wasted no time. "Butcher, would you show me your credentials? I'll only deal with someone with the power to make this deal happen. No offense."

Butcher pulled his badge and slid it across the table to the tall, muscular, very composed inmate. "Mr. Adams, have you been read your rights?"

After carefully examining the badge, he slid it back across the table. "Yea, they read me my rights and I am waiving them for this conversation. But I want to say for the record, once this meeting is finished, I will wish to speak to my attorney. Understood?" The prosecutor nodded his head.

"Mr. Adams, with your lack of previous legal problems, you could be released on bond at any time. A driving under the influence charge, is not something keeping a person in custody for a long time. And it's not a federal crime."

"I get it. I'm planning to stay right here for now."

Detective Johnson said, "I told you I'd get a fed here for you. Now it's all up to you, Adams."

Malik Adams sat and rubbed his hands together on top of the table while thoughts raced through his mind. How had he gotten to this point in life? Growing up in a housing project in Cleveland, he was blessed with a quick mind and quicker feet. He started out running track for at the Boys and Girls Club. By the time he was a student at Miles Garrett High School he had become a true track and field competitor until his body played a cruel trick on the freshman and he grew six inches and gained fifty pounds of muscle. He was no longer just fast, now he was quick and huge. Six-foot five weighing two hundred forty-five pounds at age sixteen. As he passed between classes, students cleared out of his way in the halls, teachers too. That was when Coach Long noticed the big, dark-skinned youth, and convinced him to try out for the football team in the fall of 1992. Adams spent exactly two practice sessions on the reserves squad as a sophomore when he hit a reserve running back and sent the poor kid to the hospital with broken ribs and an injured spleen from a massive defensive hit. Two years later, Ohio State University came calling for the top high school linebacker prospect in the state of Ohio.

By the first Saturday of October 1995, Malik Adams was the starting strong side linebacker for the Buckeyes. Everything looked so golden in those days. His coaches and trainers worked with him to create a tremendous force for the defense. And Adams did his part too. He went to class, stayed out of trouble, avoided alcohol, and studied Business Management. He became a regular visitor of the weight room as he traded his baby fat for football muscle without sacrificing speed. For four years, the Buckeye's locker room buzzed with talk of Malik Adams being the next big thing going to the National Football League from OSU. The problem was Adams believed he was invincible until game eight of the 1998 season against Northwestern in Evanston.

He could still see the play unfold in his mind. Northwestern was driving at the forty-five-yard line of OSU. The offensive formation shouted *pass.* Winslow, the middle linebacker called a defensive audible *"Buckeye six."* It meant Adams would blitz between the defensive end and tackle as they pushed in opposite directions on the strong side of the formation. The OSU defense had worked on this play for two weeks to hurry the offense and hopefully stop the opponent's passing game using Adams presence up the middle. With the snap of the ball, Adams flew through the opening in the offensive line and saw the quarterback for Northwestern just three steps away still holding the ball. What he did not see was the weak side guard who pulled and hit Adams in the left knee.

When he was carted into the locker room, the orthopedic specialist knew the dream had just died for this young man with so much promise. Surgery could reattach the ligaments and tendons, but no amount of rehab would make the knee right again.

As Adams lay in the hospital bed, the reality hit him. No payday. Everything he planned was over. To his credit, he returned to campus and completed his business degree. He began to search for a career but African Americans still had limited opportunities in the business world. Eventually, he was contacted by a headhunter for a financial group in Atlantic City, New Jersey. He was offered a decent position as a junior executive with New Imports Group, Inc. When he interviewed, the company was vague with answers about its business goals, but having no other real offers, Adams took the position.

It took Adams four years to finally put all the pieces together and understand his real employer was the Maguire Family - mafia. They were not the organized crime of the *Godfather* trilogy; they were much more sophisticated. But they still had their fingers in illegal activities and even more legal businesses including real estate, hotel ownership, and casinos in both Atlantic City and Las Vegas. In fact, three-quarters of the business revenue came from legal operations. New Imports Group was one of those legal operations. If your name wasn't Maguire, you knew only a piece of the story. But Adams worked hard and became trusted. His loyalty was above question until the day six months ago when he overheard a conversation causing Malik Adams to react.

No one could say Malik Adams was impetuous or rash. He spent months planning his actions, down to the smallest detail. He would take down Montgomery Maguire, only son of Benjamin. Montgomery was the threat and would pay a steep price. Today, the plan started, right here, right now.

"I have valuable information about the Maguire family. In particular Montgomery Maguire. Are you interested in what I know?" asked Adams.

"Tell me what you know and I'll tell you if its valuable or not," answered Butcher.

"It's not going to work that way. Get out your legal pad and take notes. I'll tell you my conditions. If you agree to keep them, not some of them, but every one, then I will give you enough information to bring down Montgomery Maguire. And one other thing, the video recording has to stop before I begin. Just the two of you and me. No one else. This information will be toxic to Maguire. And I know he has a long reach, a very long reach."

Butcher looked at Johnson who rose and went out to speak briefly to the shift commander about stopping the video. When he returned, he brought three bottles of water and news the recorder was off. The attorney had his pad on the table ready to take notes. This would prove to be an important day for the United States Department of Justice.

The demands of Malik Adams were centered on only two things. Where he would serve his future sentence for racketeering, and witness protection for Adam's fifteen-year-old son and the boy's mother. It took only five minutes and two phone calls to have the necessary assurances demanded by Adams. The pair would be relocated within seventy-two hours.

For most of the following two days, Adams gave information to Assistant Federal Prosecutor Jack Butcher. The accusations were so toxic a federal grand jury would be convened within a week leading to the indictment, arrest and incarceration of Montgomery Maguire along with several lower caste gangsters. It also meant an assassination contract would be placed on the head of Adams and any one he cared about.

Butcher asked Adams, "What was your role with the Maguire family business?"

Adams looked Butcher in the eye, "I over saw all the import and export business for the family. Only the legitimate stuff. I did not deal with negotiations nor with the union. Just a glorified clerk. I did my job and kept the merchandise moving."

***

The gloom of yesterday was blown east by a high-pressure system moving up the Ohio River valley. For April, the sun was bright as spring took hold of the land. Janet LeMay was getting ready for her day in the small bungalow she had owned for the past eight years in the city of Dublin, Ohio. Since her days as a student at Ohio State, she stayed in the area working hard to create a solid life for herself and her son, Cooper LeMay. Since her college graduation, Janet worked as business manager for Bright Smile Dental Clinic in northwest Columbus. By any standard, Janet LeMay was a modern, successful woman with an important career. She was pleased with how things had turned out following the deaths of her parents while she was in college. Her only sister had taken her inheritance and moved to Denver many years ago. Janet no longer missed her sister; she was simply someone from the past.

Cooper was eating his bowl of cereal before heading off to ninth grade at the middle school when he noticed two black SUV's pull to a stop in front of the house. "Hey, mom, two big vehicles just stopped in front of the house."

Janet came out of the bathroom adjusting her ear rings to see two people dressed in blue windbreakers walking toward her front door. She opened the inner door just as they were going to ring the bell. "Can I help you?"

The female agent presented her badge as she asked, "Janet LeMay? I'm US Marshall Anna Wiest and this is Marshall Paul Duncan. May we come in?"

"I'm Janet LeMay. What is this about?"

"We need to come inside and speak with you," answered Wiest.

"Let me see those badges again, please?" After carefully examining the badges and taking mental note of the numbers and checking the photos against the two agents standing in front of her, she backed up and the agents followed her inside.

"Why are you here? Has something happened? Is this about the billings from the clinic to Medicare? I can assure you everything is in order."

Marshall Duncan said, "I think we should sit down. This is going to take some time to explain. You are in no trouble from the government, let me assure you."

For the first time in the past two minutes, Janet felt herself breath a bit easier.

Nodding toward the kitchen, Duncan asked, "Is this your son, Cooper? And by chance is there anyone else in the house at this moment?"

"Yes, this is Cooper and no one else is in the house. You seem to know a lot about us."

"Ma'am, that's our job. You will want to have your son come into the room for this discussion because it will affect both of you."

Cooper, who had listened intently to every word, came bounding into the living room taking very long strides and plopped next to his mother on the couch.

"Ms. LeMay, are you familiar with the name Juan Malik Adams?"

There was an uncomfortable pause before she answered, "Yes."

Marshall Wiest asked, "Is your son aware of your relationship with Mr. Adams?"

"Well, yes. Cooper knows the man is his biological father. We have not seen him in . . . let's see, ten years. He doesn't stay in touch." Then Janet took some license with the truth. "I'm not sure where he is these days. Out east somewhere, maybe?"

"Right now, Mr. Adams is sitting in a jail in Philadelphia providing state's evidence against the Maguire crime family of New Jersey. The Maguires are one of the most dangerous and powerful syndicates in the eastern United States. As part of Mr. Adams agreement to testify against the Maguire's, Mr. Adams requested the United States Department of Justice place the two of you in federal protective custody to protect your lives."

Nothing was said for the next fifteen seconds as the weight of the Marshall's words had a chance to sink in. The agents noticed Cooper's eyes had grown larger with each moment and Janet was clearly becoming upset.

Janet LeMay asked, "Protective custody? You mean like place a guard outside our house?"

"No ma'am," said Duncan. "We mean like moving you immediately to a safe house with armed guards."

"What if I refuse? This is crazy!"

Wiest pulled out her communicator. "Arnie, bring in the photos." Ms. LeMay, I would strongly advise you to not go down that road." Just then the front door opened and a third agent entered carrying a folder of photographs which was handed to Marshall Wiest. "The people we are talking about are not nice people. I need to show you these photos. I believe you will understand once you see the brutality of these criminals."

With that pronouncement, Wiest opened the folder and handed Janet three crime scene photos. The scenes were gruesome! Wiest continued, "Eighteen months ago, a drug dealer in Newark decided to give testimony against this syndicate. These photos were taken after the sealed testimony to a grand jury. The grand jury brought an indictment against the Maguire syndicate. The very next day, the Maguire family knew all the details of the grand jury and this was the result. This is what you and your son are potentially facing. With what Mr. Adams is sharing, they will be coming after him and everyone he cares about. Remember, he is the one who requested you be protected."

Both mother and son looked slowly at the photos before handing them back. Janet felt her mouth become very dry as her stomach felt sick. "Ok, you have my full attention, now what?"

"We need each of you to pack an overnight bag. Bring two changes of clothing and any medicine you are currently taking. If you have any cash or valuables in the house, bring them with you. Leave everything else. If you have cell phones, turn them off and place them on the kitchen table."

"I need to call the office and tell them I'm not coming in today."

"We will contact the Dental Clinic."

Cooper asked, "What about school. I need to clean out my locker and return my books. I need to let Collette know where I'm going."

"Son, I hate to tell you this, but you will never be able to communicate with any of your friends, ever again. These people will move heaven and earth to find you. The people you saw murdered were in a state-run safe house. They were located in less than six hours. This is serious stuff."

"But why me, why us. We don't know anything."

Marshall Arnie said, "If these people find you, they will kill you as a sign to every other person not to mess with them. Period."

Janet asked, "What about the house? My car. The rest of our stuff?"

"Your things will be packed up and eventually it will come to you when we are sure you are settled and safe. Your house will be sold as will your car with the proceeds forwarded to you. And by the way, you need to start thinking about what your new names will be. Your current identities will be dead."

Thirty minutes later, Janet and Cooper walked out the front door of their precious home, never to return. The Marshalls placed the bags in the back of the second vehicle as they got in the lead vehicle. Every item would be checked by the Marshalls later to make sure no trail was left inadvertently. As they drove away, Marshall Wiest said, "In thirty minutes, our people will be in your house taking care of everything."

Chapter Two

Unfortunately, fifteen minutes after the government vehicles pulled away from the curb, two armed men quietly entered the back door of the house in Dublin. After checking each room, they saw no one was present. When they noticed the cell phones on the kitchen table, the shorter man made a call on his burner phone to a number in New Jersey.

"Gone."

"How long?"

"This morning."

"You know what to do."

When the federal movers showed up moments later, the fire had spread from the kitchen into the bedrooms. They could only call the local fire department and watch.

While seated in the rear seat of the black government SUV, Janet reached to hold the hand of Cooper. She whispered, "Are you OK?" He nodded. "Scared?"

"Yes."

"Me too."

***

Benjamin Maguire hung up his office phone. He could feel his blood pressure rising as the noise in his ears became magnified. "Montie, in here, now!" Benjamin Maguire was now an old man but still formidable, physically. But his only son, Montgomery, was a physical freak. At six foot, nine inches, he towered over even the largest human in any room. His wide jaw and thick black hair with dark, deep-set eyes made him look like a character from a Russian horror flick. But it was the temper of the younger mobster that made smart people get out of his way.

"Shut the door. Sit. I just got off the phone with our informant at the federal prosecutor's office. One of the prosecutors has been with Malik Adams at a lock up in Philadelphia. Adams has provided testimony to a grand jury. The government is coming after you. Do you hear me? What did you do?"

Montie hung his head at the name of the former employee. "Damn it. I was positive he would be no problem when he left here. What was it, six months ago? I had a good feeling about him."

"You and your feelings. How many times have I told you, *tie up ends when someone goes?*"

"I made a lot of money off that kid when he was a player at Ohio State. He was a defensive machine! When he got hurt, I figured he could have a future with us. I checked him out. He was a smart guy with skills we could use. Come on pop, don't blame this all on me. You liked the guy, too."

"I want you to think back to just before Adams left here. Did anything happen that might have caused him to come after you?"

Montie sat rubbing his broad chin, thinking as his eyes peered toward the ceiling. "I know I was having some doubts about the guy. I had him under surveillance but there was nothing."

"Did you talk to anyone about your suspicions?"

"Yea, I spoke to Tiny, one time in my office."

"What did you say to Tiny?"

"Something about *Adams might need to go*. Something like that."

The old man picked up his phone. Tiny answered on the second ring. "Yes sir?"

"In my office."

Tiny barely had time to sit before Maguire asked, "Do you remember a conversation with Montie about Malik Adams before Adams left?"

"Well, yes sir. Montie said, 'If Adams tries to mess with me, I'll have his throat cut and I will spit on the graves of every one of the people he cares about.'"

"Jesus Christ, Montie, could he have heard you? It's one thing to threaten someone, but their family?"

"I don't know how he could have heard me; he was down at the dock that day checking on a shipment from Central America."

"Excuse me, sir. Adams was in his office. I saw him when I left Montie's office that day. I walked right past him in the hallway."

When Maguire nodded his head, Tiny knew his testimony was complete and damning.

"This guy is coming after you, not me, according to the informant. You clean this up – whatever it takes. But don't go nuclear on me. Leave the prosecutor alone. Do you hear me? We will not go down that road."

Upon returning to his own office, Montie Maguire pulled out a folder from his desk marked, *Adams, Juan Malik.* It took less than a minute to locate the information. *Janet LeMay – Ohio.* His only call was to Mr. Johnson in Columbus, who in turn called the Marcus brothers who were on their way to Dublin in fifteen minutes. "That should take care of it."

***

US Marshall Wiest answered her cell phone on the second ring. "Wiest." For the next two minutes listened intently. "I understand." The call ended.

"Change of plans," Wiest announced to Duncan. "We need to get to Wright Patterson Airbase." US 35 exits were in two miles. As the interchange was taken, Janet noticed the other SUV stayed on the road toward Cincinnati.

"What's happening?" asked Janet.

"When our team got to your house, it was on fire."

"My God, we left less than an hour ago!"

"The team clocked in at 9:01 am, thirty-one minutes after we left. That means Maguire's people are very close behind us. Could be following us. They have no way to know which SUV you are in. So we split up. Ohio State Police will be picking us up in a few minutes and escort us to the air base."

"What will happen there?"

"Change of vehicles in a secure location."

Janet was quiet for a moment before Cooper asked, "Are we really that important?"

Duncan answered, "Our people in Washington DC are willing to do whatever it takes to keep you safe. That's how important you are to them and this case."

Two State Police cruisers pulled up next to the SUV, one going in front, the other following. They increased their speeds to ninety miles per hour and the caravan arrived in Dayton in forty- five minutes. Janet and Cooper were unaware two other State Police cars were accompanying their bags at the same time and a private single engine Piper Cub was tailing them at five thousand feet. The FAA was monitoring all civilian air craft in the area. Twelve miles to their rear, a Sheriff had just pulled over two men in a speeding white work van. They had an empty can of lighter fluid, two Glock hand guns, and two sniper rifles. The FBI, now involved, was confident these were the fire starters. They would learn nothing from the Marcus brothers. But the attempt was enough to get a federal warrant for a wiretap on the headquarters, homes and cell phones of Montgomery Maguire.

Air base security waved the government SUV through the gates. They headed to a remote airplane hangar on the edge of the air base. The SUV entered the hanger and the doors closed behind them. Duncan said, "This is where we get out. Restrooms are to the left. Probably be a good time to use them. And when you come back, we'll talk about what's coming."

A wood picnic table was near the service door of the hanger. The US Marshalls were waiting for their charges. Wiest said, "Come on and sit down. I got you some water. It has been quite the morning. Let me bring you up to speed on what we know. There is nothing salvageable from your house. The fire took everything by the time the Dublin Fire Department could get it under control, but the garage was untouched."

"Is there anything I should do? I mean, we have lost everything," responded Janet with tears forming in her eyes.

"You have home owner's insurance?" She nodded. "The government will place a claim for you so you will be reimbursed for your furnishings, and the dwelling. You can pay off your house. We handle all of that. And we will sell your vehicle and anything else of value in the garage, too. Is there anything in the garage you need us to collect for you?"

Janet LeMay felt as if the world around her was spinning out of control. She shook her head to answer the question. Then as her heart was sinking, she heard herself say, "That makes me feel a little better the way my business is being handled by you. I just can't believe this is real."

Wiest went on, "the thugs who torched your house were apprehended."

"Here is what will happen next." The motorhome by the airplane over there will be your next ride. The LeMay's looked up to see a Winnebago Recreational Vehicle. "Two agents will be taking a plane out towards New York as a decoy in about ten minutes. We can't be too careful. Then the black SUV you were riding in will head toward Indianapolis at the same time driven by agent Duncan. Standing over by the motorhome is US Marshall Mavis Brown. She will be with us. Marshall Brown will be staying with you now for at least the next forty-eight hours. We will wait ninety minutes before we leave heading in the direction of Lexington, Kentucky. We should arrive by mid-afternoon. It will be pretty hard to track all of the different vehicles even for the Maguire family with their resources."

"Once you arrive at the safe house, we will have two teams in place for you. One team will be strictly for your security. The other team will be working with you to de-program you, or at least study your past so you can be erased from your past lives. And then, that team will help you take on the new identities we will create for your future."

"I don't understand," said Cooper. "What do you mean by 'erase our past?'"

"That's a great question. Cooper, where were you born?"

"Columbus."

"When the federal government finishes erasing you, there will be no record of Cooper LeMay ever being born in Columbus, Ohio or anywhere else, either. There will be no Cooper LeMay ever being a student in the Dublin School system. Your physician will have no record of you, neither will your church, your bank, dentist or the public library. Cooper LeMay will disappear, every trace will be gone. That way, you can't be followed or found by anyone. Does that make sense?"

"I have a Social Security number. And, I have friends, they won't forget me."

"That number will disappear from the Social Security database. We will monitor your friends to make sure they can't tell anything that would lead to you. Cooper, you need to understand the government has been making people disappear since 1970. We have learned to do it very efficiently. Do you watch news on the television?"

"I do. Well not every day."

"Have you ever heard of a lost person being found after ten years on the news?"

"There was the Nazi guy they found in Cleveland."

"He wasn't in our program. When people understand how dangerous this business can be, they appreciate the federal relocation and protection program. We save lives. Protect people."

"Where is the safe house?" wondered Janet.

"For your safety, all I will tell you is you will be in Kentucky. The less you know, the better. We need to get into the camper before the doors to the hanger are opened. It's time for the plane and Marshall Duncan to be on their way. We have done this 'hand off' behind closed doors so no one can see you. Notice no one else is here in the hanger with us?"

Before the motorhome left the hanger, lunch had been brought in by another Marshall. Cooper and Janet were surprised to find two computer tablets waiting for them in the RV. Brown told them, "The tablets will let you watch videos and surf the internet, but you will not be able to use them to communicate. Don't even try to retrieve your email. Way too easy to be tracked that way."

"Sweet!" was all Cooper could think to say. "Video games, here I come."

***

Janet LeMay's mind was running at top speed as the RV rolled down Interstate 75. *A new start? What does that mean?* She wondered as she looked over at her boy who was quickly becoming a man. She never planned to be a single mother but the events of fifteen years earlier had taken unexpected twists. The days of romance between the football player and the attractive, tall brunette were magical. Janet never saw Malik as a "black" man. She saw him as a handsome, intelligent, sexy man who swept her off her feet with his dark eyes and bright smile. When she stood next to him, she had felt protected, desired and loved. His strength was more than physical. When she sat next to him, she relished every word that came from his pure heart. And when she lay with him, she discovered physical desire shaking her understanding of human sexuality. *Those were exciting times,* she remembered.

Malik's injury changed their relationship in a single day. He withdrew into himself as depression settled in upon his life. He no longer was able to express love or any emotion except anger. Janet could not live in such a toxic environment. They tried to keep the relationship going but by New Years, it was over: they both knew it was true. They went separate directions.

By mid-February, Janet suspected she carried a child near her heart. Graduation came in May even though neither she nor Malik attended. She took time to give birth to her son, Cooper Jordan LeMay in Columbus before beginning her position with a local bank. She was apprehensive of raising a child without spousal help or family support, but she was confident. She was strong, she was hard working and she believed in her ability to create a loving home for her baby boy.

Malik had known of her pregnancy but with his football dream smashed, he saw no value in his involvement with Janet or son. When the boy was born, Malik had left the area trying to find something, anything to make sense of his injury. He carried no bitterness towards Janet or the little one. Adams never knew his father, and there was no reason in his mind to even attempt to be part of his son's existence. He laid awake nights thinking of what might have been which transformed into *someday, I will help them.* But they would never know his efforts to secretly keep tabs on them. He had photos taken secretly by acquaintances and friends and the new thing called social media.

Janet looked over at Cooper. The man/child was growing. His mind was sharp. His bronze skin covered a substantial frame with good muscle tone for a mid-teen. He laid the tablet on the floor of the RV as he dozed. And then, Janet started to really worry about her son. Could she protect him, guide him, love him the way he needed? She wasn't so confident at that moment as the motorhome exited the interstate heading towards an area known as Bighill, Kentucky.

"Are we getting close?" Janet questioned the Marshalls.

"Won't be long, now." She reached over and tapped Cooper on the arm. He sat up looking out the window at a rural setting in Madison County, Kentucky. Rubbing his eyes, he noticed the three board, white fences, enclosing pastures for horses raised on the famous Kentucky blue grass. Within two miles, they turned off the county road stopping at a closed metal gate.

Chapter Three

Marshall Mavis Brown lowered the driver side window and pushed the buzzer. She said, "Delivery from Sagamore." The black metal gates opened and closed again when they had passed through. Cooper noticed a roof in the distance but could not see the buildings until they crested the small hill and started down toward a sight that impressed both members of the LeMay family. Two barns bracketed the residence, a tool shed and two grain silos. But the residence, more than a house, sat in the center of the compound. It appeared to be both old and remarkably new in the same glance. Twelve windows, six on the first level and six above the porch roof peered out over the property. The porch wrapped around the first floor and down both sides of the structure. Behind the motorhome, across the road, Big Hill rose up over seven hundred feet covered in trees and forest.

As the RV inhabitants stepped out, a middle-aged couple wandered onto the porch, smiles on their faces to welcome their visitors. Janet asked, "Is this the safe house?"

Marshall Brown responded, "This is one of many safe houses. Welcome to your temporary home. It's called *Vincennes.*" As the four stepped onto the porch, "and these will be your hosts, Jim and Lisa Allen. Jim and Lisa, this is Janet and Cooper LeMay." Pleasantries were exchanged before entering the house.

Lisa Allen was small with dainty features and a few streaks of gray in her brown hair pulled back in a ponytail. "Jim and I are here for the two of you. We have three purposes. First, we want to answer your questions. Second, we want to keep you safe and secure. And finally, we will help you prepare for your new life in witness protection. So, let's start with questions after I pour us some lemonade."

The group took seats in the living area. Cooper found the room warm and inviting with pictures of landscapes and horses. The furniture was comfortable showing polished wood feet and resting arms. Somehow, the residence seemed to fit in rural Kentucky.

"I have to confess, my head is spinning from what's happened today," said Janet. "I just can't fathom our lives are gone. I mean, we are here with you but someone we do not even know wants to kill us. They destroyed our home, according to the Marshalls." Jim slid a packet of photos across the table for the LeMay's to view. Twenty-four shots of the burned house in Dublin from every conceivable angle. There was no doubt their past had gone up in flames.

"Do you and Jim own this place?"

Jim answered, "No, we are the caretakers for the safe house. Been here for two years. Before that, Lisa and I were career military security for twenty-five years. We are married and have two grown daughters living in Virginia. We were recruited for this position by the Department of Justice because of our security backgrounds and clearance. In fact, we have the same training and clearance as every member of the Secret Service." At that statement, Cooper's brows rose, clearly impressed.

"How much does this cost?" asked the teenager.

Lisa laughed out loud. "This cost you nothing. Your friends in DC will be picking up the tab for everything while you are with us." There is one thing we need to show you before we send you off to explore your space on the second floor. Come this way." Lisa led the troop through the kitchen to a small hallway on the rear of the house. A plain wood door was opened to reveal a second open door looking like a vault door to a bank standing open. Stepping in, Lisa said, "This is the safe room. In case of an emergency, you come here, close the door, throw this handle, push this red button, then sit down and wait for the calvary to let you out. This room is totally secure with twelve-inch steel and concrete reinforced walls, floor and ceiling. It has its own air system separate from the rest of the house and an auto generator to provide power. If you have to use this room and you are together in the house, you go in and shut the door. Do not wait for one of us. We will be battling the bad guys for you. If one of you is in the house and the other is out on the grounds, come in and shut the door. There are safe rooms in each barn. We'll show you when we're out there."

"On the wall you see multiple monitors. When the red button is pushed, those screens will go live and be available for you to monitor the camera system on the grounds. There are thirty-six high resolution cameras on the property. Using the joy stick under the monitors, you can see through the eyes of the cameras and move between scenes. Also, when the red button is pushed, it will send a remote signal to our partners in the area. They will come fast and ready for war. Behind the door at the back, is a half bath with a sink and toilet for your use. Also, there are emergency provisions for up to three days in the trunks. Questions?"

"What if they manage to set the house on fire?" Cooper wondered.

"That scenario happened at a safe house in Idaho. The temperature inside the safe room went up eight degrees as the building burned to the ground. The bad guys got more than they bargained for that night. They made the mistake of thinking a force of fifteen was big enough to take out our witness. They were all terminated within ten minutes. It never made the news because that's our mission. We have never failed. We won't start with you!"

"How do we let ourselves out of the room in case of an emergency?" Janet wanted to know.

"You don't. In fact, there is no way for you to let yourself out once the handle is closed. Okay, enough of that. Lisa will take you upstairs so you can see your rooms. Supper will be served at six-thirty."

They did not have two rooms on the second floor, they had the entire floor with four bedrooms, bathrooms, living area with desks and computers and television. Even though their packed items had yet to arrive, they checked the various drawers, closets and medicine cabinets and found everything they might need for the next couple days including clothes. Janet thought, *this is like a five-star hotel on steroids*. And, out the window, there was nothing because there were no windows. Just window sized monitors giving a live picture of what scene was outside the building. Janet realized the outside windows were fake, all for show.

Janet sat in the living space looking around. "Coop, what are you thinking?"

"I'm confused. What happened to us? Is this real or am I dreaming?"

The LeMay's were surprised to see the Marshalls still in the house when they came down the steps. Supper smelled fantastic. Brown said, "We will stay the night in the control room monitoring your security. In the morning, another team will be here to replace us."

Cooper slept well but not Janet. Too much anxiety. She felt like the floor had disappeared beneath her feet. It wasn't the accommodations; those were wonderful. And, it wasn't sleeping on a strange mattress. She never had a problem going to business conferences at various hotels. It was the uncertainty of her future. Her time with Malik seemed so far in the past. And suddenly it came back to change her entire life and future. She noticed from the window monitor the day was dawning as a beautiful one. At seven o'clock, she knocked on Cooper's door to make sure he was ready for breakfast.

"Come in."

"Hey Coop, ready for today? Got to be better than yesterday, right?"

"Give me ten minutes, okay?"

She closed his door and decided to check out the news in Columbus on the computer in the living space. The article was on page two of the Columbus Dispatch headlined, "Residential fire destroys home in Dublin." The article had no picture but the description matched with every detail from the US Marshalls. Appeared to be an arson fire. House totally destroyed with possessions. No one was in the house. Attempts to locate the owner, Janet LeMay were unsuccessful as of publishing deadline. Neighbors were not interviewed. She thought, *maybe I should call the Francis family just to let them know we are safe.* She dismissed the thought as Cooper walked in.

"Time to eat. I'm hungry."

"You're in a perpetual state of hunger," replied Janet as they headed for the stairway.

***

While the LeMay's ate breakfast in the safe house, Montie was again in his father's office. "They are gone. The kid never went to school and the mother did not show up for work. I had surveillance in both places."

"Witness protection would be my guess, Einstein," said the older man. "Can you get to Adams?"

"The feds have him now in a facility in Philly. He's out of county lock up. No access for us at this point. I'll know which place by noon. Might have to wait until he is transported to court for an opportunity to get to him. Johnson, my contact in Columbus says his guys were on their tails when the sheriff pulled them over. Weapons, vehicle were both legal and permitted. They'll be out in twenty-four hours. They won't say anything. They're pros."

"Are you sure," asked the older Maguire. "Remember you had a good feeling about Adams, too."

"All right, I'll call Johnson and have him take them out."

"I'm going to make a call to get the locations of the safe houses within a five hundred radius of Columbus. Maybe we'll get lucky. But the information is going to cost us and I'm taking it out of your account."

"I'm going to find 'em. Adams will suffer for messing with me."

"Just remember, you started this mess."

Meanwhile, two county prisoners were on the move. The two had awakened in London, Ohio county jail. Now they were on the road towards Columbus where they had a date. The van driver and the other deputy were not in a talkative mood. As they entered the city limits the van headed toward the downtown. These two had long histories of criminal activities and for the most part, they stayed away from law enforcement. But this time, a sheriff deputy had pulled them over for a tail light violation and speeding on the interstate only to discover the van had weapons and an empty gas can. When they could not talk their way out of the ticket, the deputy discovered the vehicle matched the description of one seen leaving an arson fire in Dublin just ninety minutes earlier. Willis and Pauly were confident they would be free, soon. When they arrived at the Federal Courthouse in Columbus they were confused.

Entering through the basement parking garage they were met by two security personnel without normal identification badges. They were taken to separate cells where they waited, and waited. There had been no charges, no rights administered, no arraignment. It was supper time before they were taken to interrogation rooms. Willis would meet two interrogators as would Pauly. The conversations were so similar, they must have been coordinated.

Willis: "I want an attorney."

Interrogator: "Mr. Willis, you're not under arrest, yet. We would just like to speak with you. Do you understand?"

Willis: "Go on."

Interrogator: "We know you and Mr. Pauly were involved in an arson fire in a residential property in Dublin this morning.

The first one of you who cooperates with us will get a sweet heart deal. Second place will be charged with the Federal Crime of Witness Tampering and attempted murder."

Willis: "Did you say Federal?"

Interrogator: "That's correct."

Willis: "What will the charge be for the first to cooperate?"

Interrogator: "Criminal Trespass."

Willis: "Oh, shit! Who are you?"

Interrogator: "I'm US Marshall Duncan and this is FBI Special Agent Nunez."

After only seconds of contemplation, there was a race between Willis and Pauly to give up every piece of information requested. Pauly won the race. Within an hour, a federal magistrate granted a warrant for telephone records between a burner phone purchased in Ohio and Montgomery Maguire. Telephone records and two legal depositions by Willis and Pauly were sent to the Federal Prosecutor's office in Philadelphia.

***

The two new US Marshalls arrived and were sitting at the table with Jim and Lisa. Lisa told her guests, "This is Waker and Tutor. They will be running security for you, but they have asked you to keep your distance. They want to stay focused on your safety not on making friends."

Cooper just nodded at the two men while eating a stack of pancakes with sausage. Janet was surprised at the depressing way the news was delivered and how young these two Marshalls appeared. She poured a cup of coffee before asking, "So, what's on the agenda for today? Hand to hand combat training, video surveillance introduction or target practice?"

Jim put his fork down and the biggest smile crossed his face. "Janet, every person who we have hosted has asked some form of that question. I know you weren't being serious. See, your biggest job while you are here is to become your new self and, in a few minutes, someone will walk through the front door who will be guiding you on that journey. If you will excuse me, I need to go outside to handle some chores. Cooper, if you'd like to join me, grab a hat by the back door and put it on before you come out. I'll be in the barn on the right." A signal sounded in the control room announcing a visitor at the front gate. Waker rose to answer the call and returned in less than a minute. He said to Lisa, "She's here."

A petite woman swept through the front door like a whirlwind. She was less than five feet tall in her very high heels. She wore a light green dress with no jewelry -maybe size 2. Her red hair looked like it was burned to her head by getting too close to the sun. She opened her mouth and from her red lips poured the sweetest little girl voice dripping with enthusiasm. Lisa spoke up, "Janet, Cooper, this is Dr. Wendy Florence. She is a behavioral psychologist who will help you get ready for the rest of your lives. She works for the United States Department of Justice."

"Oh, just call me Wendy. I am so pleased to meet you both and have been carefully studying your profile information. Then she gave each of the people around the table a hug.

Lisa whispered to Janet, "This is why Jim went outside. Not a hugger!"

Cooper looked at his mother and asked, "Can I go outside with Jim?"

"You go right ahead," answered Wendy. "You might enjoy what you find out there." As Coop got to his feet, Wendy commented, "He is going to be a very big man someday. And he's going to break hearts along the way."

Cooper had a decision to make at the back door: which hat, baseball or Stetson? He never wore a Stetson, so he planted it on his head and went out the door. It was a nice morning with cool temperatures and a light breeze bringing in the various smells associated with rural Kentucky. He could see dew sparkling on the pasture grass. As he entered the barn, he realized it was more a stable than barn. There were ten pens on the right and ten more on the left each with a beautiful horse, except for the last pen which also had a foal sticking close to the mare. No Jim. He walked through the far door and saw Jim up ahead with a large breed dog. It looked a little like a German Shepherd but Cooper was sure it was something else. The dog's face was mostly black with gray and brown markings.

The dog noticed Cooper first. Jim said, "Come over and meet Nikita." Cooper hesitated just slightly. "Not much experience with dogs?"

"Not really."

"Just come up to Nikita and let him smell you starting with the back of your hand. That's how he will get to know you. Just stand still until he's done sniffing."

Cooper could feel the breath of the dog on his hand and then hear it while he sniffed his pants and shoes. The dog stuck his nose right into the teenager's crotch. "Nikita, no," commanded Jim. The dog stopped and sat down looking up at Cooper's face, clearly on alert. "Put your hand out to Nikita again but this time after he smells you, turn your hand over so he can smell your palm. See how his ears went down when you turned your hand, means you can pet him. He is accepting you as a member of the pack."

Still tentative, Cooper reached over and stroked the head of Nikita who was sitting very patiently. "You said *he's accepting me as a member of the pack*?"

"All dogs are pack animals. There is always a leader and then followers. One is the alpha and all the members of the pack follow the alpha's guidance."

"Is Nikita the alpha?"

"Oh, no. I'm the alpha. All the dogs here are followers in my pack."

"Other dogs?"

"Do you want to see them? Check out the kennel building." Cooper had not noticed the smaller building behind the barn. It was half the size of a small house. As they walked toward the kennel, Nikita stayed put and only watched the humans walk away until Jim turned and made a click sound. Then the dog ran to catch up. In the kennel were twelve pens but not all had occupants. There were six dogs, all the same breed as Nikita.

"Are these all your pets?"

As Jim reached to open one of the pens, he said, "Nikita, home." The dog went into the pen and Jim locked the gate. These dogs are not my pets. I train these dogs for the United States Military. They are bred and trained to accompany troops in combat. Mostly security but some actually go to combat zones with their handlers.

Before I retired from the military, one of the things I did was train dogs and oversee their training. They come to me as puppies about ten weeks old and then I start the training process. When the dogs reach about nine months, they go on to further training or if they flunk out, they go to private homes."

"What breed are these?"

"Good question. Most people look at these dogs and think they are German Shepherds but they are actually a breed called Belgian Malinois. Some refer to these as Belgian Shepherds. They were originally bred in Europe. They are a little smaller than German Shepherds but they are great for military use. They are very hard working, loyal, intelligent and strong. Nikita is my dog as well as the one in the next pen, Sasha. Nikita and Sasha are about three years old. I bred Nikita and Sasha and these other four are McArthur, Nimitz, Grant and Lee, and they're Sasha's pups. They are about six months old. There were two other pups but they did not meet military standards at four months so I sold them to private citizens."

"When you came out, I was working on Nikita's advanced training. I need to make a decision about his future soon. He can go into service before he turns five or I can keep him for breeding. Haven't decided yet. A veterinarian from the military will be here in about six weeks to assess each of the dogs. They will make the decision about which dogs move forward."

"That is really cool," Cooper exclaimed. "What about the horses? Those are beautiful animals."

"Have you ever ridden a horse?"

"No, but I would like to," he said with as much enthusiasm as he could muster.

"I am raising them for the military, too. Those horses are a breed called Morgans."

"I didn't know the military has horses. I thought that was gone with General Custer and the cavalry."

"The military owns about five hundred horses. Most are used for ceremonial duties but a few years ago, some were sent to Afghanistan for a military operation against the Taliban. So, there needs to be horses in the queue that can be drafted for use as the current ones are retired or die. When the vet comes to check the dogs, he'll check all the horses, too. And you only saw half of the herd. The rest are in the other barn. There are forty horses."

"So, you have to train the horses, too. Do you ride them?"

"Part of my job is to break them so they can have a rider. Wouldn't do much good to have a horse that could not work."

"Do you have to, ah, like shovel all their poop out of the barn every day?"

Jim laughed. "No that will be your job." He paused waiting for the statement to register in the kid's brain. "Just kidding. We have two hands who come here to help care for the horses. But I do train them. It's just part of my job for the government."

"Cooper, this is Lisa. Come inside, please?" came across the loudspeaker in the barn.

Jim said, "We'll pick this up another time. Sounds like you are needed for learning about your new life."

***

Chapter Four

Assistant Federal Prosecutor Jack Butcher sat across the table from his prize witness, Malik Adams. "You did a great job on the witness stand. The indictment for Montgomery Maguire was a "no brainer." You really had the right evidence for this case. Have you studied law in the past?"

"No. I was a business major in college. But I kept my eyes open while working for the Maguire's and my mouth shut. You can learn a lot that way."

"Are you certain you don't want to help take down the old man, too?"

"No. Mr. Maguire never did anything to me nor to my family. He was kind to me. It will be hard enough for the old man to watch his son go away."

"Don't you think he will try to get to you once his son is behind bars?"

"I've thought about it, a lot. I can't punish the man for what he might do. And I told you if Montie had not made the threat, I would not be here talking to you. That is how I work and how I think." Adams asked, "What is the status of my request for a location to serve my sentence?"

There have been several conversations about your request in the upper levels of the DOJ. Actually, there is quite a bit of reluctance to send you away at all based on what you are giving up on Maguire. So here is the plan as it stands now."

"Once Maguire is convicted or pleads, you will be placed in witness protection and eventually be transferred to the Federal Prison at Oxford, Wisconsin. It's a one thousand bed, medium security facility in the middle of nowhere. A couple high profile prisoners have been there over the years without incident. One was a congress man. Few violent offenders are imprisoned at the facility and only a handful of assaults have ever been recorded. Also, we have checked and there is no one there now with any connection to the Maguire family."

"Your plea deal will specify five years or until the death of Benjamin Maguire. Naturally, the second part will not be in writing, but we are convinced that once the old man is dead, there is no obvious successor with Montie in prison. He won't be able to run their operations from where he will be staying."

"Do you think this case will actually go to trial?"

"Hard to say. But my gut says he would be a fool not to try to make some type of deal. No matter what, I don't see him out in less than ten years."

Adams asked, "What is the status of my family?"

"They made it to the safe house with only a small issue. Their house in Ohio was burned down just after they were taken into custody by the US Marshalls. They weren't hurt. The perps have been caught."

"I have to admit, that scares me. Obviously, someone informed Maguire about what's going on."

"That was our thought, too. We back tracked to a secretary. She's being interrogated by the FBI. She's going to give up Maguire or she will be paying a steep price. All because her daughter couldn't stay away from cocaine. Sad. Tampering with federal witnesses is a serious offence."

"Have the wiretaps turned up anything?"

"There has been a request by the family to locate all witness safe houses in the area of Ohio. We'll keep monitoring activities. Let me ask you, are you okay?"

After thinking for a moment, Adams asked, "Any chance you can get me a picture of my boy?"

"Not a good idea. It could fall into the wrong hands and all our work hiding them would be compromised."

Adams sighed and looked at the floor. "You're right. I get it."

***

Benjamin Maguire knew it was only a matter of time before police would be serving a warrant for the arrest of his son, Montgomery. His insider had let him know the grand jury had indicted the younger man. *How can the boy be so stupid? This isn't the 1960s. You have to be careful of what you say, continually.* The old man remembered how his only boy had gotten into trouble his whole life because he could not shut up. *Here we go again.*

His legal team from New York were already moving at top speed attempting to stop this storm from coming forward, but until they saw the charges, they were not sure what they might be facing. Richard Swartznicki, chief partner, had warned the old man four years earlier Montie needed to be moved out of the central business. Maguire just could not bring himself to separate his son from the family business. And it had caused no end of trouble. There was the sexual assault. Good thing she was young and didn't understand how much leverage she had at the time. A million and a half was a small price to get her to recant. Then there was the assault case when Montie went all "kung fu" on a delivery driver who put a nick in Montie's Mercedes. It cost a thousand dollars to fix the little ding. But it cost thirty-five thousand to fix the driver's nose. But, on the reverse side of the troubles, Montie never hesitated to dole out retribution when it was necessary.

The old man thought it wouldn't be bad if these were the only incidents but Montie kept doing these kinds of things and the New York lawyers got paid big bucks to fix the problems. Swartznicki had already warned the senior Maguire there might be no fixing this time. If this had been anyone else, this would be the time to cut the man loose. But Montie was a kid in a fifty-two-year-old body. The phone on the desk rang. "Yes."

"Mr. Maguire, I have that information about the tree houses you requested. I will be sending it to you by courier this afternoon. Is there any other information I can get for you?"

Maguire simply hung up.

When the courier arrived, the envelop contained the locations of seven safe houses within the area specified. Maguire looked over the list. One in northern Ohio, one in southeast Ohio, one near Indianapolis, one in Louisville, one near Lexington, one south of Lexington and one on the border with West Virginia. He sat back in his office chair and closed his eyes contemplating all the information he currently possessed.

White woman, bi-racial teenager. Where could they go and be unnoticed? Has to be somewhere skin color is mostly ignored. He picked up the phone. "Montie, here is a contact for you to make. This man specializes in finding people who don't want to be found. And this envelop has a list of places they might be hiding."

Montgomery Maguire made the phone call. "Jasper, I have a little job. Can you stop by my office, tonight?"

First thing the next morning, federal law enforcement showed up at Maguire's office to take Montgomery into custody. After that circus left the building, Benjamin Maguire hung his head. *Have I failed you, or have you failed me?*

***

An encrypted message was received in the control room of the safe house. *Beware. Intelligence says you can expect a viewer within the next three days. Put all anti surveillance measures in place.*

Janet and Cooper sat in their sitting room with Dr. Wendy Florence, their new mentor. Coop had never been in the presence of a human who he thought might explode, but this little woman had more energy than he had ever seen. He remembered when one of his friends had taken too many energy drinks and almost vibrated from the caffeine overload. Cooper was convinced he should keep his distance so the coming explosion mess missed him. "Cooper, your mother and I have had a chance to get to know each other. Now I want to get to know you. Okay?"

"Sure," was his answer without any enthusiasm. She made a note.

"Tell me what it was like to grow up with just your mother?"

"It's the only life I have ever known – just me and mom. I love mom and she loves me, too."

"How do you know she loves you?"

"She tells me every day. And I believe her. I tell her, *I love you, too.*"

"Is your mother your best friend?"

"It's either her or my friend, Curtis. We have been together in school since second grade. There are some things I tell Curtis that I can't tell my mom." Janet made a funny face at the answer.

"You will be done with high school in three years. What would you like to do when that time comes?"

"I'll probably go to college like mom and my father. I don't really know what I want to do as an adult. I like to read and play video games, but I don't want to design games for kids. I want to do something useful."

"What do you mean?"

"Something that benefits other people or maybe the whole world."

Wendy said, "That is a very selfless answer. I hope you're successful. Now, if you could be anywhere in the entire world at this moment, where would you go and why?" she asked.

With no hesitation, "Back in my room in Dublin. It was my space. I felt safe there."

"Do you feel safe here?"

"Not really."

"Are you saying you don't trust these people at this safe house?"

"I trust them, but I don't know them."

"That's a fair answer. If two school friends were here with you and then two more showed up, two girls and two are guys, what would you do?"

"Listen to music. Play games. Just hang around and talk about school."

"You like school? What is your favorite subject?"

"I like school. I like history and science. Those are both really cool subjects."

"What about school don't you like?"

"Choir. It's lame. We sing old songs. It would be okay if we sang newer stuff. Maybe some rap."

"What makes you angry?"

Here Cooper had to pause and think. "I don't like it when some big kid starts pickin' on a little kid. And, I don't like it when someone says something about me being mixed race. They don't even know me."

"Do you feel bullied at school?"

"Not really, but I see other kids getting bullied."

"Last question for now. If you could change one thing about your life before yesterday, what would you change?"

"I'd have an older brother or sister."

Dr. Wendy said, "I have given your mother a list of things to complete. I have one for you, too. I'd like you to work on it until mid-afternoon. Then we will meet again. Questions?"

"If I get done early, can I go back out with the animals?" asked Cooper.

"It's fine with me, but you'll need to check with Jim and Lisa. Permission for everything starts with Lisa and Jim."

***

Lisa went out the back door with the memo received in the control room looking for Jim who was working with the pups in the training yard. She stood and watched as he ran them through their exercises. Three were doing well but one was having trouble concentrating on the task at hand. Lisa stood and watched her handsome man remembering how he swept her off her feet so many years earlier. She never saw herself as someone's wife, but with Jim, she was a partner. It worked for both of them.

"Is that Admiral Nimitz who is not paying attention?"

"Yes. And I don't understand what his problem is. He's not stupid. He just gets distracted so easily. Maybe I need to work with him more one on one."

"Have you tried working with him and Nikita at the same time? Maybe he needs a good example to watch."

"That's a great idea. I'll start on that tomorrow." Jim made the click sound. All four pups sat and looked at him. He motioned with his hand and they began to follow him toward their kennels. He clicked again and they sat outside the cages until he opened each and said, "Home." Safely back in the cages, Jim closed the doors and walked over to his wife.

"What are your instincts telling you about our latest guests?"

"Read this. Just came in." Jim read the memo. "I'm a bit worried about these two. I know they'll be fine here but their future seems murky. I don't think they understand how vulnerable they will be once they are out on their own."

Jim said after reading the memo, "This is not real surprising. I think I will take Nikita and Sasha up on Bighill and check out the area. See if there are signs of anyone trying to spy on us."

"Will you take one of the Marshalls with you?"

"Not this time, but I will have them track me from the control room."

***

Adams was laying on the bunk in his cell reading a book from the prison library. He heard footsteps outside his cell slowing as the person stopped. Adams looked up at a prisoner who was pushing a cart of books from cell to cell.

"Interested in another book, Adams?"

Malik took a short breath before calmly answering, "No, I'm good. Thanks. Maybe tomorrow."

The inmate moved on. His message had been successfully delivered. Adams played it cool, but his heart started beating hard. No one was supposed to know who he was in this institution.

Obviously, he was outed by someone. Next time he got the opportunity, he had to let his handler know what happened. He wondered; *is there any place I'll be safe? And what about Janet and the kid?*

Twenty minutes later, a call from the prison went to a burner cell phone attached to an answering machine with the cryptic message. *This is Jones. I want to thank you for sending the Bible study materials. I was especially interested in the story of Genesis chapter two. Thanks again. Don't forget to send me the next lesson. Gives me something to do.*

Immediately the message was forwarded to Benjamin Maguire via email. When he read the correspondence, he knew the five thousand dollars he spent was a small amount to confirm Malik Adams' location. He forwarded the message to his son's voice mail. If Montie gets bail, maybe he'll want to know. Step one complete. Across town, Montgomery Maguire was standing before a judge in a courtroom with his attorneys. Judge Melissa Walker looked over the tops of her reading glasses at the accused.

The clerk read the charges. "The People of the United States versus Montgomery P. Maguire on the charges of racketeering, money laundering and falsifying import documents. The People are represented by Federal Prosecutor, Ms. Alice Williamson. The accused is represented by Mr. Richard Swartznicki."

"Your honor, the people are asking for the court to deny bail for Mr. Maguire and remand him into federal custody," asked Prosecutor Williamson.

"Mr. Swartznicki?" turning to the defense.

"Your honor, we ask that a reasonable bail be established for Mr. Maguire. He is a well-respected member of the community with many ties to the community. We would ask for bail so Mr. Maguire may help in his own defense."

"Under the current circumstances and with the charges presented, I am leaning toward establishing bail at five million dollars and the defendant must surrender his passport."

"Your honor, sidebar?" requested Williamson.

"Approach."

Williamson stated, "Your honor, the defendant has made threats against the star witness in this case. His family has the means to make good on those threats."

"Do you have evidence of this threat?" asked the judge.

"No, your honor, just the testimony of the witness and my staff. Affidavits are being gathered from two associates who tried to kill the witness's family."

"You do not have those documents at this time?"

"No, your honor."

At this time, bail stands as set. If you find evidence to substantiate the accusation of physical threats, we can revisit bail in the future. Step back."

Thirty minutes after the hearing ended, Montgomery Maguire was free after posting bail.

***

"Mom, how are you coming with your homework? I think it's funny you have to do homework. I was just thinking of all the times you sat with me while I memorized math facts. Now I get to watch you. Definitely funny," chuckled Cooper.

"They want to know everything about our past. There is a question here about where we went on vacation last year. What sized socks do you wear? When was the last time you took a bubble bath?"

"What?"

"Just kidding, they didn't ask that. I thought it was funny!"

"Hilarious, Mom."

"Did you look over the family names we get to choose from? Dr. Wendy told me the list is the top fifteen surnames in the United States."

"Let's see, Smith, Johnson, Williams, Brown, Jones, Garcia, Miller, Davis, Rodriguez, Martinez, Hernandez, Lopez, Gonzalez, Wilson, Anderson: what do you think? Anything call out to you?"

"How about I'll be Brown and you be Davis? Brown and Davis. We could be rappers."

"We have to be the same."

"Okay, I'll be Speedy Gonzalez, but I don't know about you? You could be Chica Gonzalez! Or Momacita Gonzalez."

"You're really enjoying this, aren't you?"

"Yup. I haven't had this much fun since they burned down our house."

"Come on, son. No sense dwelling on the past. We can't change it. Which name should we pick?"

"I think we can eliminate all the Mexican names." After a few seconds of thought, Cooper blurted out, "Wilson."

"Yeah, simple, easy to remember and I can spell it."

"Mom, you never had trouble spelling. What are you talking about?"

"Just pulling your leg, Master Wilson."

Cooper got to his feet and walked over to Janet. He threw his long arms around her neck and just held on. "I love you, Mom."

"I know. I love you, too. Now, first names."

"I catch a lot of grief about being mixed. I want to take a name that sounds more 'black.'"

"You don't like the name Cooper?"

"The name is fine, it's just . . ."

"It's alright. You can name yourself whatever you want. But you will always be Cooper in my heart."

"Jamal. Jamal Randall Wilson! What do you think?"

"I think we can make that work. Now for me." Pausing and looking around, she finally said, "Ashley Martina Wilson."

"Can I still call you, Mom?"

"You better or I'll have to beat your butt, Jamal Wilson."

The pair returned to answering the questions posed on Dr.

Wendy's forms. By mid-afternoon, the questionnaires were not complete when Wendy entered the living area on the second floor. "How's it going? Are you making progress?"

Janet said, "I think so. You can start calling us the Wilson's. I'm Ashley and he is Jamal. My middle name is Martina and his is Randall."

"That's great," said the psychologist as she made notes. "I will send this information to my office and they will prepare your new identification documents. You will each receive a new birth certificate complete with all the proper information. We will register the birth certificates in the municipality which will be chosen for each of you as well as the new date of your birth. These need to be approved by a federal court. My office will also begin to construct a history for each of you. It'll take a few days but when we present it to you, it will be complete."

"All the information you provide about your past will be incorporated in some way. Then, you will need to learn your new back story so well it becomes natural. And, from now on, the names Janet and Cooper won't be used."

Ashley asked, "Can you tell us yet where we might be heading when we leave here?"

"That has not been determined yet, but I can tell you our goal is to have you in your new place before the start of the new school year. It will be much more natural for Jamal to enter the new school with the start of the year rather than as the only new kid. Does this make sense to you?"

Ashley nodded her head in agreement.

***

Jim Allen put his head in the control room. "I'm going to take the dogs across the road and up onto Bighill. I want to check out the terrain and look for signs of activity. Do you have all the tracking equipment ready to go?"

US Marshall Tutor said, "I've got two dog collar tracking fobs and a walkie-talkie with a tracking GPS built in to the case. We should have no trouble following you. Remember you also have the panic button. Do you want us to put the drone up in the air?"

"I don't think so. This is really just a practice run for the dogs. I need to make sure they won't get too excited if they pick up a rabbit or squirrel. I expect I'll be up there a couple hours. Oh, and can you notify the property owner I'm going up there?"

"Will do."

Jim went out the back door and stopped at the pens of Nikita and Sasha who were excited for the chance to work with Jim. As they crossed the road there was no traffic. The tree line began about one hundred yards from the road as the landscape began to rise. The dogs were smelling everything as they scampered from place to place going into the woods and upward. Jim had a good idea how high someone would have to go on the hill to see anything on the government compound. He decided to start at the west end of the hill and work back to the east. He had already decided if someone with a long-distance lens came to spy, they would approach from the east since the route would be easier than from any other direction. Jim noticed an old campfire pit about a quarter mile up Bighill. It was at least a year old but when he turned to look back across the road, he knew he was still not high enough to have a good view of the house or grounds. Jim and the dogs kept climbing. When they got within a hundred feet of the peak, the angle was sufficient to see the entire house, the west barn, and the grounds in front of the barn and house. His walkie talkie squawked. He grabbed it off his belt. "Yea, what's up?"

"Someone is coming over the peak about three hundred yards to your east."

"Copy." Jim clicked and the dogs came to sit next to him. "Work to do." They moved quietly toward the coordinates provided. When they got within seventy-five yards, the dogs spotted the person walking down the hill in their direction. Jim recognized Smitty by his limp and the big hat he always wore. "Hey Smitty, how ya' doing?"

"Great Jim. You giving the dogs some work or is something else happening?"

"A little of both."

"I understand. You don't have to tell me anything more."

Chief Warrant Officer Jose "Smitty" Smith retired from the US Navy intelligence fifteen years earlier and had come to be the owner of Bighill with a little help from the US government who paid him a fee each year to keep the property free from hikers and hunters. It was amazing how a few well-placed *No Trespassing/No Hunting* signs could keep people away. Although Smitty no longer retained his security clearance, Jim Allen trusted the salty sailor, completely.

"Without saying too much, we have intel saying we should expect visitors with binoculars and cameras."

"Good to know. I'll keep my eyes open on the backside of the hill. I'll put up some extra signs, too. I noticed someone tore down a few of the signs last year. People just don't respect property rights."

"You know, I could breed you a couple of these guys," motioning to the Belgians who were sitting with their ears at attention taking in every word. "You could train them to repel visitors and they'd be good company, too."

"I'll think about it. Good to see you, Jim. When you're not busy, come by the house for a beer. I don't like drinking alone."

"I'll do that." Jim and the dogs continued east until he could no longer see the house. Then they returned to *Vincennes*. For the next few days, this would become a daily trek. It was all about vigilance.

***

Chapter Five

"God that was embarrassing! The whole court thing made me feel like a common criminal," Montie said to his father in the office.

"You need to start listening to me."

"Do you know the feds raided our dock warehouse operation and seized all the records? Did you hear me? I heard about it on the way back here from the court house."

"Of course, I heard you. Once I heard Adams was turning on you, I knew that was going to happen. And, it happened because you are pig-headed and won't listen to me. You should have moved those records off site years ago. Being in this family means you can't trust anyone except yourself."

"Damn it. I will get him."

"That thinking gets you into trouble. Use your head."

"What are you doing to help me?"

"I sent you a voice mail. Listen to the message. We know where Adams is being kept, and don't get any grandiose idea of sending an assassin in to take him out. Show some patience. He'll be there for a while if we don't spook him."

"Jasper is out looking for Adam's family. Maybe he'll know something in a few days. I'm going home. Got a headache." But instead of heading to the Maguire estate, Montgomery Maguire headed to Lucky's Casino just off the Boardwalk. The Maguire family, through several shell companies, owned the casino and profited from its visitors. Montie pulled in to valet parking flipping the keys to one of the young employees. He headed to the bar where he was greeted by the long-time bartender, Willie.

"Mr. Maguire, haven't seen you in a while. Good to see you."

"Thanks, Willie. Get me a double scotch and send it to the table over by the band stand."

At this time of day, the bar was pretty empty. It would pick up after the supper hour. Montie had no thought of being in the bar that late. His legal woes left him restless. He needed some excitement to clear his mind. Back at the bar, Willie readied the drink and motioned for a waitress to deliver it.

"Double scotch, sir?" Montie looked up and saw the dark eyes and beautiful face of the woman delivering his drink. She was stunning.

"Are you new here? I don't remember seeing you here before."

"I've been here seven months. I work the early shift. Hard to make much in tips when the place is quiet like today. Other waitresses get the later shifts when the tips are better. I understand, being the new girl."

"You'll get your chance. Come back and check on me in fifteen minutes. What's your name?"

"Rosalee Lopez, sir."

"Come see me later."

As Rosalee walked back to the bar, Montie watched her movement. He felt a familiar stirring in his loins. *How long had it been?* he wondered. Too long. He knew he could walk to the front of the hotel and order a hooker or a couple hookers for some special fun, but Rosalee had caught his attention. He wanted her. He wanted to wrap his fingers in her beautiful long black hair and have his way with her.

Montie rose and started wandering toward the front desk. On the way he said to Willie, "I'll be back in a minute." He showed his identification to the desk clerk who handed the large man a key card to the owner's suite. Pocketing the key, Montie returned to his table in the bar. Right on time, Rosalee approached the table again.

"Sir, can I get you something else?"

"Yea, I'd like an order of the pretzel bites with the mustard sauce and a ginger ale."

"Anything else, sir?"

"How late do you work?"

"My shift ends at four, sir." Montie nodded his head at the information. As she walked away, he looked at his watch. *Thirty-five minutes*.

Rosalee told Willie she was going to take the customer's order to the kitchen, personally. Willie gave a glance at her as she walked away. After placing the food order, she made a quick trip to the women's lounge. Stepping into a stall and closing the door, she took her cell phone from its hidden holster. She keyed in a text. *Positive contact made*. She flushed the toilet and washed her hands before continuing to the kitchen. She waited the six minutes it took for the pretzels in the fryer and returned to the bar to pick up the ginger ale.

"Your order, sir."

A couple patrons entered the bar and took a table on the other side of the room. Rosalee went to greet them and take their order. The couple, both in their forties, ordered Miller Lites.

Benjamin Maguire's phone rang. When the old man hung up, he called Tiny. "Take me to the casino, right away." It took eight minutes to get to the front door. The older Maguire went straight to the bar where he saw Montie talking to a waitress and paying his bill with a one-hundred-dollar bill. He made his way to the table. "Time to go home."

"That's where I was planning to go," he lied. As he passed Willie, the bartender had his head turned away washing glasses and the front desk clerk had stepped away, too.

***

Maguire's man, Jasper, was a cautious man by nature. In his line of work, guessing was not acceptable. He was expected to get the information requested and to leave no doubt for his employer. He was compensated well for his work. Many years earlier he had been a private detective, but finding people who wanted to disappear was much more satisfying and lucrative. He remembered his very first case. It was a woman who left her husband in the middle of the day while he was away on business. *Her name was James,* he remembered. It would not have been so bad for the deserted husband except she also took their five-year-old daughter. The dad worshipped the little girl. Jasper had to admit the little girl was adorable.

It took fourteen weeks to find the pair hiding in a run-down motel in western Kansas. The mom had done everything the right way. She changed her identity and modified her looks and the appearance of the little girl too. She tossed all her credit cards and avoided calling family members and friends. The mistake was a visit to a small-town emergency room to treat the child's asthma. When Jasper received the lead, he drove across country and staked out the motel until he got a clear photo of the woman and girl. He got the information to the husband who joined him outside the motel two days later.

Jasper drove away with one hundred thousand dollars in cash. He was almost sad the next day when he read in a local paper a female body was discovered in a creek twenty miles south of the little motel. The article said the victim was not identifiable as the hands, feet and head were missing from the nude body.

Jasper decided the best way to check the government safe houses was to take them one at a time starting with the largest city working toward the most rural location. He started in Louisville where he spent forty-eight hours watching the comings and goings. He determined the residents of that safe house were all males based upon the groceries that were being delivered. He went on to Indianapolis but within eight hours he knew no one was being sheltered. Next was Lexington. Whoever was in that house was a college aged student who was starting to venture forth to the University of Kentucky for classes.

Jasper could not decide whether to check the safe house at the West Virginia border with Kentucky or the one at Bighill. He finally decided to go to Inez, Kentucky, first. He reported his findings to the contact, daily. By the time he found the rural setting, he had a bad feeling. He could not quite put his finger on the trouble he sensed but it was real. He was unaware the US Marshall service had been tracking him ever since he left New Jersey. They knew someone was coming and they were ready to intercept him before he even got close to his targets.

As he drove into Inez on state road forty, he passed the Kentucky Fried Chicken, the bank, and the community center. It was a quiet, sleepy hill town. But when he passed the Baptist Church, a sheriff's car pulled out of the parking lot and immediately put on its emergency lights. Jasper pulled to the edge of the narrow road, turned off the ignition and waited for the sheriff to approach. He lowered the driver's side window.

"Good morning, Sheriff."

"Driver's license and registration, please," as he patted his service revolver.

"Yes sir. What did I do?"

"You were speeding. Doing twenty-five in a fifteen mile an hour zone.

"I must have missed the sign," as he handed over the documents.

"I'll be right back," as the sheriff headed back to his cruiser.

Three minutes later returning to the driver's window, "There is a problem with your vehicle's registration. You will need to follow me back to the Sheriff's department so we can straighten this out. The Vehicle Identification number does not match the record provided to us by the State of New Jersey. Just start up your vehicle and follow me back into town."

Seemed like a minor problem but the uneasiness would not go

away. Jasper followed the officer into the parking lot of the sheriff's office and Martin County Government center. They parked near the entrance. The sheriff walked to Jasper's car, located the VIN on the car and with his phone, took a photo. "Let's go inside." The deputy led him into the inner office where he opened a door to a small interrogation room. "In here sir. Have a seat. Be with you in a minute."

A few minutes passed before a man and woman wearing windbreakers entered and introduced themselves as US Marshalls Wiest and Duncan. Jasper asked, "What's going on? Why are you here? I was told my VIN has a problem. US Marshalls don't have any interest in my vehicle, do you?"

Wiest said, "We'd like to have a little talk with you, Mr. Jasper."

"You know who I am. I'm honored."

"The US Marshall Service knows all about you, Mr. Horatio Jasper." Looking at her notes, Wiest added. "Let's see. Before you were here in Inez, you were in Lexington, and before that Indianapolis, and before that, Louisville."

Jasper was now getting uncomfortable. The chair he was seated in began to feel awfully hard. "Do I need to get an attorney?"

"You're not under arrest, we just want to have a discussion with you. Interested?"

Jasper hesitated. "Maybe."

***

The syndicate families up and down the east coast watched the problems of the Maguire family in New Jersey with great interest.

They understood Maguire's problem stemmed from the lack of a long-term plan of continuity. Ever since the days of the mafia in New York, crime syndicates knew they could no longer afford the ease of simply passing the business down the family line. Those days were gone. The federal government was too big, too intrusive. But Benjamin Maguire somehow had missed that lesson. Now he was paying the price of depending on his son to take over the family operation, some day. A son who was in deep trouble, meaning the older Maguire was in deep water, too.

The Power's family of Baltimore decided it might be time to make a major move to the north. Opportunities like this just did not come along very often. They were reviewing the current state of the Maguire family holdings. If they could annex the Maguire's territory, they could potentially grow their own operation by fifty per-cent. Teddy Power decided a frontal attack could be the cleanest way. Speak with Benjamin Maguire, face-to-face. Make a reasonable offer. See if he would be willing to merge. It would be to his advantage. He picked up his burner cell and made the call to his attorney.

"Alex, Teddy. I need you to make a trip to New Jersey. We want to make an offer to the Maguire family. Come by my office tomorrow and I'll give you the details."

***

Dr. Wendy Florence was carefully reviewing all the information provided by her newest clients, the Wilson's. They would pose no real problems as long as they followed the procedures developed by her employer, the United States Department of Justice. She could see having them relocated to their final destination in sixty days. They needed to get comfortable with their new back story which was being formulated for them in Washington by others in her department. Dr. Wendy walked into the sitting room where she found Ashley and Jamal both engrossed in computer programs. Ashley was watching YouTube videos and Jamal was playing a combat game. "Are you ready to do something else for me? I would like you each to take a personality test. It will help us fine tune your new back story. I'll give you the website so you can do it right on the computer."

As she gave the address, both mother and son, typed in the address. After giving each a username and password, they began the test. Wendy turned to leave, but stopped before she opened the door. "You are doing great. This is going to work. You'll see."

When the door closed, Jamal turned to his mom. "Do you think this is going to work, mom?"

"I still don't know what to think, but we've made it this far. We just need to keep moving forward and trust these people to do their jobs so we have a future. And by the way, after breakfast, when you were out with the horses, they gave me our new bank account information. We have received the insurance payments for the house, and the car was sold for a nice profit. I got my pension money from the clinic. I have never had this much money in the bank. They are doing exactly what the Marshalls told us."

"That's good, right?"

"Yea."

***

The days were dragging for Malik Adams spending twenty-three hours each day in solitary confinement, but he knew he was as physically safe as he could be. He had given all his information to the prosecutor. No more daily visits from Butcher. But, since he told Butcher about his interaction with the inmate from the library, he learned the inmate was transferred to an institution on the West Coast.

Adams had developed a daily discipline. Up at six and dressed by six fifteen with breakfast delivered at seven. The food was not as bad as he heard. Actually, it was pretty good and the government made sure he had money in his prison account so he could purchase things from the commissary. After breakfast, he read the Bible faithfully for thirty minutes. His grandmother had instilled an appreciation for the good book. Then it was time for morning exercise in his cell. Push-ups, sit ups, squats, pull ups using the bars on the door. This exercise period was for one hour. He made sure his muscles got a good work out and he was sweating.

Next, the guards took Malik to the shower. Back in his cell, lunch was followed by time reading history or fiction depending on what he could get from the library. Midafternoon meant one hour of time in the prison yard. Adams used the time for two things, running and weight lifting. Then back to his cell for craft time. He used some of his prison funds to buy yarn craft kits. He made items to be sold in the prison visiting area. He never got to go there but he felt the funds might help some other prisoner with no family or income. Craft time was followed by exactly five games of solitary cards. Then supper came followed by more reading with lights out at nine. The routine gave him purpose. Adams knew he needed that purpose while he waited for his chance to ruin the life of Montgomery Maguire.

***

Montie had agreed to keep a low profile while he was out on bail. And he agreed with his father to keep his mouth and temper under control. He spent time at the family office keeping up on the parts of the business that were his to oversee. But each week, on Tuesday, he would make a trip to the casino to spend a couple hours in the bar where he could see Rosalee Lopez. He knew she had somehow gotten in his head. She was so beautiful and seemed vulnerable at the same time. Montie found himself thinking about the woman, continually. He was having his sexual needs met by a variety of female companions set up for him by Tiny. But that was physical. Rosalee was interesting in so many other ways.

"Rosalee, if you get the chance, could you get me more of those pretzel bites from the kitchen?"

"Yes sir. Do you want a ginger ale with that?"

"Thanks for remembering."

Montie always paid his tab with a one-hundred-dollar bill. It was the best way he could express to her his interest. She saw it. She understood it, very well. This cat and mouse game went on weekly.

He learned Rosalee was divorced with no children. She was twenty-eight and lived with her parents on the west side of Atlantic City. Her parents had come to America from Guatemala when she was five years old. She had two older sisters who were living in Texas with her nieces and nephews. She gave one third of her tips to her mother each day to help with expenses. And Rosalee's smile was golden in Montie's eyes. When she returned from the kitchen, he asked, "Rosalee, where have you been all my life?"

She reached out and brushed his hand as she delivered the pretzels. "Mr. Montie, I've been right here waiting for you."

***

"Mr. Jasper, we want to make you an offer. We know who you are looking for from your conversations with Montgomery Maguire." Jasper could feel the blood rushing to his face. He was not a good liar, but he said nothing. Marshall Duncan continued. "Here is our offer. We would like you to give some misinformation to your employer. All you need to say is *you found no trace of the family*. And, we are assuming, your task is just to find them, not take them out. Have we got that figured out correctly? And, by the way, it is not a crime to find lost people."

Jasper was taking all this in and considering the possibilities. He knew the Maguire family was not one to cross. His life would be valueless if they found out his deception. "I understand what you are asking. What's in it for me? I can't do this from the goodness of my heart."

"We understand that, Mr. Jasper. Let's see. We can make sure the Kansas State Police never learn of your involvement with the Sarah James murder."

At the name, Jasper's face went stark white. *How did they know*?

"Second, we have the ability to make you disappear so the Maguire family can't locate you. We're good at that."

"And we can make it worth your while financially. You won't be rich, but . . ."

"I think it is time for me to get my attorney."

You don't trust a lawyer from our office? We are the US government. Our lawyer will give you an agreement you will be happy with. Do you want to work with us?"

***

Chapter Six

"Mr. Maguire, thanks for agreeing to meet with me." The blonde woman was in her mid-forties and looked very professional in her custom-tailored suit with matching heals. Her business card said, *Carla Franconi, attorney at law.*

"Well Ms. Franconi, it isn't often a beautiful attorney wants to come meet me. You say you have a proposal for my consideration?"

"That is correct. I am representing a party who would like to make an offer to purchase your business interests."

"Which part of my business. You know we are highly diversified."

"The party I represent is well aware of all your holdings and would like to purchase all your interests."

In all his years, no one had ever offered to buy out the old man. He had turned back suitors that tried to force him to leave. Maguire had the philosophy, *if they come after me with a knife, I'll respond with a bazooka.* "And who is this party making the offer?"

"I'm not prepared to share that information with you at this time. The party wants to know your interest, first."

"I see." Maguire sat back in his chair looking at the ceiling. "Do you know why they are thinking I may have interest in selling?"

"That has not been shared with me. I am just hired to make first contact with you."

"Are you prepared to share the amount being offered?"

"I am." Franconi reached into her brief case and withdrew a single page document. She slid it across the desk to the elderly Maguire, face down. "Of course, everything is open to negotiation."

"Of course," said Maguire. As he considered the amount offered, he did a quick calculation knowing his annual income from all the parts of the business. The amount was just short of one hundred million dollars. It represented five years of receipts for the business. "I will need some time to consider this offer."

"I expected that response. The party I represent says they will wait five days for a response." She stood to her feet, offered her hand.

"Mr. Maguire, you have my card. I look forward to your call. Thank you for seeing me."

Ten minutes later, the office phone rang in Montie's office. "Maguire."

"This is Jasper. I have checked each location as requested. There is no sign of activity. Are there other places you would like me to inspect for you?"

"Nothing."

"Nothing, sir?"

"I'll be in touch," as he hung up the phone.

***

When Jamal got a break working with Dr. Wendy, he decided to go out with the animals. He liked the horses but was intrigued by the dogs. Something about the dogs touched a place deep within the teenager. He enjoyed watching Jim train the dogs and put them through their paces. He was disappointed Jim was nowhere to be seen as Jamal went through the horse barn heading toward the training area of the canines. When he entered the dog shed, he saw Nikita and Sasha's cages were empty. *Jim must be working the older dogs.*

As he turned to leave, Nimitz began to whine and scratch at the door to his enclosure. Jamal decided it was time to get to know the pups. He put his hand out to Nimitz who sniffed him before licking his hand through the bars of the gate. This was a new experience for Jamal. He was never allowed to have pets. He didn't know why. The idea had never come up. The only neighborhood pet he could remember was the golden colored cat that belonged to the woman who lived three doors to the north. But the cat never seemed very friendly so Jamal kept his distance. As Nimitz continued licking his fingers, Jamal started to smile. *He likes me.* The other three dogs were all at the doors to their cages now, too. Grant was whimpering so Jamal went to him and got another round of doggy kisses.

Jamal had an idea. He walked to the door of the shed and pulled it closed. *Maybe I could let one of the dogs out of their cage.* He opened the door and Nimitz came rushing out and proceeded to jump up on the boy. He was uncertain what to do next so he leaned down to pet the dog who was enjoying his freedom – tongue out, tail wagging in circles. Jamal was surprised at how strong the dog was when he jumped and pushed on the human. "Nimitz, sit!" Immediately, the dog was sitting on his haunches looking up to the eyes of his new friend and pack mate. Jamal was impressed. "Nimitz, down!" The obedience was immediate. "Nimitz, stay!" Jamal backed across the room while the dog watched him very carefully. When he reached the door, "Nimitz come." *This is fun.*

"Nimitz, home," and the dog returned to his cage. Jamal closed the door and then opened the gate for Grant. He put Grant through the same commands followed by Lee and finally McArthur. Just as he backed to the door to call the final dog, the door behind the youth opened and in stepped Jim followed by the two older dogs.

"I'm sorry, Jim. I didn't ask your permission."

"It's fine. I'm glad you shut the door to keep McArthur in the building. I could see you losing control and running all over the forty acres trying to catch him. You would never catch one of these dogs. They are strong and fast. That's why the training is so important. Nikita, Sasha, home."

"Now show me what you were doing with McArthur."

Jamal put the pup through the four commands. The dog followed without hesitation. "McArthur was the last one. I already gave the same commands to each of the others. They were great."

"Even Admiral Nimitz?"

"Yes sir."

"Show me. McArthur, home."

When Nimitz cage door opened, the dog looked at Jim but ran straight to Jamal where he jumped.

"Down," commanded Jim. The dog stopped jumping. "Did you notice how he looked at me and then ran straight to you? Looks like he wants to bond with you rather than with me. It might answer why I've had some problems with Nimitz training. Okay, show me what he did for you."

Jamal put him through the commands, each obeyed properly. Jim said, "Looks like you'll need to be more involved in his training from here on. Are you willing to help me?"

"You bet. Show me another command I can use with him."

Jim showed the silent commands done by getting the dog's attention then motioning with the right hand. As Jamal demonstrated each command, his pupil obeyed.

Jim said, "We have a little time before supper, let's take all of them into the pen. I'll stand on one side and you stand on the opposite side. You vocally call them to come to you. Make them sit. Then I'll use silent commands with the clicker for them to follow."

Jamal could not remember the last time he felt this useful. And the dogs clearly liked him. Jim asked, "Do you like to run?"

"A lot."

"I want you to run around the perimeter of the pen. Any speed you want. In fact, it would be good if you varied your speed. The dogs should run with you. Not in front of you, nor behind you, but abreast with you. That's how working dogs run with their handler. I'm getting a bit old to be running with the dogs. Don't get me wrong, I can still do it."

"I know, I have younger legs, right?"

"Exactly. So, start running and I'll command them to join you, one at a time."

It did not take long before Jamal was running with four dogs all watching his every move and getting a good work out. Supper was getting close so the dogs were returned to the kennels and given fresh water. Jim said as they were walking to the house, "you're going to tenth grade. What do you want to do in high school?"

"Maybe join a club or two. Not really sure."

"What about sports?"

"I do like track and running."

"Ever consider playing football? What are you, six foot three and one eighty? You could be a real presence on a team if you dedicate yourself."

"My father was a football player in college. He went to Ohio State."

"Really, that's some big-time football. What was his name?"

"Malik Adams. Mom doesn't like to talk about him so I don't know a lot about him as an athlete, but on the internet, I found some articles that mention him. He must have been pretty good. I know an injury ended his career."

"Seems to me I remember a player for OSU named Adams back in the 90s. I was in the Army in those days but I liked watching football when I could. Let me do some checking. I'll let you know if I find anything interesting."

Lisa hollered at the guys as they walked in the back door. "Get washed up. Supper's going on the table. We're having pot roast tonight and Dr. Wendy is staying for supper."

Jamal was the last person to sit. Ashley and Wendy were locked in an intense discussion. Wendy said, "It has to be more spontaneous.

You can't hesitate when someone asks you those kinds of personal questions. You hesitate, it puts doubt in the other person's mind. Do you understand what I'm saying?"

Ashley nodded her head but Jamal could tell from her body language she was frustrated by the interchange with the psychologist. "Are you okay, mom?"

"I'm fine."

Wendy asked, "Jamal, what's your mother's name?"

"Janet, I mean Ashley Wilson. Sorry."

"It's okay here and now, but in the wrong place, it could be a costly mistake. Both of you need to work very hard to get your identities committed to your minds. After supper, I want to work with both of you on your new backgrounds. I got them by courier this afternoon."

***

Benjamin Maguire's phone was ringing as he was thinking about the offer to purchase his operations. *Some days I'd like to throw that thing out the window.* "Maguire."

"Mr. Maguire, Richard Swartznicki calling from New York." When Maguire failed to respond, the attorney continued. "Sir, I want to know if you have any interest in my firm attempting to plea bargain in Montgomery's case?"

"Swartznicki, in your estimation what would be the possibility of securing a deal with no prison time?"

"I do not think that would be possible under the circumstances. I would think a plea deal could be proposed for say three years and a one hundred thousand dollar fine."

"What is the maximum penalty for the charges as they now exist?"

"Twenty years."

"Mr. Swartznicki, at my age, you are describing situations under which I would never see my son outside of prison, again. If there is more than one year of incarceration, my answer is NO."

"Because your son is the one accused, I feel I should also ask his opinion."

"Look, you overpaid piece of shit, I pay for your services and you heard my answer." The phone crashed in its cradle as the old man made his point. Then, reconsidering, the old man once again picked up the phone and pushed the intercom button. "Tiny, come in here."

In less than a minute, Tiny was sitting across from his boss of forty-five years. "Yes sir?"

"Tiny, have you ever known me to do something foolish?"

Tiny considered the "loaded question" from his longtime mentor. "Sir, I can only think of one mistake you ever made that I thought was foolish. That was the time you went after the police captain who was trying to blackmail you over the whores in Trenton."

"But in my defense, destroying his reputation was too easy. Even a saint can be set up for a fall if you're careful in planning."

"I'll give you that, Mr. Maguire. It turned out well for us. What's troubling you, sir?"

"Jasper went out to try and find the location of Adam's son and the kid's mother. He reported he found nothing but my gut thinks there is more to the story. I want you to find an enforcer not affiliated with us. I want that enforcer to let's say, find Jasper and interrogate him. Do you understand what I'm asking?"

"I do. I will take a couple days off and make some enquiries from a family in Tampa. I'll do it in a way that can't be tied back to you. Are you getting the feeling someone knows too much about your business? Like there is a mole?"

"Something is not right. My leg aches like there's a storm on the horizon and I can feel it coming this way. And get ahold of your computer security buddy. Have him check to see if our phones and computer network could be under surveillance? We have to be careful."

At the same time, across town, Federal Prosecutor Alice Williamson and Assistant Prosecutor Jack Butcher were meeting on the fourth floor of the courthouse with a representative of the FBI and US Marshall service. "Have you found anything else we can use to shut down the Maguire operation. I don't care about the kid, I want the old man," said Williamson. "If the kid ever takes over the syndicate, he'll be dead within two years. He's unstable."

Special Agent Roland Wilkins said, "We got all we can get from Adams. Beyond that, he's not much use to us. Jasper gave up the old man, but finding out information about someone in witness protection is not a big deal. I don't think I told you, but the affidavits from Willis and Pauly are almost worthless. Willis was shanked to death in the prison yard and Pauly was hit and killed by a hit and run driver the day after he was released. We've been monitoring the phones and computer network of Maguire, but honestly, the old man runs a tight operation. Not many places he leaves exposed."

"Do you think leaning on Adams could produce more information that he doesn't want to give up?"

"What are you getting at?" asked Wilkins.

"Here's what I see. If we infer to him, we are going to back off our protection of his family, would he change his mind about helping go after the old man?" She paused and looked each person in the eye to let the idea take root. "Or, maybe we just go after the kid. Put him away and wait for the old man to die. He isn't going to live forever. When he goes, the whole operation will collapse in six months without a new head."

Wilkins says, "But then we have a new problem. Some other family will swoop in and take over the operation. We're back to right where we are now."

"True," says Williamson. "But maybe there are other possibilities we're not seeing at the moment. Eyebrows went up around the room."

Butcher asked, "You mean like replace the Maguires with someone of our choosing?"

"I mean Montgomery Maguire is not his father. He will keep making mistakes. When he makes enough; who knows?"

***

Dr. Wendy Florence handed two three ring notebooks to Ashley Wilson, one for herself and one for Jamal. "Here are your new identities as developed by our team in Washington. Everything in the notebooks are now backed by the appropriate back ground records and documents. Your task now is to learn all this information. I cannot express how important this is for your future safety. These notebooks won't leave this building with you."

"What happens if I can't remember one of the facts about me once we leave here?" wondered Ashley.

"You will each have a private internet location where you can go to access the information. These notebooks are just too volatile for your future. If someone would find these books, you could not explain them away."

Ashley handed one to Jamal as they opened the notebooks.

"Let's start on the cover page. You will see your name as it appears on all documents. These are the names you chose for yourselves, right?" She awaited their nodding heads. "Notice the next thing is your new birthdates. The way we have handled your birthdates is to move your birth month two months back on the calendar and then three days ahead. So, if you ever have to give your birthdate and can't remember the date, think of your actual birthdate and go back two months, then forward three days. If you were looking at my date, it would say January 22 because my actual birthday is March 19. Does that make sense?" Again, she waited for confirmation of understanding.

"The next thing is your place of birth. The team had to take into consideration what type of regional dialect you speak in your natural voice. In your case, central Ohio. They had to rule out places like New York, Texas, you get the picture. So, you are now both natives of Lansing, Michigan. You will notice in the back of the notebook a tab A. That is where we have given you a background for someone born in Lansing. You will want to remember that Lansing is the state capital of Michigan but it is not the county seat for Ingham County. That's Mason."

Jamal commented, "I never imagined this would be so complicated."

"And this is only the beginning. On the next page you will see your new Social Security Numbers plus for you, Ashley, your Michigan driver's license number. These numbers are now active and have been totally populated with all the pertinent data. If you open a bank account and give your ID to the bank, when they check you out, you will exist. In the back of the notebook is a pouch containing your new cards as well as birth certificates. Ashley, there is a list of all the vehicles you have owned and the dates and of course, your driver's license."

"The next page has family history information for each of you. Ashley, your parents' names were Thomas and Helen Shipley Wilson. He worked at the General Motors factory in Lansing before dying twelve years ago. Thomas and Helen were real people who really lived in Michigan who have headstones and everything. Their records have been modified to show your birth. They moved to Arizona twenty years ago so their trail in Michigan is old. Harder to track. Helen died thirteen years ago in Arizona. You were not close after you had Jamal. You have no siblings and no cousins as both Thomas and Helen were only children. Their parents are listed for you complete with locations and dates of birth and death. You will also see the various addresses you each lived at in your lives. The names of the hospitals you were born in is listed, too."

"Jamal, you don't know the name of your father. But all the information for your mother and her parents are listed for you, too. You will need to learn this stuff."

"Do I know who his father is?" asked Ashley.

"You do, but you keep it private. It's not recorded, anywhere. The next page is all about education for each of you. Listed there are the elementary schools you attended, and the names of the teachers you had. Then you'll see the Junior High Schools and for you, Ashley, the high school you attended. You also have a transcript from Lansing Everett High School. You did not attend college immediately after high school. You joined the US Navy and were stationed in Norfolk, Virginia. That's where you met Jamal's father. You left the Navy because you were pregnant. You have an honorable discharge. All your Navy documentation is included in the back. These documents are so real if you broke your leg and needed medical attention, you could go to any Veterans Hospital in the country and get health care. No problem. Any questions so far?"

"Let's move on then. In your book, Ashley, your college information is given. Using your GI benefits, you went to Lansing Community College and then ended up at Michigan State getting your undergrad degree in Business with a minor in Art. This follows with your work history. It mirrors your actual experience with some small changes."

"Where did I work before moving to Florida?"

"Your work history is listed for you in the notebook. Let's see." Looking at the page. "You worked for Dr. Ralph Blessing DDS. His office was in downtown Lansing. He retired so you decided it was time to relocate.

"You will both find your housing history in the Lansing area. Your final place was an apartment complex in Holt, Michigan. You never owned a home. You always rented and moved around almost every year so you did not get too chummy with neighbors."

"You each have a medical history. We've included the names of your doctors, specialists and dentists. Also, hospitalizations, immunizations and dental records actually are now tied to these documents. Jamal, you broke your arm when you were five years old. All the information is listed for you. There are actually x-rays."

"Ashley, we have included banking information for you along with a list of credit cards that have been opened and closed in your name. You will be happy to know, you have zero balances right now on all the cards, except for Discover."

"I can't get over how much work was done for us," said Jamal.

"But here's the part we cannot do for you. We can't construct your relationship with each other. For example, when was Jamal potty trained? We suggest you just tell the actual story of things like that. Does that make sense?"

"I get it," said Ashley. "Things like what happened when we went to Cedar Point and Jamal got sick and threw up on the kiddy ride."

"Yea, I still gave you dandelions for Mother's Day when I was seven. Right?" asked Jamal.

Dr. Wendy continued, "So, that's it for today. Look over this information and start memorizing it. I'll be back at eleven tomorrow morning. I will be giving you your first written test on the information. We'll add more information as time goes on.

I'll be testing you until you both score above ninety-five percent. When you get to that place, you can move on to the next phase of preparation for being independent."

After Wendy left, Jamal said, "Mom, a test, really. This isn't school."

"I know how you feel but it's going to keep us safe."

***

Chapter Seven

There was a preliminary hearing in federal court for Montgomery P. Maguire with the honorable Melissa Walker. It was a plea hearing. All the attorneys were present. The charges were again read by the clerk of the court. When asked his plea, Swartznicki answered, "the defendant pleads Not Guilty, your honor."

Judge Walker looked at her notes and announced, "the date for seating a jury will be October 15, in this courtroom. Any motions, counsellors?"

Swartznicki spoke up, "Your honor, defense would like to request an extension until January. As of today, we have one hundred nineteen days. I am already committed to a trial in New York for mid-October."

"Is there any objection by the prosecution?"

"No, your honor," responded Williamson.

"And the defendant will remain out on bond." The gavel came down ending the courtroom drama.

Montie went to the casino's bar to see Rosalee, again. He had an itch and she was so special. He invited her to sit with him at his little table while he ate a Reuben sandwich, but she declined. "You know I can't sit with you. I don't want to lose my job. But I'm honored you want to spend time with me. By the way, are you married? You don't wear a ring, but you have never told me."

Montie said, "No. Divorced almost twenty years now. It was a mistake right from the start. She was more interested in my bank account than in me. It hurt."

"I'm so sorry to hear that. I don't understand how any woman could be like that. You are such a nice man. I would never treat you like that, never! Can you excuse me for a minute? I need to use the powder room."

"Of course," he replied.

Rosalee went immediately to the restroom and upon entering the stall, began to text. *Moving forward. Should be done soon.*

When she returned, she brought the bill for Montie. Again, he paid with the usual one-hundred-dollar bill for which she greatly thanked the generous man. "I was able to take my mother to buy a new dress, thanks to you. She was so excited."

Montie enjoyed seeing Rosalee with a large smile.

Benjamin Maguire was aware of the flirting going on in the bar. He got a report every time Montie visited. So far, it was all innocent on the surface, but the man's natural skepticism was making its presence known. It was time to recheck this woman, just to be safe, Maguire thought. He wrote a note to the Human Resources director at the casino requesting a new background check for Rosalee Lopez. *A deeper check, this time*, he insisted.

It was time for the older Maguire to get back to the attorney who had visited earlier with an offer to purchase his interest in the business. He slid open his desk drawer and withdrew the business card of Carla Franconi. As he held the card in his hand, he mindlessly began to turn it over and over as his mind raced.

If I was thirty years younger, what would I do with an offer like this? I think I would find out who is making this offer. Then maybe take them out or send a message that could not be misunderstood.

Maybe a fire bomb, he thought. *I'm no fool. I built this business and as long as I breathe, no one will force me out, or buy me out. But how to answer without giving away too much?*

He picked up the phone and dialed the female attorney. "Ms. Franconi, this is Benjamin Maguire getting back to you."

"Thank you for calling. I appreciate your consideration of the offer."

"I believe the offer is premature. I want to wait until I know what the outcome will be for my son's legal issues."

"I'm sorry. I wasn't aware there were any issues you or your son were facing. May I ask what is going on?"

Liar. he thought. "I don't feel comfortable discussing this with you at this time."

"Is there anything I could do to help?"

Maguire stopped and thought for a moment.

"Not at this time. But thank you for asking. I have your contact information. If anything changes, I know how to get a hold of you. Good bye Ms. Franconi."

I need to investigate this offer from the shark in high heels. As usual, Maguire turned to his trusted comrade, Tiny. He was confident in Tiny's ability to get the job done.

Franconi went to the managing partner's office and closed the door. Alex Engel was a fifty something year-old lawyer, a graduate of Yale. He was good at what he did and he won far more than he lost. His list of clients was a virtual "Who's who" of the powerful in eastern Maryland. The pictures on his office wall included Presidents, Senators, Governors, and high-profile entertainers and athletes. He chose his associate lawyers from only the best, known for their litigation skills and ability to be persuasive. Carla Franconi was as good as any lawyer in his office.

"No luck with Maguire, Carla?"

"I was only trying to lay ground work. It's clear he doesn't trust me. He probably trusts no one."

"Would you trust lawyers if you were in his position?"

"Probably not."

"Benjamin Maguire is as shrewd as any CEO in America. If you follow the legal record of his businesses, he makes no mistakes. His one weakness seems to be his line of succession in the leadership of his business. His son, Montgomery, is a loose cannon. The old man protects him like an elephant protects a calf. And, if you ever see Montgomery Maguire, he is almost as big as an elephant." Engel laughed at his own humor."

"Alex, I have to admit, you surprised me when you told me not to bring Maguire's attorney into the discussion."

"Do you know how many law firms Maguire has used in the past ten years? Six! You said it, he trusts no one."

"Do you want me to be here for your call to Teddy Power?"

He shook his head. "Teddy didn't expect Maguire to just fold up shop and go home. He won't be surprised by the reaction. We'll probably end up talking strategy. Deniability is your friend."

Franconi rose. "Do you want your door open or closed?"

"Closed will be good." He made the call. "Teddy Power, Alex Engel. The first meeting with Benjamin Maguire went exactly like you suspected. Now, I expect he will do everything possible to try to find out your identity."

"That's what I expect too. Thanks for the report. I'll be in touch."

Powers called one of his employees. "Venessa, come to my office, please."

Venessa White looked like she should be the agency's cleaning woman. Sixty years old with graying hair in a rather shapeless style. The woman looked like she did not know what make up was much less how to use it. She walked with a slight stoop, wearing dresses at least ten years out of style. That is why she was such a valuable investigator. No one gave Venessa a second look, but she knew how to get information. She sat in the same seat just vacated by her opposite, Carla Franconi.

"Venessa, I have a job for you. Benjamin Maguire in New Jersey is going to be attempting to identify this firm and our client. I just made a proposal to buy him out. He's old school and I know he will want to find out who's behind the offer. I believe he'll send an associate by the name of 'Tiny' Gerald Olf to look for us. I want you to tail him for the next week. Photos. Complete report."

"Yes, Mr. Power. I'll be on my way within the hour. You can count on me."

"I don't know this to be true, but my guess is he will start looking by going after Carla Franconi. She is the only face they know behind the offer."

***

From the beginning, Malik Adams expected the federal prosecutor's office would put pressure on him to try to bring down both Maguire's. The deposition and testimony for the grand jury was now done. When Jack Butcher showed up, Malik was not surprised.

"Adams, I've come to see if you want to give more information about the operation of the Maguires? We want to take down the operation and feel this is our best opportunity. We need your help."

"I told you before, this is all I'm giving you. You agreed to this arrangement."

Butcher squirmed in his chair. "I'm getting pressure from above. They are talking about dropping your kid and his mother out of witness protection if you refuse to cooperate. This is not about me anymore. The FBI is now involved."

"Do you know the name Gordon Banks?"

"There was a Gordon Banks who was a reporter for the Sports Network, back in the day. Is that who you are talking about?"

"That's the guy."

"Why are you bringing him up?"

"Here's the deal. Gordon Banks was my college roommate for three of my years at Ohio State. He was a reserve safety. Didn't play much but was a communications major and interested in broadcasting. Do you know what he is doing today?"

"Can't say I do."

"He is now the assistant director of news at the ABC affiliate in New York. If the government throws my family to the wolves, I contact Banks. He exposes everything. Not sure your bosses would be real happy when their whole case falls apart. Maybe you could share this with your friends and associates?"

"I hear you." Then he paused. "I do have another question for you. In your opinion, if Montie goes away and the old man can no longer run the operation, who will step up?"

"The only person I can think of might be Tiny. He knows about all the pieces of the business. I got the impression no one other than the Maguires know more than Tiny. His office is next to Mr. Maguire's office. He's closer than Montie's office."

"Hey, do you really think Banks would believe you over the US Government if we disagree?"

"Did you ever serve in the military?" Butcher shook his head. "When you bleed with another guy for three years like Banks and me, he'll believe me. And, on your way out, why don't you check with the warden's office and ask who is sending me three sports magazines each month."

"Banks?"

"Good guess."

***

Jasper decided to leave his car at the condo and take his bicycle to the pharmacy. It was only a mile in the town of Millville in the south of New Jersey. A peaceful place, that's what attracted Jasper to the town ten years earlier. Ever since returning from Kentucky, his hay fever had been acting up. He needed an over-the-counter medicine to stop the sneezing and runny nose. As he rode up Second Street, something caught his attention. Across from his place was a black Chrysler with two men sitting inside. They were casually glancing at the front door of his condo. He had a very bad feeling. He was glad he thought to grab the baseball cap as he walked out the backdoor. He got off his bike, pulled the hat a bit lower, and looked at the sprocket on the back wheel as if it was not working quite right. He had stopped three cars behind the Chrysler in a place where they would not see him as they glanced his way.

He knew he could not go home, nor could he linger long looking at his bike before someone would see him. He turned around and pushed the bike back the way he had come. At the first intersection, he rounded the corner, hopped back aboard the bicycle, and pedaled to the north. This was exactly the reason Jasper kept a bedroom at an old woman's house; just in case. When he arrived at his safe place, he went to the back door, got out his key and carried his bike up the steps.

In his room, he went to work putting on one of the disguises he used when trailing persons for his employers. He made sure he had the small camera with the 10x lens as he walked back toward the condo using a circuitous route. Jasper knew the routines of his neighbors. The couple who lived across the street would not be home. He approached their property from the alley, then let himself in the gate to the backyard.

He moved along the north edge of the house staying out of sight until he could see the rear end of the Chrysler, still parked. When he peaked to see the occupants, he was frightened to see the car was empty. He quietly backed up after taking a photo of the car. He noticed the screen door on his unit was ajar, meaning someone had recently opened it. *They are inside my place.* He knew his location was not good. Time to move.

He retraced his route to the alley where he decided he needed to get to the opposite side of the street. It was too big a risk to just cross the street within the block of his condo. Either he had to go back several blocks, or cause a distraction. He pulled his cellphone and made a call.

"This is 911, what is your emergency?"

"This is Horatio Jasper, 152 South Second Street. There are two burglars in my condo. Can you send the police?"

"Dispatching two cruisers. Are you in the condo, sir?"

"No. I'm outside where I am safe."

"Estimated time of arrival for the police is two minutes. They will approach without sirens."

"Thank you. I'll stay on the line, if that's okay?"

"Yes sir. I will keep you informed."

The cruisers came from opposite directions and parked in the middle of the street without lights. The officers approached carefully; guns drawn. Jasper again approached the scene through the neighbor's backyard.

"Mr. Jasper, the officers on the scene say the two men tell them they are your cousins and have come to surprise you."

"I have no cousins. I repeat. They are not my relatives."

Jasper knew this would end one of two ways. *Either the preps come out in handcuffs, or they try to escape.* Just as the thought went through his mind, the two came flying out the door with the officers right behind. Guns had been exchanged for tasers.

"Stop, police!" When the tasers connected with the fleeing men, they collapsed in the street as the voltage shot through their flesh. A third cruiser arrived on the scene – a K-9 unit. It was over within ninety seconds as the burglars were handcuffed and placed in separate cruisers.

Jasper needed no further convincing of the danger he found himself in. And he knew the source. After the police left the scene, Jasper went into his condo, collected his essentials, put his beloved cat in her carrier, locked the front door and left in his car. He had photos of the fleeing criminals; he didn't wait to find out their identities.

Late in the afternoon, Jasper called US Marshall Wiest from a village fifty miles away in Pennsylvania. "This is Horatio Jasper, I'm ready to cooperate with your investigation of the Maguire family."

"There was a little incident at your home, today, we understand," said Wiest. "Are you looking for protection?"

"Yes. Can you help me?"

After hearing the location of Jasper, he was instructed to drive to the local Sheriff's office and wait for the Marshalls to pick him up.

Just before supper time, Jasper was sitting in an interrogation room with Assistant Federal Prosecutor Jack Butcher providing more information for the case against Montgomery Maguire. As

Butcher said, interfering in a federal investigation was serious.

***

Jamal and Ashley sat across the table from one another. Dr. Wendy handed each a five-page test. "This is a timed test. Don't spend too much time on any one question. The goal is to achieve a ninety-five per cent score. You have six minutes. Questions?"

"I have one, no two," stated Ashley. "How many people have you shepherded through this witness relocation process. And second, what is the average number of times someone takes your test before they pass?"

"I'll only answer one question now. I have worked with about thirty-five individuals in this program. Now, ready, go."

The tests were turned over and each began to read and answer as quickly as possible. The first questions were pretty basic and both Ashley and Jamal had their names down along with their birth information. But as they reached the third page, things changed. *What significant events occurred in your life when you were ten years old for Jamal and twenty-seven years old for Ashley.* Ashley suddenly forgot everything she had memorized about her new parents. Jamal could not recall the order of the apartments they lived in. The test was not easy and when time was called, neither had reached the final page.

Dr. Wendy took the tests. "Here is the answer to the other question you asked. No one has ever passed the test on their first three tries. The most tries were twenty-eight. I'm guessing you will each need more than ten attempts. Does that discourage you?"

"It does," admitted Ashley. Jamal just put his head down on the table.

"I want each of you to take the remainder of the day off and relax. I believe Jim has an idea for you this evening. I'll see you tomorrow at lunch."

"Mom, that was really hard. Will I ever be able to remember all that stuff?"

"You will. It will take time and a lot of effort. Let's head downstairs for supper."

Lisa was busy in the kitchen. Jim was nowhere to be seen. Lisa said, "We need to practice the safe room protocols. I want you to imagine you just heard there was a breach of security and you are ordered into the room. Go!" Before they could take two steps, there was an explosion in the kitchen and they stopped and turned toward the sound. Lisa yelled, "Stop the test! You both just failed, you're dead. Do you understand? This is not a game. When you are told to go, you have to go right now. No excuses. Got it?"

Tears began to flow down the cheeks of Ashley. "I don't think I can take this anymore." She began to sob. Jamal placed an arm around his mother and held her.

"Don't you see that my mother is upset. Do you have to be so heartless?" Jamal said.

With no emotion in her voice, Lisa said, "Head back upstairs. When supper is ready, I'll let you know."

After the door on the second floor closed, Dr. Wendy and Jim came out of their observation posts. The three sat at the table. "Wendy, you called it. She is the fragile one," said Lisa.

Wendy answered, "Every human has their breaking point. We've seen hers. I just wonder when we will see his. It'll come."

Jim asked, "Is the plan still a go for tonight?"

Wendy said, "Yea, they need it to get their minds off their situation. Show them a good time."

***

"Hey pops, Tiny's tech guy reported no spyware on the computer network and no phone bugs. But he says technology has changed and spyware can be installed without touching our equipment and still not be traceable. He recommends more burner phones be used for communication and to have two separate computer networks, not interlinked," said Montie.

"Did he say anything about using pigeons? Might be the safest way to keep others from listening in."

He didn't say anything about that but Tiny said something went wrong in trying to get information out of Jasper. The two enforcers out of DC haven't checked in. Their rental was found outside Millville, New Jersey in an impound lot. No sign of the two guys. They did some investigating in the neighborhood where Jasper lives. Found a neighbor who said there was some type of disturbance outside his condo. Couple burglars were taken into custody by the local police. Jasper wasn't home according to the neighbor. But later, Jasper was seen driving away. I don't like this pop. Everything seems to be blowing up in my face."

"Stay on it, son. You have plenty of time to work on your situation since the lawyer got that continuance until the first of the year. And you need to be careful with the waitress you've been flirting with at the casino. What do you really know about her?"

"I know she has a green card, so she's legal. Her parents are here legally from Guatemala. She passed the background check at the casino so she must be okay. Do you know something I don't know?"

"No. I had the Human Resources run another background check on her. She checked out. Just be cautious."

"I am careful. She's interesting. Kind of sweet and innocent. You know I haven't been serious about any woman since Candy left me. That was a long time ago."

"I know. But you need to be thinking there are eyes and ears everywhere these days. Don't be surprised to find casino customers watching your every move. You have to know the feds would love to find out more dirt about you. They won't be satisfied 'til they tear down everything we've built."

"I want to send another investigator to follow up on Jasper's trail of safe houses," Montgomery said. "Have any suggestions?"

"There is this guy I heard about in Vegas. Used to be in the air force. Got drummed out for breaking military protocols. I understand the guy is a wizard with technology spying. He uses these drones. Little ones with mics and cameras. Government is using these in the middle east to track the Iranians. I was told he is pretty expensive but very competent. Guy's name is Carmichael."

"I'll find his contact info for you. I don't want you contacting this guy. Have someone you trust make the contact. Leave your name out of it. Low profile."

"Okay pop. I understand you have Tiny out on a job?"

"Someone is making a play for our business. I want to know who it is before I politely tell them to back off."

"That's funny, pop. You using the word *politely*. It's kind of like Mr. Rogers saying *smackdown*, if you know what I mean. A bit out of character. But why did you send Tiny. It's not his expertise."

"I know, but the person I wanted to send is no longer available."

Montie understood the reference as soon as it was uttered out loud.

***

Chapter Eight

After supper, Jim went out and got the Ford 150 pickup from the garage and brought it to the back door. Lisa hurried their guests to the back seat while she rode shotgun in front.

Ashley asked, "Where are we going?"

"Going for a little ride into Big Hill," said Jim. "Time for a little fun."

"Is this a good idea?" Ashley asked.

"It will be fine," said Lisa. "We do this with all our guests."

Seven minutes later, the truck pulled into the parking lot of the local Ice Crème shop. Jim said, "Cones for everyone. What flavor do you like?"

Jamal wanted strawberry while Ashley wanted butter pecan. When Jim returned, he had four double dip cones and plenty of napkins. "With the tinted windows, nobody can see your faces. You are totally safe. And we will just sit here in the parking lot and enjoy our cones. People saw me, but they've seen me before and now don't even take a second look. We just blend right in. Hiding in plain sight."

Fifteen minutes later, they were getting out of the truck behind the house. As Jamal started for the back door, Jim said, "Whoa. Another surprise." US Marshall Waker came out of the east barn leading four saddled horses. "How about a ride around the property?"

Jamal's eyes lit up instantly. Ashley said, "I've never been on a horse."

Lisa said, "We are just going to walk. It will give you a chance to get some fresh air and clear your head."

Lisa led the way on the back of Biscuit. She dismounted and opened the gate to the back forty acres. Ashley was on Tulip, Jamal on Racer and Jim brought up the rear on Thunder. For the next hour they just walked around the pasture and felt the strong muscles of the horses as they effortlessly carried the riders. The view of the Kentucky countryside was calming and spectacular as the sun was heading toward the western horizon. Few words were spoken but peace was communicated to the souls of the Wilsons who knew only fear and anxiety these days.

When they returned to the house, Jamal volunteered to help Jim walk the horses back to their stalls. The boy was in his glory. He did everything for the horse he rode that Jim did for the other three. Removed the saddle, blanket, and harness. Brushed the horse, gave him fresh water and some new hay. Jamal liked this life. He wondered, *could this be my life*? He wanted to dream, again. And that night he did.

Jamal was not one to have memorable dreams. But around three in the morning, he woke from a nightmare. He remembered the details. He found himself covered in sweat. He went to the bathroom and wiped his face, used the toilet, got a drink and headed back to bed. He was fully awake and decided to do something he hadn't done in the longest time.

Knocking on the door, "Mom? Can I come in?"

He could hear her rustling in the bed. "Come in."

"What's going on, buddy?"

Sitting on the edge of her bed, "I just had a really bad nightmare."

"Do you want to talk about it, or just crawl under the covers with me? It's been a long time since you came to bed with me. I kind of miss it." Ashley held the blanket up for Jamal to slide in. She lay on her side facing her son, head on her hand. He lay on his back with his hands under his head, elbows sticking outward.

"I was back in Dublin at school. The fire alarm went off but when I went into the hall, I saw someone I did not recognize coming straight toward me with a knife. I turned and starting running away but he was catching up. I pushed some of my friends in front of him as I kept going. Then, ahead was a second guy but I couldn't see his face. He had a mask. I turned and went into an empty classroom but it wasn't a classroom, it was the dog shed out back. They were catching up with me so I released the dogs. The young ones ran to me but Nikita and Sasha went straight for the bad guys and took them down. They were growling and snarling. I could hear it. Then Jim came and made the dogs stop and sit. That's when I woke up."

Ashley said, "I'm no psychologist but it sounds like you don't know who to trust. And it sounds like you have a lot of fear hiding inside of your mind. How do you feel now?"

"The nightmare is fading and talking about it helps. Thanks for being here for me, mom."

"I can't promise this, but I always want to be here for you. You are the most important person in my life. That's not going to change. Come over here." She wrapped her arms around her precious boy holding him until he began to relax. She heard his breathing slow and get steady. She decided it was time to whisper a prayer for them. She realized this was the first prayer she offered in many years. Soon, she joined him in peaceful sleep.

***

Tiny Olf checked into a hotel two blocks from the office of Carla Franconi in Annapolis. Tiny earned his nickname because of his diminutive size. At five foot, three inches, no one thought he would have much to offer the world. But his lifelong friend, Benjamin Maguire saw potential when he realized how much "street smarts" the boy, his buddy, possessed. The first time was when the two were shoplifting candy from a small grocery in the neighborhood they lived. When the owner grabbed Maguire by the collar, Tiny calmly explained it was the kid walking up ahead who was the real thief. When the store owner confronted the other kid and found eight packets of Kool-Aid in his jacket pocket, Maguire and Olf were free to go, still possessing the candy in their own pockets. Later, Tiny explained, "I set the kid up. I put the Kool-Aid in his pocket – insurance!"

As Maguire grew his crime world business, Tiny was there offering whatever was needed. Advice, contacts, or just common sense, Tiny had them all. Maguire trusted him, totally.

Tiny decided the best way to find out who was behind the Franconi offer, was to bug her office. But once he understood she was just one of many attorneys in the employ of Alex Engel, he changed his target to the senior partner. Tiny had already discovered the cleaning crew entered the building at nine each evening. Tiny would simply follow them in the building, place a bug under Engel's desk and then return to listen.

That night as the cleaning crew's van pulled up to the service entrance, Tiny stepped from the shadows. He picked the lock in fifteen seconds knowing the security system would already be turned off. He quietly made his way to the top floor listening intently to noise trumpeting from the vacuums. With gloves on, he went directly to the main office suite. Door plaque said *Alex Engel.* In three minutes, Tiny was back in the alley, task complete. He walked back to his hotel passing several people walking on the street. He took little notice of the old homeless woman he passed just outside the hotel's front door.

Venessa White got a good look at Tiny's face. She liked using the homeless woman costume. With her plain looks, it worked every time. She returned to her old Dodge Minivan. She pulled her tablet from under the front seat and went through the photos she had earlier downloaded of the known associates of Benjamin Maguire. As she went through the photos, from the edge of her vision, she saw movement. By the time she turned her head, whatever had been there, was gone. It was the fourth photo. She blew up the image of Tiny Olf. *Got ya!*

Every player had a task to complete before evening rest could begin. Tiny needed to contact Maguire. Venessa would call Power, who would in turn call Engel. Engel would wait until morning to notify Franconi.

Inside the flower delivery van across from the minivan, Agent Fry asked Agent Paul, "Did you get the pictures?"

"I got pictures of White as a homeless woman, and pictures of Olf entering the building of Alex Engel."

"Our tech guys are reporting they're picking up a listening device planted in Engel's office. Funny, it's only a few inches from the one we planted."

"Do you want to make the call, or shall I?"

Fry sent a text to Special Agent Roland Wilkins. *Things are in place.*

Within the hour, Federal Prosecutor Alice Williamson had received a warrant from a federal judge to wiretap the offices of Engel and Power. She thought to herself, *Things might just work out.*

***

Jamal was eating a bowl of cereal when Jim came in the back door. Jim said, "You're up early today. What time did Wendy tell you she'd be here this morning?"

"Late morning. She wants us to keep going over the story she gave us."

"Heard you took your first test, yesterday. How did it go?"

Jamal gave no answer. He just rolled his eyes.

"That bad? Where is your mother?"

"She's sleeping in."

"I found something for you. Remember we were talking about your father playing football for Ohio State?" He walked over to the refrigerator and pulled a magazine off the top handing it to Jamal.

"Every year, the college football magazine put out an issue before the season starts highlighting the top players. Take a look at page twenty-two."

A full-page picture of Juan Malik Adams. On the facing page was his name, statistics from his junior season, along with a brief description of his potential impact for the coming season. "This article was written before his senior season. Have you ever seen this?"

"No." Jamal forgot about his food and was reading the information and gazing down at the picture of the man he did not know. "Can I keep this for a few days?"

"Few days, you can keep it. I'm glad I hung onto it. That magazine has been around the world with me. Never thought I'd meet his family."

"Thanks. I'm taking this upstairs. I'll be right back."

Jamal asked, "Are you working the dogs this morning?"

"I planned to start in about ten minutes. Want to help?"

"You bet."

"Once you finish eating, go let the dogs out into the pen. Grab the six leashes. I'll meet you there."

Jamal was running with the pack when Jim joined him. "Enough running for now." He clicked and the six came and sat by his feet. "Today, I want to use the obstacle course. Help me set it up."

When they finished, there was a tunnel, balance beam, a long teeter totter and a line of orange cones. Jim said, "This is how it's done. Nikita, come." The dog went to Jim and sat. He pointed to the tunnel. The dog ran to the opening, and crawled through to the opposite end. Jim pointed to the teeter totter and the dog slowly began to walk up the incline until it shifted from the weight, then Nikita ran down the board to the balance beam. He jumped up and carefully crossed the four-inch board, three feet off the ground.

Approaching the cones, Nikita ran like a skier down a slalom course. Jim then reversed with Nikita so the dog did the course the opposite direction. Jim praised the dog before taking Sasha through the same exercise.

"Nimitz has never done the course. Take him to the tunnel and see if you can get him to go through."

Jamal thought for a minute. He took the dog to the opening of the tunnel and had him lay down. Then the boy went to the opposite end where he laid on his stomach and looked through the tunnel at the dog. When he called Nimitz, the dog ran around the tunnel and jumped on the prone human.

"Nice try," said Jim. "Try using treats."

Jamal started over with the dog at the opening. He let the pup smell the treat but did not give it. Then, Jamal went to the opposite end and showed it. He pitched the treat into the tunnel and called, "Come." When the dog hesitated, he threw a second treat into the tube. The dog crawled in to get the tasty morsels. Jamal placed another just inside his end and the dog continued until he exited where he gave one more treat and much praise. Jamal had a big smile as he looked toward Jim. He was smiling, too.

"Good job, kid."

The next half hour was filled with getting the four younger dogs familiar with the obstacles. By the end of the session, all four were following Nikita through the course.

"Jim. This is all important, I get it. How do you teach the dogs to attack?"

"Next time. Now you best get inside for Wendy or she might attack me. I'll get the dogs back in their kennels."

Ashley, Wendy and Lisa were sitting at the table enjoying coffee as Jamal entered the room. "Morning everyone," he said.

"Ashley was telling me about your nightmare. How are you feeling this morning?"

"I'm fine."

Wendy responded. "It takes your mind about forty-eight hours to process current memories and move them into your long-term memory. Sometimes it causes a conflict. That is where most nightmares start."

"Let's head upstairs to get started."

Dr. Florence gave the test results to each. It was clear they were unhappy by their scores, both under sixty. "I want you to review the test for the next fifteen minutes. Read every question again, and the answer you listed. Say to yourself *right* for the ones you got and say the word *wrong* for the others. It will help your mind reinforce what you have learned."

The following hour was used to review with the psychologist their new histories as she asked questions and they took time to answer. *They are making progress* she told herself.

After lunch, Wendy administered a second timed test. She could tell from body language the stress of the test was less than the previous day. When the test was complete, Wendy had news for the Wilsons. As she handed each a thin packet of materials, she said, "We have chosen your new destination. It's an area called Pines in Dade City, Florida."

"Where is Dade City, Florida," wondered Ashley. "I'm not very familiar with Florida."

"Is it anywhere close to Mickey?" Jamal joked.

"Dade City is a small community of about sixty-five hundred residents located maybe forty miles northeast of Tampa. And, it's about the same distance to Mickey."

"Oh boy, oh boy! Can we go see Mickey, mom? Can we, please?" clapping his hands like a toddler.

"Go sit down," as Ashley took a play swing at her son's behind.

Wendy continued, "If you look at the information, you will see photos of the house you will occupy. The address is listed for you on White Fir Road. It's a lower middle-class area, working families with a fair number of seniors. The area is well integrated so you will fit in. You'll need to get familiar with the information about the area. Jamal, you will be attending Pasco High School. It's about a mile from your house. You'll be able to walk to school. Wendy, a job has been secured for you as a clerk with the US Post Office in Dade City. You will be working in the back. You might occasionally be on the front desk but for the most part, you'll be out of the public eye."

"Will I have an opportunity to look for other employment, eventually?"

"You will have a contact with the US Marshall's office who can work with you on those type things as time moves forward. Do you have feelings about working for the Postal Service?"

"It doesn't seem like a job for a college business major, that's all."

"Remember this is about keeping you in a safe environment. And to be honest, a place to hide in plain sight. And the pay is decent.

Lots of military veterans choose to work for the post office."

"What about the high school, what can you tell me?" Jamal questioned.

"There are about seventeen hundred students. How does that compare to Dublin?"

"About the same."

"I suggest you check out the school on the internet. There is information in your packet on Dade City. And, high school football is huge in that part of Florida. Many kids have started out playing football in the area and end up playing in college and even into the pros."

Ashley stole a look at her son to see how he reacted to the football comments. But he just nodded his head, saying nothing.

Wendy said, "I think I'll take these tests downstairs and score them so you see how you did. Besides, my boyfriend wants to take me out this weekend. So, I made an appointment to get my hair done tonight."

Ashley said, "Boyfriend, do tell. Anything you want to share with me? This is the first time you've mentioned a boyfriend."

"Move along. Nothing to see here. And don't mind the man behind the curtain." Then she laughed all the way down the stairs.

"Mom, I need to show you something." Jamal went into his room where he picked up the football magazine. "Jim gave me this today. Page. . ."

"I know, page twenty-two."

Jamal had an incredulous look on his face. "Mom, really? Were you ever going to share this information with me?"

"Well, to be honest, do you remember the big, black trunk in the basement I wouldn't let you explore?"

"Yea."

"I had a copy of this and a lot of other things about your father that I was saving for you. Now, poof, gone in the fire. I wasn't trying to keep you in the dark. I was waiting until you wanted to know about your father."

"Well, I want to know! You want to tell me now?"

***

Chapter Nine

Malik Adams was just falling asleep during his morning time of Bible reading when a guard's voice interrupted. "You have a visitor."

Adams got to his feet, slipping on the sandals. He placed his hands behind his back for the handcuffs to be placed on his large wrists. The guard commented, "Your exercise program is working. Your muscles are getting more definition."

"Helps keep me busy," he replied. When he arrived at the interview room, Adams was surprised to see Assistant Prosecutor Butcher accompanied by two women he did not recognize. Each was dressed in business attire.

Butcher said, "Guard, you can remove the cuffs." Once the guard left, Butcher said, "This is local prosecutor Wanda Grimes, nodding to the young African-American woman, and this is Patty Lee. She is a court recorder."

Grimes took over the conversation. "Mr. Adams, the federal judge has asked the city to take over the Driving Under the Influence violation. The Judge wants that issue resolved before having you deal with the federal charges pending against you. Do you wish to have an attorney present for this hearing?"

"No."

"Mr. Adams, you were cited under statute 3802 (a)(1) Incapable of Safe Driving. This is punishable by probation of six months and a fine of three hundred dollars. This is a misdemeanor. Do you understand this violation and the penalty?"

"Yes."

"How do you plead on this single charge?"

"Guilty."

"Your probation will be dated from the day of your arrest since you have been incarcerated. You will receive a letter from the court for you to pay your fine. Do you understand these penalties?"

"Yes."

"Thank you, Mr. Adams."

"I would like to speak to Mr. Butcher alone, please."

The women gathered their things and stood at the door until the guard opened for them.

Butcher asked, "I know this was a little unusual but the judge wanted this out of the way."

"It's fine. Do you have any word on Janet and the boy?"

"I spoke with the Marshall's office yesterday. They are doing fine. They have chosen their new identities and are working with staff to assume the identities. Also, they now know where they will be relocated to. Of course, I can't share any of this information with you."

"You told me before some intelligence was intercepted about someone trying to find them. Any change in that situation?"

"The FBI investigated and stopped the threat. However, we have now learned a second investigator has been contacted about trying to locate them."

"Is this coming from Montie?"

"I won't answer that question. Sorry."

"Just keep them safe. It's all I'm asking."

"We are. The Marshall's office assures me they are being handled by their top team."

"What's happening with the case against Montie?"

"They requested a continuance into January which was granted."

"Is Maguire being held?"

"No. The judge granted bail."

"Shit! That means he won't stop coming after them."

"We know that."

***

Bradley Carmichael received an inquiry about his services through an ad he placed on the Dark Web. It wasn't that his surveillance service was illegal but law enforcement wanted him kept away from anything they were investigating or hiding. He tried to "weed out" the wacko requests by demanding a five-hundred-dollar fee before he would consider taking on a job. It helped but just last week a guy paid the fee wanting Carmichael to send a drone over certain coordinates in the southwest. He wanted pictures over Area 51. What a moron!

Since Carmichael was former military, he knew better than to mess with military targets. They had much more sophisticated equipment than he could procure. He wanted to stay in business.

There was plenty of business for him just from private detectives. He even got a few jobs from small municipalities around Las Vegas. He wasn't rich, but he was doing okay. Last month a rural county in northwest Nevada hired him to help search for a lost child. It was an easy thousand dollars and it made him feel good, too.

He was pretty sure this latest inquiry was from a private eye. The message accompanying the payment was short and cryptic. But the money was deposited into his account via Pay Pal, just the way he requested. The requestor wanted to meet with him face to face at a casino bar in Vegas; ten o'clock tonight.

Carmichael arrived ten minutes early and took a seat at the crowded bar. A man tapped him on the shoulder. "Carmichael? I'm Larsen."

"I have a client who is interested in your services of surveillance."

"Before I agree to take the offer, I need to know more about the purpose of the job," said Carmichael.

"This is a case of a run-away wife with a teen aged son. My client wants to find their location. What he is asking of you is photo confirmation. Then he will take it from there."

"Sounds simple enough. Where?"

"He believes they are staying at one of four locations in Kentucky."

"Kentucky, that will affect my fee, greatly. Has he looked for someone closer? It would be much cheaper."

"He turned this over to me. I checked around and found your

reputation to be excellent. So I'm coming to you. Larsen slid a business card to Carmichael."

"Let me get some additional information." When Carmichael and Larson walked out of the casino, they each got what they wanted. Carmichael would get five thousand for the trip to the Bluegrass State plus two thousand for the photos of each location. There was also a bonus for actual photos of the woman and kid, and for getting the job done within thirty days.

***

Montie was feeling confident. He had just over three months to find Adam's family to make the son of a bitch suffer. He cared about little else. When the email arrived from Larsen, Montie felt even better. *Safe house, won't be safe when I hit it.* But he knew better than to share this part of the plan with his father. He would find something wrong with the plan. He always found fault with plans. *When the old man kicks the bucket, this place will run a lot differently.* Montie envisioned himself with a big Cuban cigar, sitting in his new office, feet up and Rosalee sitting over on the couch in a yellow sundress, low cut, lots of cleavage. The image made him smile.

Tiny wasn't back in the office and Montie wondered what was going on. Tiny only went out on real important matters. The man had no family and no interests outside of the Maguire business. *What isn't the old man telling me,* he wondered? His desk phone rang startling the younger Maguire from his day dream.

It was Yapelski on the phone. He was a low-level snitch Montie used on occasion. "Mr. Maguire, I have some information you might find interesting. I don't want to tell you over the phone. Can

I come by?"

"How soon can you get here?"

"I'm outside right now."

Yapelski had yellow teeth from too many cigarettes. Montie was sure the guy was going to die from cancer any day. He coughed up a wad of phlegm and spit it into a dirty rag. "I found a way for you to get to Adams." He had Montie's full attention.

"I know this guy who is locked up in the same place as Adams. He was a nurse until he got caught stealing pain pills. He works in the prison infirmary. He said if we can get Adams to the infirmary, he'll take him out. He said it would be an honor since the Maguire family has been good to him."

Yapelski went on. "This guy said his cellmate works in the kitchen. He would be willing to put laxatives in Adam's food. Enough to send him to the infirmary."

Montie responded, "I don't like it. Too many hands involved. Too many places something could go wrong. What if the wrong inmate gets the food? There's no guarantee it would get to Adams. Out, just get out. I don't want to hear from you again unless you've got a better plan. Dumb ass."

Montgomery Maguire knew he had one chance to get to Adams. If that failed, there would never be another opportunity.

Benjamin Maguire walked into Montie's office. "Who was that?"

"He's a snitch I know. He thought he figured out a way to get to Adams. I told him to hit the road."

"How did he know you would be interested in getting to Adams?"

Montie had not thought about that. "I don't know, I didn't tell him."

"Have you told anyone?"

"Not outside of this office."

"Somebody is bugging us. Has to be a bug somewhere."

Teddy Power dialed Yapelski. "Good job. There will be a little reward in this for you. Expect your reward, real soon." Later that evening there was a little incident at the Acme Motel where Yapelski was staying. Someone got in his room and slit his throat and took his cell phone. The police found no leads and no suspects in the murder.

***

Rosalee was doing laundry when her secret cell phone buzzed with a text message. *Llámame*

This was unprecedented. The handler had never asked her to call. She stepped out onto the back porch away from the others in the house. She dialed, when the connection was made, she said, "Es Rosalee."

"English. The plan needs to move quicker. Can you move things along?"

"He seems afraid or maybe just careful."

"Use your atributos físicos. Understand?"

"Yes."

It was Tuesday, Montie would be visiting the bar in the afternoon. Rosalee's shift at the casino bar was uneventful. Only a handful of customers entered the bar and most were around the lunch hour. She spotted Montie enter the bar at three o'clock. She met the large man with her sweetest smile. He responded in kind as he took his usual table near the bandstand. Over the weeks since she first met him, she had learned bits and pieces about him from the others working in the building. Then she supplemented the information with things he had volunteered to her. "Mr. Montie, it is nice to see you, again. What can I get for you today?"

"Afternoon, Rosalee. I will take a lite beer and an order of nachos. A little extra hot sauce would be nice."

"I'll be right back." She walked toward the kitchen and waited for the order stopping at the bar to get the lite beer in a glass from Willie. As she delivered to the table she said, "I could make you some real nachos and I make my own sauce too."

"I bet you could."

"No, you don't understand. I would like to make nachos for you."

Her words caught his full attention.

"Are you still off at four?"

"Yes. But these walls have eyes everywhere."

"I've noticed. I would really like to sample your nachos and some hot sauce, too. When you get done with work, walk to the casino across the street. Go to the second floor of the parking garage, and I'll pick you up in my Mercedes. Interested?"

"You do not know how much I am looking forward to being by your side."

At four-ten, Rosalee slid into the front seat of Montie's roadster. Montie drove southwest on Atlantic Avenue past the multitude of high-rise ocean front condominiums. At North Jerome, Montie turned right and continued on Margate, heading towards Northfield. He eventually pulled into the parking lot of the Holiday Inn.

Montie turned to Rosalee, "Are you certain this is what you want, I certainly want to be with you."

She leaned to him placing her hand upon his leg and whispered into his ear, "I am so ready for you. You will experience real hot sauce!"

***

Tiny checked in with Mr. Maguire. "The listening devices are in place. In the morning I will be monitoring and recording the conversations from Ms. Franconi's lead attorney. His name is Alex Engel. You should be able to have him checked out from your end. When I realized she worked for Engel's law firm, I decided to bypass her and try to get the information through him."

"That makes sense. Plan to stay through the day today. After the office closes this afternoon, pack it in and come back. Keep the recording going. Never know when a bit of information might be helpful."

"That's what I will do."

Teddy Power was choosing his words carefully as he spoke with Alex Engel about the information, he received from Venessa White. "I'm confident your offices have been bugged, so be careful of what you say over the next couple days. I need to decide how much I want Maguire to learn. Might be a good time to spread some misinformation. If you shut off all conversation, Maguire's going to be suspicious. He is a cagey old man."

Engel asked, "What if I called one of the competitors. Make it sound like that competitor was the one making the bid. Then you could sit back and watch the action without trouble coming your way."

"You're making the assumption Maguire is going to be bringing some heat to the buyer."

"Isn't that what you're assuming, too?"

"That's exactly what I suspect. Now let me see. Who do I want to implicate? Who's been a pain in my ass, lately? Hmmm. I know. The Cordova family in Cleveland. I used to be able to work with them reasonably, but recently they have tripled the cost of heroin and I know the wholesale price has been steady. Seems to me everything changed when Enzo turned the day-to-day operation over to his brother, Butchy. Serve 'em right to have to spend some of that profit to fix a warehouse or distribution system. If I work this right, maybe I could start an old-fashioned war among the families. That could be interesting. Haven't seen an old family war for years."

Engel said, "Teddy, call me early in the morning to tell me exactly how you want me to play this. You know how to reach me?"

"I'll do that. Say seven am?"

Special Agent Paul took the headphones off and rubbed his ears. "Fry, can you believe what we are hearing?"

"This is like a soap opera. I'm making an audio file of the

conversation and sending it to Wilkins. Not sure how they're going to react to all this."

"Depends on whether they want a war. There are always winners and losers in war. Hard to tell who will survive and who we want to be left standing at the end." Half hour later, a message was received from Wilkins. *Keep listening. Getting interesting, now.*

***

It was ten o'clock when Montie walked with Rosalee back to his Mercedes. Both were pleased with their performances for very different reasons. Montie showed the woman how strongly his feelings were for her beauty and sensuality. He had not felt this satisfied in years. This was not just physical; this went far beyond to almost a spiritual level. He was restraining himself not to simply pick Rosalee up and return to the room and its bliss. He knew she had to get back to her parent's house before it was too late.

Rosalee had enjoyed the physical lovemaking, but more than that, she was moving the relationship in the direction it needed to move. She had a job to do. Under different circumstances, she could have feelings for this man, real feelings.

***

Two days of driving were required for Carmichael to get from Vegas to eastern Kentucky with his equipment. He was able to get everything into his Toyota Sienna minivan. He brought two drones as well as various cameras and lens to find the missing mom and teenaged son. He decided to start at the safe house in Inez, Kentucky then work back to the west. He had good maps on his computer. He already knew where to set up to monitor the drone's surveillance. He would begin the operation using the infrared lens to check for body heat in the house. His equipment was sensitive enough to pick up each human signature in any normally constructed building. He remembered using this exact camera and software in Iraq to track some high value terror threats. He was able to count how many were in the house, even the three in the basement. His intel led to a successful capture of three Iraqi's who now called Guantanamo Naval base prison, home.

It was two fifteen in the morning as he drove through the sleepy village of Inez. He expected to see not a single moving person or vehicle. He pulled his van to the base of the community water tower and set up his equipment. It was always a challenge to put the drone up on a dark night in an unfamiliar place, but that is precisely why he had night-vision goggles for himself. He put the drone up and circled the water tower to get a feel for the night air currents. Then, satisfied there would be no surprises, he entered the coordinates for the safe house. He made sure the drone was high enough so its propeller noise would not be noticed. He programmed it to fly at five hundred feet. No one could see it at night, and in fact, at that height, it would be a miracle to see it during the day.

The infrared images came up on his computer screen. It appeared there were two sleeping individuals in the house. He circled to the south going counter clockwise. From every angle, there were only two people. This was not the place anyone was hiding. He recorded the video feed for Larsen, brought the drone back, packed up his stuff and decided to catch some sleep before he headed to Big Hill, Kentucky. He would send the copied video in the morning as an email attachment. *Streaming would be better* he thought to himself.

***

The day started out warm with dew on the pasture grass. The horses began grazing at dawn. The hired hands were busy cleaning stalls. Jim was sitting on the back steps with coffee while Jamal was working with the dogs on the obstacle course. The boy was pleased with the progress the canines were making with his oversight, and so was Jim. *The kid's a natural.*

Ashley was inside using the laundry equipment. It was the one service the safe house did not do for the clients. Ashley did not mind. There was something calming about doing domestic tasks. She had just started the second load of laundry which today was linens and towels. She was going over her new history as she did her task.

On the back steps, Jim's cell phone rang. "Hello."

"This is Smitty. Heads up. Somebody is trying to send up a drone over Big Hill."

"I'll call you right back."

He shouted, "Jamal, safe room, now." The boy ran at full speed into the room in the barn, shut the door, threw the handle and hit the red button. His heart was racing as he went to the monitors to see what was happening.

Lisa had heard the warning Jim gave and ushered Ashley from the laundry area to the safe room where she followed the procedures, just like Jamal. She too went to the monitor to see what was happening.

The Marshalls were intently looking at their screens for the source of the alert. Nothing yet. Then Jim's phone rang a second time. "Yea."

"Smitty. Come to my place. There is no problem but get here as soon as you can."

Jim got Nikita and Sasha into the pickup and left for Smitty's house. He pulled into the gravel drive and saw Smitty standing down the road about two hundred yards with his shotgun pointed at a guy standing outside a minivan. The guy was unknown but appeared to be holding a drone.

"Hey Smitty, what's going on?"

"I was standing out on the front porch when I saw this guy getting out with the drone from the van. I don't appreciate anyone spying on my hill."

Jim pushed his panic button three times in quick succession which would signal no imminent threat and would summon one of the Marshalls. Jim walked to the drone owner making certain he never got in the shotgun's path.

"You might want to stay calm. My friend is a crack shot with that twelve gauge."

Bradley Carmichael did not appreciate looking at a loaded shotgun aimed at his midsection. "Who are you guys?"

Jim answered, "Why don't you tell us who you are first? Law enforcement will be here in less than two minutes."

"What did I do?"

"You are about to fly a drone over government property, which is a crime unless you have a permit."

"I didn't know this was public land. I saw the No Trespassing sign so I was going to stay on the edge of the road."

Marshall Waker arrived on a four by four. He took charge of the questioning. He started by identifying himself as a US Marshall; showing his badge.

Carmichael asked, "Can I put my drone back in the van so I don't have to hold it?"

"No," said Waker, "place it on the ground next to your feet. Now show me some identification."

Carmichael put the drone down and removed his wallet showing his Nevada driver's license.

Waker looked at the identification making sure the photo was the man standing in front of him. Then he called the control room and transmitted the information to his Partner. "Now, tell me Mr. Carmichael, what are you doing in Kentucky with a drone."

Pausing for a moment to consider his options, Carmichael decided the best way was just to be honest about his presence. "I was hired by a private investigator to search for a woman and her teenaged son who ran away from her husband. The investigator heard about my drone business and offered me the job of trying to find the missing pair. He gave me the location of several places he thought might be safe houses. I was in the process of checking out a place on the opposite side of this hill."

Waker spoke again to the other Marshall conveying the information he received. Tutor responded, "Bradley Carmichael is the owner of a drone investigation business in Las Vegas. He is a former US Army drone tech. The story he is relaying could be true but Washington wants him to be detained for questioning by the FBI."

Waker said, "Mr. Carmichael, a local sheriff's deputy will be here in five minutes. You will be detained until the FBI has a chance to question you. Do you understand?"

"I understand, but the FBI, really? Am I under arrest?"

"No. We are part of a federal task force. Once it is determined what you know, and if you are willing to help in our investigation, I'm confident you will be able to walk away. Now, if you would like to place the drone in your vehicle, go ahead. But do not get into the vehicle."

Carmichael placed the drone into the back seat and closed the door just as the Sheriff's cruiser pulled up followed by a tow truck. The deputy placed Carmichael in his car and the tow truck loaded the minivan on its platform. Then they headed to the county jail to await the FBI.

Jim smiled at Smitty. "Thanks buddy." He introduced Waker to Smitty before the agent returned to Vincennes. "Smitty, how do you feel about a morning beer?"

***

Chapter Ten

It took two days before the listening device planted in the office of Alex Engel provided the name of the Cordova family in Cleveland. Benjamin Maguire had no reason to believe he was being played. "Montie, come in my office," he ordered. With Montie's presence, the elder man continued. "I have learned the Cordova family has its eye on our business interests and actually has made an attempt to buy us out. I am not happy with this situation."

"You know, pop, I expect to someday be sitting in your chair running our operations. I'm glad to hear you have no interest in selling us out."

"I want to give a proactive response to the Cordova's. Kind of like the Navy puts a shell across the bow of enemy ships." Montie nodded in understanding. "But with your recent legal issues, I'm reluctant to ask you to head up our response."

Montie became livid with instant anger. "What do you mean by that? Suddenly you don't trust me? That is bullshit! There is nobody working for you better at retribution than me, and you know it's true. I'll take care of this. When I'm done, they will know they should never mess with us again."

The older Maguire did not respond. He just watched as his only heir got to his feet, and went to his own office without another word. Benjamin Maguire bowed his head and just shook it even though no one would see his action. *The boy is digging his own grave. He doesn't listen to anything I've said to him.*

Montie sat at his desk for the next fifteen minutes thinking of an appropriate response. He had dealt with the Cordova family in the past and had a natural dislike for them and their methods. The two mob families tended to use the same drug pipeline from Columbia. Occasionally, their paths would cross which caused certain difficulties for each side. Montie knew, that was where he would hit them. Pipeline.

He picked up the phone to call his chief logistics man, Carlos Montez. "Carlos, I need you to carry out a little action. I want you to set up a government interception of a shipment of drugs to the Cordova family. I need you to do it in a way that hurts their finances, maybe a few mules. And, I need you to do it in a way that they know it is coming from me. Can you do that?"

"Of course, boss. When does this have to happen, how soon?"

"Let me just say, the sooner the better."

"It will be done by the weekend."

"Good."

Thirty minutes later, Federal Prosecutor, Alice Williamson and assistant, Jack Butcher were listening to the recording of the call from Maguire's office to Montez. Williamson said, "Montgomery Maguire just keeps digging a deeper hole for himself. If we get him on this, plus the attempt to find our witness protection family, he's going away for a long time. Get a hold of the FBI. So, they can keep tabs on this. And, by the way, is there a deposition from Carmichael, yet?"

Butcher said, "the agent interrogating Carmichael is still working out the details to assure his cooperation."

"What's he asking?"

"He wants his military record wiped clean so he can pick up jobs with government agencies."

"That doesn't sound too difficult."

"Department of Defense is not keen to help us. Carmichael pissed off some Lieutenant Colonel who is on the White House promotion list."

"Keep me informed."

Meanwhile, back in Kentucky, Bradley Carmichael was trading information with the FBI for the one thing he wanted more than anything else. He was a loyal soldier. He just wanted his reputation repaired. He realized it could mean some better paying jobs down the road.

Special Agent Roland Wilkins stepped into the hallway outside the room where Carmichael was waiting to answer the call from FBI headquarters in Washington DC. He returned, "Carmichael, the deal has been approved. Now, who was your contact?"

He reached into his pants pocket and pulled out the business card he received from Larsen only days earlier. "And one other thing," Carmichael said, "I didn't give you permission to search my vehicle, but now that we have a deal, I'll give you a copy of the video I sent to Larsen. Naturally, his email is active and should help you find him."

"I don't think that will be a big problem, but thanks for your cooperation."

Carmichael never knew the identities of the mom and son he was seeking nor the real story behind their situation, and it did not matter. He also never got paid for the trip to Kentucky. A small sacrifice for a bigger payday in the future. But when Larsen filed his report saying the drone guy was missing, Benjamin McGuire was not a happy man.

***

When Marshall Waker returned to Vincennes, he arranged to open both safe rooms so the Wilson's could return to their tasks. He made sure they understood Jim would answer their questions when he returned. Both Ashley and Jamal had watched the monitors with great interest and with adrenaline pumping through their veins.

"Mom, did you see anything?"

She just shook her head. "Let's ask Jim when he gets here. See what he will tell us."

"I'm going back out with the dogs."

Drinking a beer with Smitty took most of thirty minutes. When he pulled the pickup behind the house, Jamal was ready for an answer. He put the dogs in their kennels and went inside to find Jim, Lisa and Ashley sitting at the table.

Jim started, "You two did great in getting into the safe rooms. Any issues while you were in the rooms?" Both shook their heads. "Well, that's good. Here's what happened."

Jim relayed the story of Carmichael attempting to fly a drone over the compound to take pictures. Smitty, the neighbor was the hero of the story. The FBI was interrogating the man to get more information. Jamal could feel himself settling down from the earlier rush of adrenaline. All this excitement before ten in the morning.

As Dr. Wendy was not scheduled to return before late afternoon, Jamal wanted to return to working with the dogs. The pups were excited to go through their training regimen with the young man. Jim came out of the house to watch. "Jamal, do you want to learn about training dogs to attack?"

"I've been waiting for you to teach me. I sure do enjoy working with dogs. This has been the best part of staying here."

"I can tell you enjoy this and you have natural ability. I'm going to show you what the end product looks like. Then I'll show you the parts that need to be in place for a dog to understand what you are instructing them to do. Get the pups to sit and stay while I get the equipment from the shed."

When Jim returned, he flipped a braided yarn ball with an attached handle to Jamal. He also had an overstuffed sleeve under his arm which he put on his own arm. Nikita was instructed to sit and stay across the pen from Jim. The dog was clearly at full alert, ears up, watching every move of his alpha pack member. Jim slid the sleeve over his right arm, held it out horizontal to the ground and said, "Target!"

In an instant, the dog was running at full speed across the pen until he launched toward the sleeve clamping his teeth around the sleeve and trying to rip Jim's arm from his body with all the strength the dog possessed. When Jim said, "Sit," the dog stopped and followed the command releasing the bite grip.

"Wow, that was impressive," said Jamal. "If I was a bad guy and saw Nikita coming at me, I think I might poop my pants."

Jim said, "It's about twenty-five yards across the pen. Nikita can cross the space in less than two and a quarter seconds. No human can move that fast. And when the dog hits the target with its full weight of eighty-five pounds, it can take down a human weighing over three hundred pounds. Nikita will not release until the handler gives the command. Now, I want you to experience the sleeve." He removed the padded protection from his arm and tossed it to Jamal. "Put it on. Go stand on the other side of the pen but not too close to the fence."

"That's great," Jim said. "I'm going to command Sasha to attack. She's about ten pounds lighter than Nikita. But I warn you, be prepared to get hit. Understand? Ready?" With Jamal's nod, Jim said, "Sasha." Then he made a motion with his right arm like a chop of an axe. Sasha hit Jamal with so much force that he lost his footing and went down on his back. Sasha began to pull and tug on the sleeve with such force Jamal felt helpless until Jim called, "Sasha, sit." That quickly, it was all over. Jim walked over to Jamal and offered him a hand to get to his feet.

Jamal exclaimed, "I think I was hit by a truck! You didn't even give a command to go, or anything."

"That's because a dog working in combat must be able to move silently. The handler must know how to command the dog with as little vocal sound as possible. It can mean the difference between life and death for both the dog and the handler. I want to ask you a question."

"Okay."

"If you were a bad guy and you saw Sasha coming at you, would you have enough time to raise a weapon and shoot the dog before the dog takes you down?"

"I don't think so."

"Possibly a well-trained soldier could get a round off but for the majority of those who confront these dogs, there is no time. There are many recorded incidents of dogs taking a direct round and still taking the shooter down."

"So, how do you train these pups to get to this point?" asked Jamal.

"You have to think of it in terms of the various parts involved. First, the handler must have command of the dog."

"You mean, like sit, stay, down?"

"That's right. And that's why all the work I do with the dogs seems to be so repetitious. You go over the basics until the dog understands there is no hesitation."

"So, the first thing is *sit*. Then *stay*, then the attack command. Right? But with Nikita you didn't say *Attack*, you said *Target*."

"That's the code word I use with Nikita. With Sasha, the word is *farm*. That's on purpose so I don't lose control if I have both dogs working together. But the visual command is the same for both dogs."

Jamal asked, "How do I start with Nimitz? Is it with the yarn ball?"

Jim responded, "Let me show you how to start. Throw me the ball." Jim then commanded all the dogs to lay down. He called Nimitz who followed Jim away from the group. Jim stopped the growing pup with a *sit* and *stay* command. Jim walked on about ten feet, then turned and faced Nimitz. He gripped the ball by the handle holding his arm to his side letting the ball swing, easily. "What you do next is play a game of tug with the dog, like this."

Nimitz was intently watching the ball swinging from Jim's hand. "Nimitz, come" and the dog ran to Jim where he allowed the dog to sniff the ball until the dog was interested. Then Nimitz grabbed the ball with his teeth and instinctively began to try to pull the toy away. Jim held on for about five seconds before releasing the stick. The dog shook the toy and started to run away when Jim commanded, "Sit, drop. That is exactly what you do, over and over until the dog understands to come from anywhere in the pen to get the ball. It's a game for the dog. Eventually you then introduce the sleeve, and finally, the padded body suit. Remember, always let the dog take the toy from you."

"Take your time, but use the ball with each of the pups ten times today." Jamal found it was a bit slow getting the dogs to want to play with the toy, but by the tenth repetition, each wanted more. He would start repeating the lesson, tomorrow.

***

Illegal drugs cross the southern border of the United States using various modes of transportation. The most expensive way to bring drugs in is on commercial airline service with the cheapest being on the backs of young men called mules, crossing at night. Carlos Montez knew more about being a mule than most DEA agents. When he was fifteen years old, he crossed the border in west Texas making his way to a prearranged location forty miles north of the border in Pecos County. He carried twenty pounds of cocaine packed carefully within his backpack. There were eight mules that night. After the "hand-off" Carlos continued north eventually landing in Oklahoma City.

Four years later, he was working in the drug trafficking business in central Pennsylvania. But with his past, Carlos worked as a roofer during the day. He kept his ears open to other immigrants coming through the area to learn the latest news. He knew routes changed almost daily along with drop off locations but the direction did not vary, much. It was south to north. Juan Rodriquez, a young man from Chihuahua, Mexico had made a number of drug runs before deciding to try his fortune in the States. When he met Carlos, they became business partners and shared experiences. Juan said there was a rumor of a processing location outside the little town of Marfa, Texas. The processing was being done at a ranch raising cattle for hides used in boot making, a major industry in Marfa.

Carlos explained to his partner, they could have a major payday if they could confirm the location to a syndicate in Atlantic City. Juan made inquiries of his family and former compadres. Within hours the exact location was communicated to the Maguires and Montgomery took over the operation. It only required one anonymous contact to the Drug Enforcement Agency before the ranch was raided cutting the supply line of the Cordova family. The loss to the Cordova family was just over eight million dollars in product and the use of the ranch. It was enough to get the attention of the Cordova's. Then Montie sent a pair of used cowboy boots to the family from himself as a gift.

The Cordova's, having no idea why they were targeted by the Maguire family, fire bombed a brothel in Ohio owned by the Maguire's. An eye for an eye. While these events were happening, Teddy Powers smiled knowing his plan worked. The Department of Justice also watched and noted the events and the personnel involved.

Teddy Power decided it was time to make a direct contact to Benjamin Maguire and change his offer. "Benjamin Maguire, Teddy Power. I would like to have a meeting just with you. It was my offer to buy your interests that was brought to you by Carla Franconi and I'd like to have a chance to meet with you, face to face."

"So, it was you! We thought it was the Cordova's."

"I wanted to see how measured your response would be before moving forward."

"I see. Well, I'll meet with you on the condition you let the Cordova family know it was our mistake brought on by you. I don't want a war with them. That helps no one."

"I agree and I will be certain to work out an acceptable deal with them. When can we meet? Someplace neutral. Just you and me."

"How about meeting at Citizen's Bank Stadium in Philly. I know someone with a luxury box we can use. Let me get out my schedule to see when they are playing at home. They have a seven o'clock game on Friday, August 4. Will that work for you?"

"I will see you there."

***

Dr. Wendy Florence could see the stress of being in the safe house was causing negative effects on Ashley Wilson. Dr. Wendy knew isolation could cause problems for people who lost their freedoms, and Ashley was showing those signs. "Ashley, I think you and I need a chance just to talk. Does that interest you?"

"It does. What's the chance we could go somewhere away from

here and have a cup of coffee. These walls are starting to close in."

"Sure. We can do that. We'll leave Jamal here. He likes working with the dogs."

They got into Wendy's Sentra and she drove to a roadside truck stop south of Lexington. As they went, Ashley said little, but seemed to relax watching the scenery pass by. The women took a booth looking out on the parking lot as trucks came and went. Wendy said, "You are coming to the end of this ordeal. How are you feeling about everything?"

"I'm not nearly as fearful as when we first arrived. I think Jim and Lisa and the team have done a great job helping us. And Jamal is settling into his new identity. But I'm still worried about him."

"As the parent, you set the tone for him. If you're calm and relaxed, he will be too. And likewise, when he is stressed, you will be, too. You feed off each other, emotionally."

"Jamal has taken great interest in learning about his father since Jim gave him a bio from an old sports magazine. Now he says, he would like to play football when we get to our new home. And daily he asks me questions about Malik. Sometimes, I can't remember. It's been a long time."

"Makes sense. You closed that part of your past so things will get fuzzy in your memory. But your son is just starting to create his father in his mind. Up until now, his father has been a blank space. He wants to fill that void. Have you thought about ever allowing Jamal to meet his father?"

"I didn't think Malik was interested in us until this started."

"But now, it's the son who wants to know the father. Whole different dynamic. Would you let them visit?"

"If Jamal wants that someday, I don't think I could stop him."

"Ashley, if Jamal decided he wants to meet his father, you will have to be supportive? Anything less than supportive, Jamal will see as you interfering. He could resent you forever."

With the coffee done, the woman rose and returned to the safe house. Dr. Wendy said, "Tomorrow, I'll be back for the final test. Well, I think it should be the final test. You're both so close."

Jamal asked, "Do we leave then?"

Wendy paused, then said, "You need to know there has been discussion about moving you to a different safe house since the drone incident. There is thought the Maguires might be able to pinpoint your location based on the information they have gathered already. I convinced the department to give me a few more days to have you ready to leave."

"There is one last test for the two of you ; not a written test. It will be an interview with two psychologists from headquarters. They do an interview to make sure I have not missed anything in getting you ready for witness protection."

***

The military veterinarian arrived at Vincennes to check out the dogs and horses. Dr. Sin Cho was stationed in Washington DC and travelled widely to check on the many animals in service to the United States government. Jim met the doctor years earlier while he was still in the active military. It was Dr. Cho who recommended

Jim for the training program for both dogs and horses and Jim never forgot the support.

"Dr. Cho, good to see you again. Do you want to start with the horses or with the dogs?" asked Jim. Jamal was standing in the background eavesdropping. "Jamal, come over here and meet the doctor. Dr. Cho, this is Jamal Wilson. He and his mother are guests here at Vincennes. Jamal has a great interest in the dogs and has been working with me in their training."

"Nice to meet you," as he looked up at the tall teenager. "It takes patience to work with animals being trained. Is this something you are interested in doing in the future?"

"Before I came here, I had never thought about it but I enjoy it, very much."

"Well, you should know, the military, and the government, are always looking for talented people interested in working with and training animals. Since you have the interest and seem to have ability, according to Jim, you might want to consider it in your future. Let's go look at the horses," said the doctor.

The three walked first to the west barn. The doctor examined each horse checking for injuries or signs of soreness in the legs or hooves. When the assessment was complete, the vet pointed out two studs and a mare. Those three would be moving on in the next week. But he also pointed out one gelding who would be dropped from the program due to arthritis. "Jim, your crew is taking great care of the horses I've seen so far. Be sure you tell the hands they do a great job."

Jim replied, "Will do, doc."

In the east barn, Dr. Cho expressed concern about the development of the foal. Then he pointed out two mares which would be joining the three from the west barn plus a stud who would be moving on to a different farm for stud service. Jim asked, "I'll be losing seven horses. Will they be replaced, here?"

"I'm not sure what's happening at this point. You know, it's about the military budget. Never know which way the political winds are blowing in Washington. But, just a guess, your horse hotel will probably be full by the first of the year."

"Good to know."

Dr. Cho said, "Let's see the dogs. Have you made up your mind about Nikita?"

Jim said, "It's been a tough decision, but I'm keeping Nikita and Sasha for breeding purposes. Both have such solid temperaments. I'm hoping Sasha can have two more litters in her life. She's a great mom to her pups."

"I think you're being wise. They come from quality bloodlines. You are raising the best Belgians the military has in the program. Bring out the four youngsters and let me watch you work them."

Jim and Jamal released the four from their kennels, then Jim called them to the pen, with Jamal following. Jim put them through their exercises. The dogs looked healthy, smart and fast. Jamal took the four on an unleashed run around the pen. Last they were sent through the obstacle course. Dr. Cho noticed a slight limp in the back leg of Nimitz. He examined each dog finishing with Nimitz. "Jim, I hate to tell you this, but I have to "wash out" Nimitz from the program. It's not hip dysplasia, but there is something wrong in the rear right hip that is causing him some problem. Sorry. The other three appear ready for the next training phase. I'll arrange transportation to Lackland Air Force Base. There's a rumor going around the dogs at Guantanamo are being retired. Who knows, maybe your three will end up in Cuba?"

Jamal was more than anxious about the future of Nimitz, who Jamal loved greatly. "Dr. Cho, what about Nimitz? He is really a good dog. I've been working with him."

"It will be up to Jim."

Jamal turned to Jim with a questioning look. "We'll talk, after the doctor leaves."

When the doctor's vehicle passed through the front gate, Jamal was ready for the "talk."

"You told me before, dogs that fail, you sell to good homes. How much do you get for a dog?"

"Usually twelve hundred dollars."

"Would you consider selling Nimitz to me?"

"I have a feeling you won't be making the final decision."

"I've got some money. Let me see if I can convince mom."

"Good luck! Let me know. I won't sell him before you let me know." Jim broke into a huge smile as Jamal ran to the back door of the house. "Mom!"

***

Benjamin Maguire allowed Teddy Power to arrive first to their meeting place during the Philadelphia Phillies game with the San Diego Padres. Power rose to greet the elderly Maguire. There was no one else present except for two small microphones placed by a technician from the Department of Justice. Even the refreshments were in place before the principals arrived. The luxury box's owner had arranged for the catering to take place midafternoon.

"Mr. Maguire, I did not want to offend you when I sent Carla Franconi to visit your office several weeks ago. I often forget you and I come from different eras in our leadership style of our respective family businesses."

"Explain that statement, Mr. Power."

"Sir, people my age live more by the rule, live and let live. But your generation believes in the mindset of bring the biggest stick to a street fight. Am I making sense?"

"I'm not sure I would say it quite like that, but I understand what you're saying. Can we get to our business?"

"Of course," said Power. "Mr. Maguire, as I see your current position, you have built a very fine business. However, you have one large problem. Your plan of succession is not secure, if I can be frank."

Maguire rose and got a beer for himself. "Would you care for a drink?"

"I will take a cola."

Maguire returned to his seat. "I'm not sure I see my succession plan as a problem."

"With your son's legal issues, you can't be very confident of his ability to succeed you as the head of your business."

"First of all. He is not in custody. Second, he has a gifted legal representative. And third, he is not my only chess piece."

"Now you have my full interest. Could you elaborate at all?" Maguire took a long drink of his beer but remained silent. "I'll take that to mean you're not going to show your hand. Let's move forward."

"No, Mr. Power. Let me say something. The offer you made to buy my business interests was almost fair. If I wanted to get out, I might have negotiated based upon your offer. That however is not my ultimate desire."

"Go on."

"How would you react to a sort of merger between your business interests and mine?"

"What do you propose?"

"There are parts of both of our businesses that have larger rewards but also larger risks. As you have noted, I am no longer a young man, but I am not ready to ride off into the sunset, either. I would propose to sell to you all the parts of my business that are left off the balance sheet submitted annually to the Internal Revenue Service."

Power paused to take in the weight of the offer. "Is there more?" His eyes swung toward the field as the crowd roared.

"Yes, there is. Once we come to a mutually agreed upon figure, you allow me to buy into your legal side business with the dollars you pay to me. According to my research, my off the book's revenue is worth about thirty-two percent of my total business. And that value should be about twenty-two percent of your legal holdings. Are my numbers close?"

"Probably within a percent, one way or the other." Each man took another drink.

Maguire continued, "I'm tired of trying to outsmart the FBI. If I can eliminate the part of my business that catches their interest, I can concentrate on growing my legal holdings. There is one other thing and it is not negotiable. I would like an agreement that we would come to the defense of each other in case of a war."

"That is an interesting proposal!"

"Once word gets out within the other families that you have bought out my old interests, someone will be coming after either you, or me, or both of us. It could get very messy. Do you agree?"

"I believe you are correct. And, I have a feeling I know who will be coming first."

"Who are you thinking?"

"Tijuana Cartel."

"That is the same name I come up with. How interesting."

"They seem to be posturing to come across the border and establish a major presence in the eastern US. We know they already have a west coast presence. Even if it is small and they are making overtures to the Puerto Ricans in New York City."

"Yes. And they need to make the move before the Sinaloa Cartel goes to war with them over territory in Mexico."

Power asked, "Tijuana versus Sinaloa could be a blood bath.

Do you want an answer from me today? Frankly, this proposition sounds very attractive, but I would like to run it by my legal team."

"You mean Alex Engel? You might want to be a little careful using him. I know you trust him but he does not watch his flank, very well."

"I suppose he is as reliable as Richard Swartznicki."

"Very good. Touché."

While Power and Maguire were in their high stakes' negotiations, Montie and Rosalee were sharing a bed at a hotel in Atlantic City.

"Mr. Montie, could you ever love a woman like me?"

"What do you mean by the question?"

"Well, I am so common and you are a gentleman. You are a man of means and I am a poor woman from a poor family. You are educated and I am simple."

"But Rosalee, that is the wrong question. The real question is what do you think of me. Do you love me?"

Rosalee bent down over his massive body and whispered in his ear, "Mr. Montie, can you feel my love for you? It is real and my love has captured your love. She squeezed ever so gently as he began to become aroused once more. "I love you, Mr. Montie. I could love you the rest of my life. You believe me, don't you?"

Montie only answered with moans as he responded to the rocking movements of the senorita.

***

Chapter Eleven

"Come on, mom. It's only money and you told me your bank account is in good shape since we came to the safe house. I've never asked you for anything even close to this. I would like to buy Nimitz from Jim. I helped train the dog. I feel like he is mine as much as Jim. I will spend all my savings first so the dog won't cost you everything."

"You've never had a dog before. How do I know you will take care of it? You'll be responsible for feeding it, bathing it, taking it out. If I agree to this, I don't plan to do any of those things. And don't forget cleaning up the dog poop. In about three years you'll be going off to college. I'm not keeping the dog for you."

"Mom, you never let me have a pet, ever. Not even a little gold fish swimming around in one of those little bowls. Why not, mom?"

"I don't know. I never had a pet growing up. Didn't cross my mind. And, how are you going to pay for the dog's food and veterinarian bills? Have you thought about that?"

"I'll have to get a job. I'm sure people in Florida need to cut their grass. And maybe I could work at a grocery store packing bags and pushing carts in the parking lot. I don't see myself having much of a social life when we first move to Dade City."

"Twelve hundred dollars is a lot of money. How about waiting until we get to Florida and then we get a dog from the shelter? It will cost lots less than twelve hundred."

"But, could a shelter dog protect us?" Jamal had hit upon a weak spot in Ashley's logic. "Are you going to get a gun when we're in

Florida? Would you even know how to use a gun? You know you are scared of guns. The dog could be a friend for me and protection for both of us."

Jamal continued, "Mom, you've never seen me work with the dog. Come outside and let me show you what Nimitz can do now. He is not even fully trained and he could make a bad guy piss his pants."

"Language!"

"Okay, but come see what the dog can do before you shut me down. I really want this dog."

"No kidding."

Dr. Wendy walked through the front door and announced, "Final exam time. Are you ready?"

Jamal said, "Your timing stinks."

Ashley said, "No it doesn't stink. You saved me from having to witness Cujo out back."

"Mom, his name is Nimitz, Nimitz!"

Wendy said, "Now I'm seeing how you two really interact. This is interesting but I have an appointment in three hours in Lexington. We need to get this test done so I can set up the final interviews."

As Jamal and Ashley started answering the questions on the test, the psychologist could tell they were going to be successful by the speed they were turning the pages. Ashley finished first followed by her son a half minute later. While they sat at the dining room table, Wendy started checking their answers. She did Ashley's first.

She mumbled to herself as she turned the pages. "Hmmm." She made a couple notes on the forms then switched to Jamal's papers. The more she read, the bigger her smile became. "Perfect. Two perfect papers. Congratulations you pass. Both of you. Tomorrow my colleagues will be here to interview you. I don't anticipate any problems. What did your names used to be? Doesn't matter. You are Ashley and Jamal Wilson now. That's what we wanted and you've done it." She gave a big hug to Ashley followed by one for Jamal. "Stand up, young man. I do believe you have grown since you got here. Can I ask you a question?" The teenager nodded. "Have you ever thought of dating older women; maybe one who is kind of short with red hair? You know a professional?"

Ashley was certain Jamal was blushing at the question.

Lisa and Jim walked in from the back door. "Jim, could you help me show mom how well-trained Nimitz is? She's not agreeing to buying the dog. I'm trying to convince her the dog can help protect us."

Jim said, "Jamal, you do understand the dog is not completely trained yet?"

Jamal dropped his eyes to the floor feeling like he might end this conversation in tears. Then Jim continued. "You will need to continue his training. But I'll show you how to finish."

"Really?"

"Yes. And I've been thinking about the price of Nimitz. Since training is part of the price I charge, and since you did much of his training, I'll discount my price to reflect your help."

A smile was starting to appear on the boy's handsome face.

"I'll help you demonstrate Nimitz abilities. Come outside."

Lisa and Ashley followed to the dog pen as Jamal went into the shed to get the dog and a few training tools.

Jim said, "Jamal it's your show. Go."

Jamal instructed Nimitz to greet Ashley and Lisa. "Mom, let me put Nimitz through the basic commands."

The dog moved flawlessly through the basics watching Jamal intently. Jamal then went for a jog around the pen with the dog right at his side. Then he commanded the dog to *stay* while Jamal continued to the other side of the pen. He directed the dog with silent hand signals, left, right, forward and back. Standing, sitting, laying on his side. Then he walked to Ashley and called the dog who came and sat looking up at the young woman.

"Mom, I want you to start walking away from Nimitz. When you get ten steps away keep walking but say *Nimitz, come*. Okay?"

When Ashley uttered the words, the dog trotted to join her and walked with her until she returned to the starting point. "I'm impressed," she admitted.

Jim said, "I'm going to put on the padded suit. When I come out, Jamal, take Nimitz across the pen and let's test out the latest training."

When Jim returned, he looked like a gray snowman with all the padding. Nimitz was watching very carefully. Jim said, "Lisa, come stand over by me. I'll make a threatening movement toward you and Jamal will use the silent command to send him to attack me. Everyone ready?"

Jim raised his arm like he would strike Lisa and immediately, Jamal made a chopping motion toward Jim. The dog was at full speed within three steps and hit Jim with such force, the ex-military man was on the ground with the dog trying to rip off his arm. Jamal commanded, "Nimitz, sit." The dog stopped and sat.

Jim got on his feet and started to run away. Jamal said the word, "Spider," and the dog caught the fleeing man taking him down. Jim did everything he could do get the dog to stop, kicking, hitting and thrashing about. The dog kept up the attack until Jamal commanded, "Nimitz, sit."

Ashley's mouth was open in disbelief at what she had just witnessed. "I'm more than impressed. How much do you want for this dog, Jim?"

"My discounted price for Jamal is one hundred dollars."

"I'll pay that from my own money," said Jamal.

"I feel like you two manipulated me," Ashley responded.

Jim said, "Who us?" Jim and Jamal bumped fists. Jim had a word of caution. "Nimitz is not house trained. You'll need to work with him. And, I suggest you start now."

Jamal could not contain his joy and Ashley loved to see her son so happy.

***

Montgomery Maguire had a bad feeling after conferring with his legal team. Richard Swartznicki, the lead attorney seemed uncomfortable in his thousand-dollar suit of clothes with patten leather shoes. It was something about the way he would not look the mobster in the eye. When their strategy session ended, Montie told himself, *I better do something drastic or I'll be sitting in a cell the rest of my life.*

When Montie returned to his office, he refused to see the elder Maguire, instead, he went to his safe and got out the super-secret file he kept. He chuckled to himself as he read the tab on the file – Top Secret. He remembered writing the label out when he was nineteen-years old. There were only three sheets of paper in the file. Each had a cryptic number listed, nothing else. He starred at the three for a few seconds before taking the second page and placing it on top. The numbers, 26 – 17 – 9 referred to the combination of a small box at the local Pack and Ship store. He knew the box number was 114. He never received mail there, he just kept the information he now needed. After placing the file back in the safe, he took the top page and left the office for the small business on the west side of town. When he arrived, he opened the box and removed the only thing within the box, a single unmarked key. He drove to the storage facility on the north side of the street just up the block. There he used the key to open the unit only he knew about. It contained one small box. He opened it to see the three hundred thousand dollars in unmarked cash and two phone numbers with a burner phone.

Montie called the first number. After two rings a woman answered, "Smith."

"This is Jones. I wish to place a want ad."

"One minute." The line went quiet until it was answered by a second voice.

"Johnson."

"This is Jones. I wish to place a want ad. This is for an open-ended contract."

"I will meet you at the diner at Third and Shell Street in ninety minutes. Bring the details." The line went dead. Montie placed the cash in a gym bag and deposited the phone in the dumpster at the back of the storage facility. He did not bother to take the key from the lock. He no longer needed the unit. The meeting at the diner took less than five minutes.

***

Alice Williamson, Jack Butcher and Roland Wilkins were meeting to strategize the Maguire situation over breakfast. Williamson said, "Wilkins, your agents have done a great job in putting together a much broader case against Montgomery Maguire. You should make sure they know their work is appreciated."

Wilkins responded, "The agents are just doing their jobs. If I praise them too much, they might stop trying so hard. Don't want that."

Butcher asked, "Alice, do you have enough to move forward with expanded charges? Seems to me if we leave Maguire out of custody too long, we may have other problems to clean up."

Williamson took a bite of her bagel savoring the flavor before responding. "I think we have enough to go back to the judge. I just don't know how the judge will respond. I've had problems with this judge. It's like an airtight case is not good enough for her. Makes me wonder who's side she's on?"

Wilkins said, "We trailed Maguire to a self-storage unit yesterday. We're not sure what he was doing but he went in alone, and left alone. Surveillance said he carried a small bag. Gym bag. When he left, the agent checked with the storage owner. By the time they figured out which unit he visited, there was just an empty cardboard box. We asked when the unit was rented, but the current owner said it predates him. He bought it ten years ago."

"Any intercepted cell phone calls afterwards," asked the prosecutor.

"None."

"Could have been a handgun," offered Butcher.

"I doubt it," said Wilkins. "What reason would he have for a weapon at this point. He doesn't know where his targets are and there are no others we know of."

"No pun intended," said Williamson, "but my money is on cash. The question is, why would he be hoarding cash?"

"Think he'll try to run?" questioned Butcher. "How big was the cardboard box?"

"He'll never get out of the country without his passport. Legally, anyways. And Maguire doesn't strike me as devious enough to try to flee quietly. How would you flee quietly when you look like him? He can't disappear in a crowd. Too big, he stands out everywhere. I think the cash is to purchase something," offered Williamson. "Wilkins, I just thought of something. In all the surveillance, are there any clues on the trigger man he might engage if he finds his targets?"

Wilkins looked carefully through his notes. "Nothing about a killer."

"That's it. He's funding a contract. Butcher, when you get back to the office, call the organized crime section in DC and see if they know who the Maguires have used in the past?"

"I'll check but I bet he uses someone new. And my question would be *one killer or three*?"

"Wilkins, you keep listening for clues with the wiretap. I'll be contacting the judge's clerk to set up a meeting as soon as the paperwork is ready. If we're lucky, maybe he will be off the streets in the next twenty-four hours, before he can do any damage."

Butcher made the call to Washington DC. After the phone call, he knew he struck out. Three times Maguire's contracted a killer in the past. Two were now dead and the third was in prison for murder. There were no links between the three. One was from Chicago, one from Los Angeles and the third from Brussels. Butcher wished he had a "yellow page" for contract killers. When he expressed his exasperation to the agent, Don Ward, in the organized crime office, the agent offered, "Do you want me to check the dark web for recent activity?"

"Yes. Look for activity which might be soliciting multiple deaths."

"Do you mean mass casualties?"

"No. Three separate contracts for three individuals."

Federal Prosecutor Alice Williamson placed her call to the clerk of Federal Judge, Melissa Walker. "I will be sending over a petition to amend the bail order for Montgomery Maguire, this afternoon."

"I will notify the judge and send copies to the defendant's attorney. Anything else?"

"Do you have any idea how long before the judge can get us on her schedule?"

"Judge Walker does have time available next week, but it will depend upon the availability of the defense attorney."

"I understand. Thank you."

Special Agent Roland Wilkins called his superior in Washington to explain the current situation and the changes which were happening in Atlantic City. "It's a long shot we can stop this killing before it happens. We have no leads on the shooter or shooters at this time. Hopefully one of the wiretaps will produce something."

"We did receive a request from Assistant Prosecutor Butcher to open an investigation on the Dark Web just minutes ago. Maybe we'll get lucky."

***

Chapter Twelve

Montie headed for the casino. He wondered if there would be any more chances to meet with Rosalee. He doubted it would ever happen again. Rosalee knew Maguire would come. She had no stomach for what she needed to do. She had broken off with several men over the years but she took no joy in ending relationships. She wished this relationship had a future but she knew from the beginning it was impossible.

Montie walked into the bar and headed straight to his favorite table. As always, Rosalee greeted him with her best smile and welcome. "Mr. Montie, so good to see you today. What can I get you today?"

"Just some regular pretzels and a lemonade."

"Is everything all right?"

"Got a lot on my mind today, that's all."

"I see. I will get those things for you right away." Rosalee served the man and noticed two older men walk in the bar sitting at a table near the bar. There was something about them, she could tell.

"Excuse me, Mr. Montie. I need to check on the men who just entered. I'll be back."

When she finished taking care of the new customers, she returned to Montie's table. "Anything else I can get you, sir?"

"I'd really like some of your hot sauce."

"If you would like to get your car and meet me across the street,

I will meet you when I'm off in ten minutes."

He rose to leave after paying his bill. She watched him walk away. She checked on her new customers. One of them asked her, "The same meeting place?" She nodded once.

***

When the FBI agents showed up on the second level of the hotel parking lot, they found Maguire's Mercedes parked across from the stair way, idling. Prosecutor Williamson had convinced Judge Walker to revoke the five-million-dollar bail based upon the information they now had acquired from so many sources about Montgomery Maguire's intent to kill the LeMay family.

Guns drawn; the agents approached the car very carefully hoping there would be no incident. The parking garage exit was blocked by an FBI vehicle, just in case. As they got closer, there was no movement. "Montgomery Maguire, FBI. Shut off the vehicle and get out with your hands in full view." Nothing.

When the agent on the passenger side stooped to look in, he saw it immediately. Blood running down the face of the mobster. He holstered his weapon as he called the commander. "We need an ambulance at our location. "Maguire's been shot. I repeat, Maguire has been shot."

By the time the second agent opened the driver's door and shut off the ignition, an FBI vehicle pulled up in front of the Mercedes. The agent checked for a pulse but knew from the placement of two shots in the back of the head, Montgomery Maguire was no longer among the living.

Within the hour, Rosalee Lopez, also known as Yvette Hernandez was heading to Pittsburgh for a flight to Mexico City and on to

Bogota, Colombia. She was not the killer so no one bothered to track the woman. She had accomplished her mission. Her handler in the Tijuana Cartel was pleased with her performance, but he too had to produce results. Rosalee would be dead within two days in Bogota along with her parents in Atlantic City. This was no game; this was business.

***

Selena Patel was already two levels up from Maguire's car in the parking garage. Here she would cross the skywalk into the hotel. She needed to change from her clothing into the maid's uniform she wore earlier in the day. Slipping quietly into the housekeeping room on the fourth floor of the hotel, she changed, put her blouse, slacks, gloves into her oversized bag along with the 9 mm Sig Sauer with the SRD9 silencer, she slung the bag over her shoulder and headed for the staff elevator. Down to the first floor, no one noticed when a maid went through the kitchen and out the delivery entrance to the alley as she put on the oversized sunglasses. The key, move at a normal pace and be calm. At the second intersection, Patel waited for the cross-town bus.

Back in her room, she told Miguel it would be best to go immediately to Maguire's office and finish the job. But as usual, Miguel thought he knew better. This was his big play. He instructed her to stay in her room until the time was "right." They had set up the younger Maguire, now to set up the old man. Then the territory would need new leadership and they would have their opportunity.

The phone in Alice Williamson's office began to ring as she was heading to the washroom. She almost let it go to voicemail, but decided to pick up, instead. "Williamson."

"This is Wilkins. Montgomery Maguire was just assassinated in the hotel parking lot across from the casino. It was a double-tap to the back of his head. Looks professional."

"Oh my God! Any clues as to the killer?"

"Agents are on scene. The medical examiner has not even arrived. I'll let you know when we know something."

She hit the intercom button. "Butcher, now!"

When he arrived, she told him to sit while she used the restroom. Butcher could see something happened. "You look awful."

"I am. Just sit here and listen in while I call the Department of Justice."

"Organized crime director, French." Her call was taken by Gerald French, one of her many bosses. "This is Williamson. I was just informed by the FBI; Montgomery Maguire was assassinated. Within the past thirty minutes, sir. Yes sir, that would be an understatement. How do you suggest we proceed?" She made notes while Butcher sat feeling like the floor had just disappeared beneath his feet. Five minutes passed before she hung up and looked at her assistant. "Damn, what a mess!"

"What do we do?" Butcher inquired. "Our case is gone."

"The director wants us to back off until the investigators figure out what happened. He did say to cut Adams loose but leave him sitting until we have a clearer idea what is happening. We need to let the investigators go back to work. But the way he sees this, there is no way Adams can be involved."

"What does this do to all the intel we uncovered about the Powers, Maguire, Cordova, Tijuana syndicates?"

"I'm not sure but we'll leave that to the FBI to figure out. I need to call the clerk for the judge and Swartznicki to let them know. I think you should go have a little talk with Adams. And, sooner is better."

Across town, two Atlantic City detectives met with Benjamin Maguire. They relayed the news to the next of kin. Maguire showed no emotion and felt nothing in the moment. He would need time to process the loss of his son and heir. His mind started going at top speed with questions?

Who? Why? What's next?

Then he told himself the obvious. *Stop asking questions and get ready for war.* He knew there were three things that had to happen right now. First, he called Teddy Power to give him the news and remind him they had a mutual protection pact. Second, he talked to Tiny to get the protection level for the family's interests set to the highest level. And third, he needed to write a quick note and get it to his second in command.

***

Late in the day, US Marshall Anna Wiest was on her way to meet with the Wilson family at Vincennes. When she arrived, she noticed the transformation of the mom and son. Ashley's hair was now very short and instead of blonde, it was now dark brown. Jamal had grown what seemed to be at least two inches and looked to be a little more filled out: ten pounds she guessed.

Wiest gathered the entire team along with the Wilsons in the front room. "You all need to hear what I have to tell you. There has been a change in your situation," she directed to Ashley. "The man

Malik Adams was helping to prosecute, is dead. His name was Montgomery Maguire. He was assassinated yesterday in Atlantic City."

Jamal asked the obvious question, "If he's dead, are we free to leave? Go back to Dublin?"

"I wish I could tell you it's all over, but I can't do that."

"Why?" asked Ashley. "Can you tell us what's going on?"

"I'm not sure anyone can tell you everything that's happening. Here's what I can tell you. We were able to stop each attempt to find you, we believe. You don't know about all of them. But Maguire is believed to have put out a new contract on you and Adams before he died. If it's an open contract, it will remain in effect until the task is complete. If it's other than an open contract, it will end with his death. We will keep investigating. I know you are in the final stages before moving on to your new lives in Florida. Once you have passed the final exam, if you insist on moving on, you can. It's your call. I would like to ask you to stay an extra, say, week. It should give us time to figure out this assassination of Maguire."

"I don't understand," said Ashley.

"Again, I don't know this to be a fact, but it appears the Maguire killer was a professional. If that's true, we need to know the motive. We suspect the motive may be to over throw the Maguire family. If that is true and they are successful, they will take out the entire leadership of the Maguire family. That would include Malik Adams as a former lieutenant in the family. Again, if that's the direction this goes, you will be in peril again. I'm asking for a little time to sort this out and to keep you safe in the meantime."

Ashley sat back in her seat and starred at the ceiling. "Wow. Two months ago, we were just living our lives in Ohio and now we are targets of who knows who? Yea, I think we can wait a few more days."

Lisa said, "And you know we will do everything we can to keep you safe."

"We appreciate everything you have done for us." With that, Ashley looked at each person in the room and thanked them with a smile and a nod.

***

Agent Don Ward was relatively new to the FBI but was a veteran of computer investigation. He had been with the St. Louis Police working on both missing children and internet child porn investigations. After four years of looking at the cesspools where perverts went to try and satisfy their sexual gratifications, he decided to do more to help the government take control of societal filth. Ward was the son of a long-time cop in suburban St. Louis. He wanted to be in law enforcement but a motorcycle accident while he was in the community college left him a paraplegic. It affected his legs but not his analytical mind nor computer love and skills. Ward proved to be an excellent investigator, thorough and detail oriented. He caught the attention of the bureau when he located two young boys who were sold into sexual servitude in western Illinois.

But, relocating from Missouri to FBI headquarters in Washington proved to be a challenge. It seemed none of his earlier accomplishments meant anything in Washington. He knew, he would have to work harder than before to establish himself in the new environment. So, when Assistant Federal Prosecutor Jack Butcher called, Ward was ready to show his abilities.

Ward reviewed the warrants which were in force for spying on the communications of the organized crime families Butcher was investigating. Ward started by looking at Dark Web advertisements about murder for hire. Much was just bragging, but some were legitimate. He began to cross reference the advertisers with unsolved murders within one hundred miles of the advertiser's base location. Using those parameters, he found six possibilities. Then using telephone locations triangulated on cell phones, he found two persons who were in the proximity of Montgomery Maguire on the day the storage unit was entered. The two names were Erik Johnson and Mattawan James.

Ward did a background check on each. In the process of investigation, he found the vehicles registered to each man. More background information showed Johnson was a known associate of a white supremacist organization in western Pennsylvania. He owned five registered weapons including a sniper's rifle. Definitely a possibility, Ward thought.

When he switched his focus to James, something did not feel right, immediately. The background check was totally empty prior to four years earlier. There was simply no record of Mattawan James, anywhere. Ward got the identification picture from the man's driver's license and ran facial recognition against the FBI records which included military and incarceration records across the country.

After twenty minutes, matches were found in both the military and prison records. Mandan Hillman was thirty-nine years old. He was a trained US Army sniper who was dishonorably discharged seventeen years earlier. His record was full of confrontations with fellow soldiers. When he was deployed to Saudi Arabia as part of Desert Storm, he tried to shoot out the tires of a Saudi prince's vehicle from twelve hundred yards. That was the act that got Hillman sent to Leavenworth Prison for three years.

Records said he stayed away from gang activities in prison. However, his cellmate for two years was Ronnie Junior Jasper. Jasper was serving a life sentence for attempted murder of a local prosecutor in New Jersey – a contract murder attempt. When Ward dug a little deeper and saw the prosecutor's notes from the trial. He found Jasper failed to admit who had purchased his services. The notes pointed to a single suspect, Montgomery P. Maguire.

Ward was not satisfied with circumstantial evidence, so he got the Department of Motor Vehicles information on Hillman/James F-150 Ford pickup. It was a quick check of the street cameras in Atlantic City before he positively located the truck driving on Third Street. Ward watched his monitor as the truck moved from camera to camera along Third until it pulled up at a diner on the corner of Shell.

Ward picked up the phone and called Special Agent Roland Wilkins. When Wilkins came to Ward's cubicle, he watched Hillman exit the truck and enter the diner. Just moments later, Montgomery Maguire entered the diner. The two men left the diner five minutes later. "Great work, Ward. You have some impressive skills. Start looking at video around the Maguire murder scene. See what you can find."

***

Once again, Malik Adams sat across the table from Prosecutor

Jack Butcher. Adams was totally in the dark about the purpose of the current visit.

"Did you come to ask me one more time to turn on Mr. Maguire, cause if that's your question, you can leave right now."

"No. That has nothing to do with my visit. Montgomery Maguire is dead. He was assassinated yesterday in Atlantic City while sitting in his car."

"I don't know what to say. Somebody else didn't like him. Can you share any details?"

"There's not much to share. It appears to have been done by a professional. Whoever it was, they got into the back seat of his car and put two rounds in the back of his head. The initial investigation found no clues about the shooter."

"Professional, you say? Hmm." It was clear to Butcher; Adams was thinking about what he had learned. "So, where does it leave me? And what about Janet and the boy?"

"That's the other thing I wanted to discuss with you. The Department of Justice has decided to drop all charges against you. They wanted the Maguires, not you. Do you have an attorney?"

"I do not. Why?"

"When the government goes into court to have the charges dismissed against you, the judge will want you to be represented."

"What about a public defender?"

"If that's what you want, it can be arranged, but in your case, you might want someone a little more seasoned in the law," said Butcher.

"That's good advice. I'll check the law library here in the prison. There has to be someone local I can find," answered Adams. "Now, what about Janet? Will the government simply throw her out of witness protection?"

"No. We have an agreement and we'll honor it. Of course, she'll have more freedom to reveal her past if she chooses. But, for the moment we are encouraging her to stay in the safe house. We believe Maguire put an open contract on all three of you before his death. We're looking into it, right now. If we can identify the murder for hire individual, we may be able to do something. The FBI and the Marshall service are working on it."

Adams asked, "What's next?"

"I imagine you'll be here another week or two until the court hearing. Then, you'll be free to go. Any idea what you'll do?"

"Probably go get a beer and a steak. After that, no idea."

Butcher smiled at the answer. "Yea, I'd probably go do the same in your shoes."

***

"Jamal, come outside with me. The transport is here for the dogs." The two went out the door to meet the truck which looked like a vehicle used by any animal control unit. Jim Allen was carrying a large envelope.

"What's in the envelope?" Jamal wondered.

"These are the legal documents for each dog. You realize these are registered Belgian Malinois."

"What does that mean? Never heard of dogs being registered."

"The American Kennel Club keeps records on all pure-bred dogs. It ensures when a person buys a dog, they get a dog with a pure blood strain. If you wanted a French Poodle and you pay more than a thousand dollars, you would want the dog to be one hundred percent poodle. Right? It means both parents are registered, too. I also send all the records of their medical care. Dogs need vaccinations and puppies need to be dewormed."

"Okay. Isn't it a long trip for the dogs?"

"This truck takes them to the airport in Cincinnati. They will fly to their new home in Texas."

"How do you get paid?"

"When the dogs reach Lackland, they will be checked out and then I receive a money transfer. Just like when I get my paycheck. Let's get leashes on the three so they can go." Jim went to the driver who accepted the paperwork and opened the three kennels in the rear of the truck. When the dogs were loaded and gone, Jamal went back to the kennels and looked at the empty cages with some sadness. Those were his friends, his dogs. Jamal asked Jim, "Don't you miss them?"

"I do. But soon there will be more puppies and it starts all over."

As Nimitz was in the house, Jamal asked, "Is it okay to bring Nimitz out to the pen?"

"Of course. As long as you're here, use the pen anytime. And that reminds me, there is one other training I would like to do with you and Nimitz since you're here."

Jim met with Jamal and the dog in the pen. Jim was holding what looked like a shotgun and a pair of hearing suppression headphones. "Take him through the obstacle course so he'll know he's training."

When the dog was fully working, Jim said, "Put these over your ears and stand on the other side of the pen with the dog. Make him sit and stay." When they were in place, Jim raised the gun pointing it away from any target and pulled the trigger. *BOOM.* The dog flinched but did not move. "Tell Nimitz he's a good boy and give him a little love." Jim reloaded, walked half way across the pen and repeated. *BOOM.* Jamal repeated the attention to the dog who did not flinch this time. Then Jim reloaded once more, walked right up to the dog and pulled the trigger over the dog's head. *BOOM.*

Jim handed the three spent shells to Jamal. "I want you to let Nimitz smell these. He needs to learn when he smells gunpowder residue to give you a special signal. Remember how I showed you to make the dog speak? I need you to teach him when he recognizes this smell, to give you a little "yip.""

"Got it." Jim returned to the shed to clean the four now empty cages while Jamal continued to train Nimitz.

***

Tiny stood in the doorway to Benjamin Maguire's office. "What will you do about a funeral?"

"No funeral. Too exposed if the killer's waiting. I called the undertaker. He'll handle everything and keep it private. He took care of my wife. That was twenty-two years ago. Hard to believe it was so long ago." Tiny could hear a faint shake in his friend's voice.

"Teddy Power sent a contingency of six security people up from Baltimore to help out. I gave them an orientation and they are working alongside our people. Are you going to keep travelling back and forth to your home?"

"No. I'll stay here until this is over. Who do we know that can get a message into the Federal Lockup in Philadelphia?"

"Adams?"

Maguire nodded. "I always liked the kid. He was like a better version of Montie, and was respectful, loyal and careful."

"Do you want to make peace with him?"

"No, I want him to come back. Only you and Adams know this business and you're the only two I really trust. If there is a war, I want my two-best people by my side."

"Do you think he might be carrying a grudge against you? It's not a picnic being locked up for two months in solitary."

"I don't believe he holds anything against me or you or anyone but Montie. If it was anyone except Montie, he would have talked to me. And, he did not try to take Montie out. I think he was looking out for me. If he wanted to get to me, he knows enough about our business to put me away. That's not his game."

Tiny said, "Let me check to see who we have on the inside that could get a note to Adams."

Maguire called Teddy Power. "Are you checking with the other families to see who might have set up my boy? I figure that waitress must have been a plant. She ran right after he was gunned down."

"My people tracked her to Pittsburgh where she got on a plane to Mexico City. She used the name Rosalee Lopez on the plane reservation. Lost her there. She was running but wasn't trying to hide. You know, her parents lived here with her. They were murdered in their home last night. Someone broke in and cut both their throats while they were sleeping. The Medical Examiner told my detective it was professional. No wasted effort. Just enough to make sure they did not wake up."

"What about the other families?"

"I have personally spoken to the heads of every family east of St. Louis. No one had reason, desire or motive. They respect you, too much. I've made contact with the larger families on the west coast: it's none of them either. I'll speak to the rest. Also, I'm having them listen for chatter. The half million reward will turn up something. No one will turn down such easy money."

"Tijuana Cartel?"

"I still think it's possible, but until we have a lead, it's just a guess."

When Maguire hung up the phone, the FBI was reviewing the information from the call. It gave them a new possible target in Tijuana. Tiny stuck his head in the door. "Boss, I have two possible contacts to get your message to Adams. One is a guard. We've used him before but he can't go too fast because he moves from place to place in the prison. He could take a while. The other possibility is a chaplain. He has run of the entire institution. He will only take information in or out. Nothing else. He uses the money to help with a school in the ghetto."

"Are you talking about Father Angus Murphy?"

"The same."

"He doesn't support a school, he uses the money to buy Irish Whiskey, the good stuff. I've known him forever. I've shared whiskey with him, years ago. Father Murphy it is!" The memory of the Irish priest brought a rare smile to the face of Benjamin Maguire. "Oh, and Tiny, if this is an attempt to take over the business, watch your backside. They could come after you, too."

"I'm taking precautions. Just like the old days."

***

Chapter Thirteen

The FBI intelligence gathering team notified Don Ward of the new voice recording between the Maguire and Power families. Rather than use the transcript, Ward wanted to listen to the recording, personally. His supervisor made it happen. He picked up on the Rosalee Lopez information and started checking back in time and following the flight from Pittsburgh to Mexico City.

Utilizing video cameras at the airport, he watched Lopez enter the terminal with a single bag. She was moving at a fast walk like she was afraid of something. She rode in the economy section of a Delta 737 and deplaned at eight in the evening. He watched her move within the Aeropuerto Internacional Benito Juárez from the Delta area to the Aeromexico airline area. There she purchased a ticket under the name of Yvette Hernandez to Bogota, Columbia. Although video quality was not as good as in Mexico City, he watched her exit the airport and get into a cab. The trail died there.

Next, Ward accessed the database of murders for Atlantic City. He located the report for the murder of Ferdinand, age fifty-two, and Juanita Lopez, age fifty-four, on the north side of the city. He copied the reports and crime photos. Then he checked immigration records. He found they came into the country from Tijuana twenty-three years earlier. They entered as farm workers, nationality, Mexican. They came with two daughters, Amelia, aged six and Yvette aged five. He found them returning to Mexico at Tijuana each year except for the fifth year when he found farm workers. Ferdinand and Juanita Hernandez from Guatemala with Amelie, Rosalee and Maria. He made copies of everything. Ward told himself, *be thorough. No stone unturned.*

Ward was not done. He checked civil records in New Jersey and found Rosalee Lopez working at a café in Trenton. It showed her as twenty-three and divorced. No record of any marriage in New Jersey registered for a Rosalee Lopez or Yvette Hernandez. He expanded his search to include the entire United States.

***

Aldis Freeman had agreed to be the legal representative for Juan Malik Adams. Adams was impressed by the fact Freeman started his legal career as a public defender, then did work for minority business owners and represented the local teacher's union. He had argued before the New Jersey Supreme Court and he clerked for a federal prosecutor back in the 1980s. Freeman liked the idea of having a case in Federal Court. It was difficult for an African American lawyer to build a well-diversified portfolio of cases for a variety of clients.

Adams was again sitting across the same metal table from an attorney. For a moment he wondered if this would ever end. "Mr. Adams, tell me what you need me to do for you?"

Adams began his story with the threat made by Montgomery Maguire against his family and himself. He ended the tale with the news which had been delivered by Prosecutor Jack Butcher stating the charges would be dismissed with the death of Maguire.

"It sounds straight forward. I'll need to contact the prosecutor's office for discovery and then represent you at the hearing with Judge Walker. I will be pushing for dismissal with prejudice. That way these charges can never be brought to court against you in the future. Is there anything else I can do for you?"

"Yes. Could you draw up a Last Will and Testament for me? Nothing complicated. All my possessions would go to Janet

LeMay and her son Cooper of Dublin, Ohio at my passing."

"Of course. The cost for the two things will be twenty-five hundred dollars."

"I don't have that kind of money in my prison canteen account but once I'm free, it will be no problem."

"That's fine. I trust you, which I don't do very often. But I have a final question. Is it true you worked for the Maguire family of Atlantic City for many years?"

"Why do you ask?"

"Over the years I've done work for many clients and I had to go up against counsel for Maguire at one point. It was a good learning experience for me at the time. If you get the opportunity, maybe you could put a good word in for me?"

"Mr. Freeman, I'll keep that in mind."

While Adams was meeting with his attorney, Benjamin Maguire was sitting with Tiny. He was writing out a draft of the letter he wanted to get into the hands of his former employee. When he was finally happy with the wording, he began to copy the words onto one piece of toilet tissue. It could be easily taken into the institution without notice.

Dear son by another set of parents:

I hope you are well. Please consider forgiving me for the sins of your big brother. I did not support his actions. You know how I feel about family. I look forward to your quick return and restoration. You will be welcomed like a returning hero. Your skills are desperately needed at this time. Come quickly. BM

As Tiny read the simple note, he nodded his head. "He'll understand what you're trying to tell him. I certainly hope you're right."

***

At Vincennes, Dr. Wendy was introducing her two colleagues to the Wilson's. Psychologists Henry Morton and Victoria Cotton would be the testers. Morton started by saying, "This will be very informal, so just relax and answer our questions."

"Cooper LeMay, where were you born?" There was no answer and no reaction from either. "Jamal, who was your sixth-grade teacher in Ann Arbor, Michigan?"

"Excuse me, I went to sixth-grade in Lansing, not Ann Arbor," said Jamal.

"Ashley, did you ever date a football player?"

"I went to prom with Jake Willey in high school? Why are you asking?" she answered.

"Tell me about the father of your son."

"No. It's none of your business. And if you ask me again, you'll get the same answer next time, too!"

"Jamal, you have a very nice dog there? Where did you get the dog?"

"I knew a breeder. I helped with chores at the kennel. He gave me a great deal and I love this dog. Do you want to see what he can do? His name is Nimitz."

Cotton asked, "Does the name Malik Adams mean anything to either of you?"

Jamal said without hesitation, "Is he an actor? Did I see his name in the credits on the last Star Wars movie?"

"Means nothing to me," said Ashley.

Morton pushed back from the table, followed by Cotton and Dr. Wendy. He offered his hand to Ashley. "As far as I can tell, you are both ready to go. Congratulations and good luck." Smiles were returned by the Wilsons. Dr. Wendy wanted her final hugs.

Wendy said, "I know you can't leave quite yet, but you are ready to go as soon as the Marshall service gives the word. I'm so happy for you both."

Lisa dished up two big bowls of chocolate ice crème after the psychologists left the house. "Enjoy, you two. You deserve this treat." Jim came in carrying a DVD. This is for you, Jamal. It's an older movie, *Rudy*. It's about a kid who wanted to play football at Notre Dame. I think you'll like it. The kid was a winner. So are you."

***

Special Agent Roland Wilkins was meeting again with Alice Williamson in Philadelphia. "I'm afraid we are in the middle of a massive dilemma. We have all the families on the east coast trying to figure out which side of the coming war to be on. Our intelligence says Maguires and Power have forged some type of agreement for self-protection. Power has been in touch with all the other families on the east coast and the Midwest. Word on the streets is everyone is on edge waiting."

Williamson asked, "Is there any roll for us in this mess? I see our roll as one of control if any actors get too aggressive."

"Maguire and Power suspect the Tijuana Cartel is behind the murder of Montgomery Maguire, but they don't have the intelligence we have. They're still fishing for information. We are at least two steps ahead of them."

"What would change if Maguire knew what we know?"

"My guess, they would develop a plan to attack the Cartel to end this problem."

"Remind me why that would be a bad thing?"

"Well, I suppose they would take the war to Mexico. That could produce problems for the State Department and maybe the White House. The cartels have great influence in Mexican politics. It could mean the Mexican police would join against the US families."

"It still leaves the problem of succession within the Maguire family. There does not appear to be a clear person to take over if anything happens with the old man." Williamson went on. "What does your intelligence say about the role of Malik Adams within the Maguire family before he wanted to take down Montie?"

"We know he started out at the bottom. He was involved in the legal import/export part of the business. He worked his way up over time and eventually became the principle person in the Maguire headquarters in the logistics part of the business. We have nothing on him ever being involved with the criminal part of their business. Not one tiny piece."

"So, it's safe to assume, Adams had the opportunity to learn about other parts of the family business. Do you agree with that?"

"Knowledge yes, control no. Did you read the transcription of the new deal between Maguire and Power? All of that agreement was worked out while Adams was in custody. He knows nothing about it."

"And, he may not care. I have a tough time believing Adams will run back to Benjamin Maguire when he gets cut loose. Call it intuition. If there is a reunion, who do you think initiates it?"

"Probably Maguire. Adams has no way of contacting Maguire without us knowing. I'm not sure I totally agree with you about Adams running home," said Wilkins. "How long before Adams is out of custody?"

"Maybe another week. He has an attorney to help with the dismissal of charges."

"Any connection between the attorney and either Maguire or Power?"

"None."

Williamson stood and walked to the window of the office starring out for a moment deep in thought. "Butcher met with Adams to let him know about the DOJ's decision to dismiss the charges. Maybe I should send him one last time. He could probe to see if there is any possibility of Adams going back to Atlantic City. In the meantime, we need to send this mess up the line to see how they want us to proceed. I think it comes down to two possibilities. Either, we help keep Maguire in control, or we stay out and let the war start."

Wilkins said, "I'll write this up for my superiors and you write it up for yours. Hopefully, they will talk to each other."

"I'll send Butcher back to see Adams."

***

Malik Adams was laying on his bunk reading a novel when he heard the door at the end of the hallway open and steps coming toward his cell as the door was relocked. It took a few seconds to realize the visitor was not a guard but rather a chaplain who was going cell to cell to offer spiritual support. Adams could hear the discussion between the inmate and chaplain two cells to the north. He tried not to listen and go back to concentrating on the story in his hands.

It was ten minutes before the chaplain stood in front of Adam's cell. There was a slight Irish brogue to the voice. "I'm Father Murphy, son. I've come to visit with you and encourage you."

Looking up, there was a man in priest's clothing with the telltale Roman collar. He was in his 60s with a tuft of red hair above his round face. He looked over the tops of his glasses as he talked.

"Father, you know I'm a Baptist."

"It does not matter to me, son. I come to visit all God's children. I think Baptists are part of His family, too."

"I believe you are correct."

"How are you faring in this place?"

"I'm doing okay, for now."

"Do you want to talk about it, my son?"

"Nothing to talk about, Father."

"Well then, I'll just move along. But I want to leave this copy of our parish missalette for each man. There is a very good passage about peace on page seven. You might find comfort in the words from the Psalms."

Adams got to his feet and accepted the booklet from the priest. As Murphy moved on, Adams returned to his bunk and the novel.

That evening, after the lights were out, he pulled out the missalette. He knew if he laid facing the wall of his cell, he could make out the words without letting the security camera observe his activity. He started reading on page three and when he turned page five, a small paper fell from the booklet. It was too dark to make out the words, so he tucked it into his pants waist band to read later. Then he finished the booklet, closed his eyes, and slept.

***

US Marshall Waker delivered the news to the Wilson's at breakfast. "You'll be glad to know there has been zero chatter about anyone coming after you in the past seventy-two hours. That means, it's time for you to go."

Ashley asked, "How do we get to our new home?"

"You arrived here in a motor home, remember?" Ashley nodded. "You will leave in the same way but a different motor home. The Marshall Service will drive you to MacDill Air Force Base in Tampa. There you will have your personal items loaded into a two-year old Chevy minivan that was purchased for you. You will then drive yourselves to Dade City which is about an hour to the northeast. Then you start your new lives."

Lisa asked, "How does that make you feel?"

Ashley said, "First thought, I'm terrified. But I'm relieved, too and ready to get back to a real life."

"How about you, Jamal?"

"I'm excited. I wanna see our new house. And I need to find out what I need to do to join the football team. When can we go?"

"Tomorrow morning," answered Waker. "The ride will be here at eight o'clock."

Lisa said, "I need you to put together a list of things you will need for your house. I have an inventory of what is already in the house. And this is for both of you. Jamal, has Jim talked to you about the type of dog food for Nimitz? Other things you need for the dog need to be added to the list. Some of the things, we will go buy today. Other things will be brought to the house from the moving company. This needs to appear to neighbors like any other relocation into the neighborhood."

"Lisa, let me see the inventory. I can work off the list. We should have a list for you in an hour. Then we'll start packing up our stuff."

Malik Adams slipped the small message into the book he was reading in the late morning. He then moved to the toilet and sat, dropping the note in the water. It was the news he hoped for. Benjamin Maguire wanted him back.

A guard stopped at his cell. "You have a visitor."

Jack Butcher was waiting in the interview room one more time. "Your attorney is in the process of getting the charges dismissed. He seems competent. What will you do when you leave?"

Adams had already rehearsed an answer. "I've got an aunt living in Atlanta. I'm going to visit her. There are opportunities for a black man in Atlanta. I'll find something. Sure, glad I finished my education at Ohio State."

"Well, good luck to you."

When Adams returned to his cell, he thought, *something's going on. The feds want to know my plans. I can't tip my hand. Not now.*

***

The sun had just set on a hot, humid day near Tampa Bay when the Wilsons left the motor home. Jamal turned to his mother, "Mom, it's hot here."

"That's pretty typical for July in Florida. And I bet it rains sometime today. Rains every day in Florida during the summer."

"Going to take me a while to get used to this for football season," he retorted.

Marshall Brown had again been tasked with driving. She said, "We've arranged for you to spend the night here at the air base in visitor housing. You'll be able to start out in the morning."

"Thanks for everything," said Ashley.

Jamal took Nimitz for a short walk before heading into the overnight accommodations.

There was no urgency to get to Dade City, so they took a roundabout way east on Interstate 4 to Lakeland and then north on US 98. When Ashley pulled into the driveway, the street was quiet even at mid-morning. "Well son, what do you think of your new home?"

"Looks just like the pictures. I'm sure glad there's a fenced in back yard for Nimitz."

"That's right, and you get to cut the grass. No more hosts doing everything for us. We get to carry everything into the house from the minivan."

"Mom, a minivan, really? You should have insisted on a Corvette. I can start driving soon. I can see me driving a Vette – with Nimitz in the passenger seat!"

"Dreamer! Let's go look inside."

It was a typical house for central Florida, made from concrete blocks covered with stucco, pale green - no basement. *Storage may be an issue*, thought Ashley as she looked from room to room and checked out the cupboards and closets. The interior of the house was painted in earth tones. No accents. Kitchen was functional with newer appliances and laminate counter tops. Then she remembered most of their former possessions were lost in the fire. The floors in the living space were tiled with vinyl and the bedrooms were carpeted. The place was totally furnished, serviceable pieces, *probably picked from a catalogue*, she thought. *At least we have a two-car garage.* Someone had the presence of mind to leave some groceries both in the refrigerator and in the cupboards. It had been a while since cooking had been part of the routine but Ashley was ready and thinking about making omelets for supper.

It was after supper when Jamal announced he was going to take Nimitz for a walk. He was determined to get to know his neighborhood. It was Jim who had counselled him to know his surroundings, and "keep your head on a swivel." At the end of the street, Jamal turned and started to circle the block. In the center of the block on the far side sat a Pasco County Sheriff car in the driveway. He saw a man in the front yard checking the bushes. When he passed by, the man said, "Nice dog."

"Yes sir. Thank you. I got him from a breeder in Kentucky."

"Malinois?"

"Yes sir. Most people think he is a German Shepherd."

"May I approach the dog?"

"Yes sir. He is pretty well trained but he's not a year old, yet."

"I'm Tom Swift. I'm a K-9 officer with the Sheriff's office. My dog, Ms. French is inside. She's a shepherd." He offered the back of his hand to the dog who sniffed with enthusiasm. Then he offered his hand to Jamal. "Are you new here?"

"Yes sir. My mother and I just moved in on the next block, today. My name is Jamal Wilson."

"You know you will need to get a dog license. You have thirty days."

"Where do I get a license?"

"Animal control office."

"Is it expensive? I never bought a dog license before."

"It is one hundred dollars for a three-year license. You have the dog's shot records?"

"They're at the house."

"What's the dog's name?"

"Nimitz."

"You mean like Admiral Nimitz?"

"Yea, the breeder named all the pups after military leaders. MacArthur, Grant and Lee were the others in his litter."

"So, Jamal Wilson, what grade will you be in this fall?"

"I was in school in Michigan last year, ninth grade, so mom will be registering me at Pasco High. I want to play football."

"Great. People here love their high school football teams. Some folks say Texas has the best high school football, but I believe Florida is their equal. I usually work the home games with Ms. French. Maybe I'll see you there. Nice to meet you. Come by and meet my dog some time."

"Yes sir. Thank you, sir."

Jamal continued his walk through the area and realized he was sweating by the time he was back home. He noticed various signs along the walk indicating a diverse neighborhood. A few faces peeked out windows along the street as he walked along. "This is going to be a great place to live, mom. I met a K-9 officer for the Sheriff's department. He lives on the next street. He was cool."

***

Chapter Fourteen

Attorney Aldis Freeman met with Malik Adams to report on the outcome from court. "I was able to convince the prosecutor to have the charges dismissed with prejudice like I told you. Remember, it means the things you admitted can never be used against you in the future."

"Do you have any idea about how long it will take for me to be released?"

"Probably tomorrow."

"I need to ask a favor. Any chance you could arrange for me to get a ride from here to my apartment when I get out?"

"I'll arrange it for you. There will be a cab waiting when they let you out in the morning. I'll have the cab bring you by my office so you can sign your will. Then the cabbie can drive you home."

"Thanks for your help."

Butcher picked up his phone and called Williamson on the next floor at the Federal building. "Adams said he is going to Atlanta to see his aunt. Said he will look for a job there, too.'

"Thanks for checking it out." When she hung up, she called Agent Wilkins and relayed the information. "What's the plan going forward?"

"I'm not sure, but I'll keep you informed." When he was off the phone, he called his boss, in Washington DC and relayed the information. "Anything else you need from me or our office at this point?"

Marcus Leon had been part of the FBI for eighteen years. He began as a Field Agent in Portland and showed himself to be a fine leader and a critical thinker. He was appointed head of the Criminal Investigative Division two years earlier. When he hung up with Wilkins, he was ready for the next steps the agency had pre-determined. They would follow Malik Adams to see if he returned to the Maguire family. Organized crime was a major focus for Leon's division. He must take the lead and bypass the Prosecutor and local agents.

Leon knew it was a difficult situation. FBI intelligence believed the Maguire family was leaving the world of organized crime as they traded their old racketeering ways for completely legitimate business interests. Once the family was totally legit, he would no longer be able oversee their operations. In all his experience, he had never seen a syndicate family move totally towards being legal. And there was still a possible war coming to the east coast being led by a Mexican cartel. These are definitely not the good ole days. New problems mean new tactics.

*** *

While riding to his apartment in the cab, Adams asked the driver to stop at a convenience store. He first went to the Automatic Teller Machine and withdrew his pre-determined maximum of cash. Then, he found the burner cell phones, purchase one with twenty hours of air time. When he arrived at his apartment, he made a stop at the office and paid for the apartment past month's rent plus sixty more days, even though he doubted he would use it after tonight. When he let himself into the front door, he could tell the rooms had been searched. *Probably the FBI. If Montie did it, he would have torched the place.*

He unpacked the phone and made the only call he had planned. "Mr. Maguire, Malik Adams. Was the note from you?"

"It was."

"Do you really want me to come back?"

"I do. You know you have always been like a son to me."

"Thank you, sir. I'm sorry for Montie's death. It was never my intention to physically hurt him."

"I believe you."

"I told the feds I would be visiting a relative in Atlanta after getting out, but if you need me sooner, I can be there tomorrow."

"Much has changed. I think you should come as soon as possible."

"I will be there in the afternoon."

In the morning, he packed his vehicle and turned his key in at the office. The manager took his forwarding information so the over payment and security deposit could be refunded. Malik Adams was on his way back home. When he failed to exit onto Interstate 95 south to Atlanta, a text was sent to Marcus Leon. *Heading toward Atlantic City*. Seventy-five minutes later, Adams parked his vehicle in the parking garage next to the Maguire offices. *This would be interesting* thought Leon.

***

Miguel received a text from Andres. Andres was a lieutenant within the Tijuana Cartel. Miguel knew he didn't need to subjugate himself to this lieutenant. Miguel had watched lieutenants change almost monthly, and it was never pretty. One mistake and lieutenants were known to disappear, permanently. Benjamin Angel Felix held a vise like grip on the cartel since he founded it in the late 1970's. His word was not questioned, not even by outsiders. His power was absolute. Ruthless was an accurate descriptor of Felix. He once cut the throat of a boy for daring to ask for a peso to give to his mother as a gift.

The text message received by Miguel said simply, *find a crack in security. Eliminate the leadership.* Miguel sent a text to Selena Patel. She knew it could not happen quickly. The layers of security around Maguire had increased. It would be difficult to find any crack to exploit. But she had to start and succeed or else.

Malik Adams entered the office building of the Maguire family. He was frisked before Tiny was called to escort Adams to the administrative offices. Tiny walked down the steps to meet his former associate. He nodded ever so slightly and Adams responded in kind. No words exchanged. Tiny returned to the stairway with Adams following. When they stepped out onto the top floor, Tiny led the way to Maguire's office. Out of respect, the two men stood until they were greeted by the elderly Maguire who pointed to chairs across from his desk. Maguire began to speak until Adams held up a hand signaling, *STOP*. Adams reached into his pants pocket and pulled out a small sheet of paper which he handed across the desk. The note said, "Private Room." Maguire pulled a key from his desk drawer, stood, and moved down the hallway to a door only used by four people, and three were about to enter once the door was opened. Montie's old office door was closed, Adams noticed.

Once they were secure within the soundproof room, Adams began. "Mr. Maguire, I have much to tell you and your office is not secure."

Maguire asked, "How do you know?"

"Things said to me by the federal prosecutor. I believe they know everything that has been happening here."

"I trust your judgment. Always have, you know that."

"Yes sir.

Adams went on to deliver all the intelligence he had gathered. "I don't know what you are planning, but we need to move carefully."

Maguire said, "I have struck a deal with Teddy Power to turn over all the more lucrative parts of the business in exchange for a percentage of his legal holdings. I want out of the old ways. Everything legal going forward."

"Who knows this besides us, Power and the feds?"

"No one."

"Sir, we may need to shout it to the world. The Tijuana Cartel is trying to move in on your territory. If they find out you have made a deal with Power, they may change their focus. I doubt they are interested in the new legitimate business interests. I heard a rumor it was the cartel that orchestrated Montie's assassination. And, it's part of a bigger plan to take you out."

Benjamin Maguire stared ahead without blinking for the longest time. He wondered when this day would come and now one of his two most trusted associates delivered the news. "I'm going to need to think about this." He turned to the door as Adams and Tiny followed him back to their work spaces. Malik Adams sat at his desk with pen and paper and started developing a plan to propose to Mr. Maguire to move forward. It would need to be the best plan he had ever developed.

***

Agent Don Ward had made some progress on the murder of Montgomery Maguire. He patiently watched hours of camera footage from around the hotel parking garage where the murder took place. He checked video footage against each employee of the hotel. He catalogued each coming and going for the week prior to the murder. It dawned on Ward, there was something wrong. There was an extra maid he spotted only on the day of the shooting. He saw her come into the hotel via an employee entrance at three in the afternoon and then he watched the same maid leave about ninety minutes later. He could not get a clear picture of her face, but he saw enough to know the maid did not belong. She was not an employee. She carried a bag big enough to hold a weapon and extra clothing. He saw her get onto a bus but never saw her again. He took the information to Agent Wilkins. "I'm ninety-five percent positive the killer was female."

"Keep at it," said Wilkins. That was Ward's plan.

***

"Jamal! Can you move a little quicker? We need to get you registered for school. I can't do this without you. And, I'm supposed to go in to the post office this afternoon for my orientation."

After closing Nimitz in his bedroom, Jamal hopped in the passenger seat of the minivan as they drove the mile to the school. The school was located on State Road 52 on the edge of Dade City. "Mom, this is okay. I can walk to school if the weather is good."

"You won't have to worry about snow storms."

Ashley parked in the front parking lot and together they walked into the school administration foyer. A woman was sitting at the reception station. "How can I help you?"

"Good morning. We are here to register my son, Jamal for school."

"Are you new to the area?"

"Yes, we came from Michigan," answered Ashley.

"Welcome to Pasco High School. Jamal, what is your last name and what grade did you complete last year?"

"Wilson. I was a ninth grader."

"Here are some forms we need you to complete. You can either complete them now, over at those tables" pointing to the area behind the desk, "or you can take them with you and bring them back. You will need to meet with a counselor to pick your classes for the fall semester, either way."

Ashley said, "We'll fill them out now. Thank you."

It took twenty minutes to complete the forms as Ashley repeatedly had to check her purse for phone numbers and addresses. While she completed the paperwork, Jamal walked to the trophy case and examined the various hardware. *There aren't too many* he thought. *Maybe I can help win a few more.*

With the forms complete, Ashley returned to the receptionist who checked the information. Then, satisfied, she sent the Wilsons down the hall on the right to the sophomore counselor's office.

Mrs. Shell was waiting when they walked into the small office.

They sat at a table. In the next thirty-five minutes, Jamal was registered for English class, Algebra, Biology, Spanish, Physical Education and World History. Additionally, he would have one study period and lunch. Mrs. Shell gave Jamal a packet of information about the school. "Mrs. Shell, I would like to try out for the football team."

"Mr. Mel Stoddard is the head coach and I believe he is here today. You should go introduce yourself. I think practice starts later this week. You're done with me. Here are the room numbers and the names of your teachers. When you leave, turn right, go outside and follow the walkway to the second building. That's where you will find Coach Stoddard."

Jamal questioned, "We go outside?"

"Yes, this is Florida. Many schools have outdoor walkways between buildings. A little different from Michigan."

The door to the coach's office was partially closed, so Jamal knocked.

"Come in."

"Coach Stoddard? I'm Jamal Wilson. I would like to speak with you about playing football."

"That's great, come sit down. What grade are you going to be in?"

"Tenth, sir."

"You're new here. Have you played football before?"

"Not on a team."

"Most of the young men who play for Pasco High School have been playing organized football for several years by the time they are in tenth grade. Many start as early as first grade. So, you may have a little catching up to do as far as learning the game and techniques, but the coaches will help you, along with the upper classmen. There is a fee for playing sports, are you aware of that?"

Ashley said, "Not a problem."

"You will need to get a physical for Jamal. And, you will need to buy a pair of cleats along with the required gym suit. We start conditioning practice this Thursday at ten o'clock on the practice field. Oh, and you will need to fill out these forms. Bring them to the first practice along with the fee, your physical form completed and you should take out the optional health insurance for athletes, just in case. Oh, I almost forgot, Jamal, you will need a fitted mouth guard. You can get one at any pharmacy in Dade City."

Ashley asked, "We are new to town and don't have a doctor, yet. Can you recommend someone?"

"The road behind the school complex is Fort King Road. There are two places on the road you can go. There is the ER Center and the Family Medical Center. Each is very helpful. If you say it's for an athlete's physical, they will get you right in. There is a page in the papers I gave you with the phone numbers and addresses."

The coach continued, "There is one other thing. This school has a long history of producing some fine players. A couple brothers made it to the NFL. But that takes a lot of hard work. So, don't be disappointed if you don't make the varsity. Just do your best and give it your all. Understand?"

"Yes, Coach Stoddard. See you at ten on Thursday. I'll be ready."

***

Ashley Wilson sat across the desk from her new boss. The nameplate on the desk said, *August Fine, Postmaster*. Auggie Fine was a bald, sixty-year-old man with a large belly and a large mustache. There was a distinct smell of cigarettes coming from his presence. "Can I call you, Ashley?"

"Of course."

"I must tell you; this has been the strangest hiring experience I've ever encountered in my thirty years with the post office. I know it has nothing to do with you, but someone must be on your side."

"I don't understand," said Ashley.

"I posted the open clerk position and sent it up the chain of command like normal. An hour later, I was notified the position was assigned to you. I have never seen anything like that happen. And in one hour! I just had to shake my head."

He continued, "Well, welcome to the Dade City Post Office. I'm glad you're here. I looked over your hiring packet. I see you're a veteran – Navy. I was in the Air Force. The extra points I received for being a veteran helped me get in the door. Tell me about yourself."

"Other than my time in the military, I spent my whole life in the Lansing, Michigan area. I have a fifteen-year-old son. We have no other family, so I decided it was time to make a change. We moved here after I learned I got this job. Do many of your new hires have military experience?"

"It's not like it used to be. I think the voluntary military has led to fewer candidates. Times are changing. Let me show you around, Ashley."

Auggie continued, "Lansing, hmm, Lansing. I knew somebody from there but can't quite remember. . . Maybe the name will come to me."

"You realize the hours for the clerk's job are a little strange? Somedays you will work from six in the evening to two in the morning and other times you will need to come in at four in the morning. Most of your job will be to get mail ready for the carriers."

"I just appreciate getting the opportunity to work for the post office. When do I start?"

"Sunday night, ten o'clock." She received instructions on procedures and how to enter the building. She understood there would probably be only two other clerks in the building while she was there. At least with Jamal having Nimitz, Ashley believed he would be safe when she was away.

***

After eating supper, Jamal decided it was time to do some running to get ready for football season. He called Nimitz who was ready for some time on the leash. The two started running at a moderate pace through the neighborhood. Jamal thought it would be a good idea to run to the school to be familiar with the route. Nimitz was more than happy to stretch his legs. In seven minutes, they were on the school grounds. Jamal led the way to the school practice field. He was surprised to see three youth running on the track around the field. He stopped to watch them while standing just outside the fence. When the boys came past, they stopped.

"Hey, how you guys doing?" asked Jamal.

"We're trying to get in shape for sports, this fall," answered the shortest of the boys. He appeared to be Asian. "Beautiful dog!"

"Thanks, his name is Nimitz. He was being trained to be a military dog but he flunked the physical."

The tallest kid who had blonde hair said, "I didn't know dogs had to pass a physical to be in the Army. But I guess it makes sense."

Jamal said, "Nimitz is real smart and well trained. I got him from a breeder in Kentucky just before we moved here."

The third guy, a Hispanic, asked, "Is that where you used to live, Kentucky?"

"No, I grew up in Michigan. We picked up the dog on the way to Florida."

"Are you guys done running?" asked Jamal.

The third guy said, "I think we'll do another mile."

"Could I run with you?"

"You and the dog?" asked the blonde.

"No. I'll make him stay while I run," answered Jamal.

"Okay with me. What's your name?" asked the short guy.

"Jamal Wilson."

The short guy was CK Newman. The Hispanic guy was Andy Lopez and the blonde, Archer Swensen.

Jamal led Nimitz through the gate and took him to the grassy infield. "Nimitz, down. Stay." Nimitz just watched as the four youth ran four laps. When they returned to the starting point, Jamal said, "Nimitz, come." Five seconds later, "Sit."

CK said, "Your dog is cool. How fast is he?"

"You want to race him?"

"Sure!"

"I'll take Nimitz to the goal line and make him stay. I'll stand at the fifty-yard line. You start from the twenty. When you start running, I'll signal the dog to come. He'll beat you."

CK inquired, "He won't attack me on the way, will he?"

"He will if I tell him to." CK's eyes got huge at the answer. "Don't worry, he won't attack. He'll just run. The other two guys joined with Jamal after Nimitz and CK took their places. CK started sprinting as Jamal made a hand signal to Nimitz. CK made it fifteen yards while Nimitz completed the fifty yards, all the way to Jamal's side.

Andy and Archer were laughing hysterically at the sight of the dog flying past their friend. "Hey CK, that dog just busted you, dude!" The three boys made friends with Nimitz.

Jamal asked, "So are you all going out for football?"

"Me and Archer played on the team last year, but CK is on the cross-country team," answered Andy. "What about you?"

"I'm going to try out for the football team."

"What position?" wondered Archer.

"I haven't decided. I guess wherever they can use me."

"What positions have you played in the past?"

"I've never played in the past."

"Seriously? When you walk on the field, you need to declare a position for practice. You're pretty tall. Maybe a wide receiver. What grade are you in?"

"I'll be in tenth."

The boys looked at each other. "OHHHH! Junior varsity. Got to start somewhere."

Jamal said, "I think I might want to hit people. Maybe I'll declare for linebacker."

Archer said, "Jamal, you play linebacker, you're going to get hit, a lot."

CK said, "And remember, you can't bring your dog with you to practice." The boys agreed to meet again the next two evenings to run.

***

Chapter Fifteen

Teddy Power met with Benjamin Maguire in the sound proof room to discuss the situation. "Benjamin, I believe we have everything under control from our end. Our business transaction is now complete with one another. You sir, are now totally a legitimate business. Have all your written records sent to me in Baltimore."

"Except we are joined at the hip." Maguire laughed. "I want to make the right announcement to the other families about our situation. What are your thoughts?"

Power said, "Once word is out, the war might come my way instead of yours, but I'm willing to accept the risk. There's always risk. No risk, no reward." Power became very quiet and thoughtful. "Is there a way to use Adams to get information from the FBI about their involvement in this?"

"What do you have in mind?"

"Adams spent a lot of time with the federal prosecutor. Maybe there is information to be gathered if Adams plays it the right way."

"I'll discuss it with him."

***

Special Agent Wilkins sat across the office from Prosecutor Williamson and assistant Butcher. He began, "Thanks for taking time to meet with me. I know the whole Maguire/Adams thing has been taken away from us, but I have a concern. And it's ethical to me."

"What, the FBI has a conscience? Amazing," said the prosecutor.

"We have discovered the identity of the contract killer Montgomery Maguire hired. Should we inform Malik Adams? The Marshall service said, thanks for the information, but they plan to do nothing to protect the woman and her boy. I feel like we could at least let Adams know there is a problem out there. The problem has a name. And the name has a history."

"Quite the dilemma. From a legal perspective, the FBI could be liable if anything were to happen and the government failed to take any action. Hmm," said Williamson. "By the way, why do you think we were ordered to stand down on this case?"

"Do you know who Marcus Leon is?" asked Wilkins.

"Head of the organized crime section?"

"He is one step above that. He's over all investigations of the FBI. He has taken this as a personal challenge. I don't think he trusts anyone outside his office. Thinks he's better than us."

"Double dilemma," said Williamson. "If you contact Adams, you are going directly against an assistant FBI director." Wilkins nodded. "The Federal Prosecutors don't answer to Leon." She looked directly at Butcher.

"I get it," answered Butcher. "Funny, I had a voicemail from Adams this morning. Maybe I make contact and handle whatever his request is plus this. Wilkins, do you have the name of the guy who picked up the contract?"

"Mandan Hillman – also known as Mattawan James."

"Is there a photo I could get of the guy to pass on to Adams?"

"There is, but if I request it, word goes back to Leon I'm involved."

"I'll request it through our channels and leave you out of this."

"Thanks."

*****

Although the first football practice was supposed to start at ten, the players began to assemble outside the school an hour early. The sun was already baking the area as the temperature rose into the upper eighties. There was a feeling of anticipation as the youth waited for the season to begin. Each student carried a small backpack with shoes, mouthpiece, and gym clothes. In their other hand, forms signed by themselves, a parent, and a medical professional. Jamal looked around for his new friends, Archer and Andy. Archer motioned Jamal to join them in the line. Archer did a mass introduction to those standing nearby. "Guys, this is Jamal. He's a sophomore but he's a good guy. New to the area. Be nice to him."

One of the other guys said, "Yea, I'll be nice to him until he stands across the line from me. Then – BOOM!" Jamal just smiled.

The doors opened with Coach Stoddard giving instructions. "First table is for seniors, second for juniors, next for sophomores and the last table is for freshman. Have your paperwork ready." The line began to move forward. When Jamal reached the table, he turned his paperwork over to the woman sitting there. She didn't identify herself and he did not ask who she was. "Your locker is number seventy-eight with the other sophomores. Just follow the other guys to the locker-room."

There were about thirty guys in the room as Jamal entered. He walked to the far end of the room and found his locker. The locker had a single black helmet with the school mascot, a Pirate on the side. Across the front was a piece of white athletic tape and another across the back. A guy was walking around carrying a magic marker saying, "Print your last name on the tape, front and back. Try the helmet on to see if it fits. Let me know if it's too big or too small."

Jamal had never worn a helmet before. He picked it up, stuck his fingers in the ear holes, pulled apart the opening, and slid it over his head. He buttoned the chin strap. *Pretty good fit*, he thought. Someone yelled, "Get dressed and out on the field. Let's go ladies!"

As he was lacing up the new cleats, another player pulled out the helmet in the next locker. Jamal looked over at a black kid. The kid said, "Are you ready for this? I'm Smitty."

"Jamal. What position are you declaring for?"

"Defensive line. How 'bout you?"

"Linebacker."

"Very cool, dude. You going to hit some people. I'm not fast enough to play back there, but I love hitting people!"

"See you out there, Smitty."

As far as Jamal could tell between ninety to a hundred kids were waiting for things to start. At the far end of the field was a smaller group of about fifty. *Probably freshmen*, thought Jamal. Coach Stoddard stepped forward. "Take a knee. These first three days we will work on conditioning. Now listen carefully, if you start feeling light-headed or have no saliva flowing, you are probably dehydrated. Tell your coach and go to the water table under the tent, cool down and come back when you feel better. Understand?"

Stoddard continued, "These are this season's assistant coaches. First is Coach Byron Aldrich. He will be working with the defensive back field players and the Junior Varsity. He is new here and is from Arkansas. Next is Coach Moose Allison. He was here last year. He will be working with the linemen on both sides of the ball. He is my top assistant with the varsity. Finally, is Coach Brady Sieman. He is working with the offensive backs and the Junior Varsity. Down at the other end with the freshmen are Coaches Cotton and Smith. You will meet them later."

From there, the players spread out on the yard-lines and began the exercises to get ready for the day's practice. The players were then divided by class. The sophomores went with Coach Aldridge.

When Aldridge got the group together, he started with an announcement. "Gentlemen, no one has announced this yet, but you sophomores have the weight room reserved just for you from three o'clock each afternoon for forty-five minutes. I expect all of you to use the weights if you want to get better. Now, I want all of you on the track for two laps. Then we will run forty-yard sprints for time."

Jamal felt he was running a solid pace for the first lap. Then he noticed a few of the players were leaving the pack, running in the lead. Jamal picked up the pace and found himself leaving others behind. He felt good, he felt free. He noticed his helmet was bouncing on his head a bit too much. When they got to the final hundred yards, the group broke into a sprint to the finish line. Jamal finished third.

Coach told the players to line up one at a time for the forty sprints. Jamal knew this was the time to give every bit of energy he possessed. Players were not told their times. He did not see the astonished look upon Aldridge's face as he wrote down, *five point one five seconds*. From there the players went through agility drills, and drills in catching, throwing, and punting. By the end of the first practice, Jamal Wilson did not know he made a favorable impression. The two-hour practice went by quickly before the players headed to the showers. They would be back at four-thirty for another one-hour practice. Meanwhile, the coaches would begin to compare notes.

As Jamal was getting dressed, Smitty was too. Jamal asked, "How do you think you did?"

"About as good as last year. I think I'm a little quicker. I gained twenty pounds since last year. How are you doing? Man, you were flying on the forty. You made an impression."

"Really. I've never played football before this year."

"I have to play. Coach Smith with the freshmen, that's my dad." A minute later, Smitty said, "Dude, you looked like a natural out on the field. Did you even drop one pass?"

"No. I was pretty lucky."

"Share some of that luck with me."

***

Assistant Federal Prosecutor Jack Butcher felt like he was entering enemy territory as he walked into the Maguire office building. While waiting for Malik Adams, he glanced around the lobby, *nice place*, he thought. *Somebody's making some serious money*. Only a couple minutes passed before Adams met him. They went to a conference room on the first floor. Butcher began, "When I learned you returned here, I was surprised. You told me you were heading to Atlanta."

"Mr. Maguire made me an offer I could not refuse. I couldn't tell you everything because I wasn't sure how it would all go. Fortunately, Mr. Maguire understood I held nothing against him."

"So, did you return to your previous role with his company?"

"I did. I still handle the logistics of the company."

"All the logistics?"

"Let me stop you right there. I never lied about my involvement with the business. But something has happened since I left. Mr. Maguire sold all his interests in, let me call them, the parts of the business the FBI wants to monitor, to another family. He retained all the parts of the business I was involved with. You know, the parts that pay taxes. In exchange, he received a percentage of the legal parts of the other family's business."

"Are you telling me the Maguire family is no longer involved in organized crime?"

"I would say that's accurate. And it's the reason I wanted to speak with you. See, Mr. Maguire learned the Tijuana Cartel was responsible for Montie Maguire's assassination. It was part of their plan to overthrow the Maguire family and assume control of his interests. We would like to ask a small favor."

"What's that?"

"Could the federal government find a way to notify the Tijuana

Cartel the Maguire family no longer has anything they would desire?"

"That is quite a request," said Butcher.

"Killing Benjamin Maguire and the business leadership will gain them nothing."

"Do you want to tell me who now has this territory?"

"Mr. Maguire knows you already have that information."

Butcher sat still for a moment and then said, "We want you to have some information, too. Montgomery Maguire took out an open contract on you, Janet and her son. We know who has that contract. He slid an envelope across the conference table containing the name, alias, known locations, and photos of Hillman. "We have not tried to track him. There is no other information I can give you but I imagine you have the resources to find him. One other thing, we have been ordered to back off from you, Maguire and anything related. The final thing I will share with you is the killer of Montgomery Maguire was a female. We don't know who."

The men parted. Each had helped and played the other.

***

Jamal had enough time at home to take Nimitz out for a walk around the block before he had to return to the weight room. As he walked down the next block, Sheriff Tom Swift was exiting his cruiser with his patrol dog, Ms. French. The dogs spotted each other immediately. Ms. French stood very still and just watched the Belgian. Nimitz tail wagged but he made no move to approach. Jamal stopped. "Hey, Jamal. How are you?"

"I'm fine. Went to my first football practice today."

"How did it go?"

"Great. I need to go back in a little while."

"Two a day practices?"

"Yes sir, and they expect us to put in time in the weight room, too."

"Some things never change. Jamal, is it time for the dogs to meet?"

"I think I'm ready," answered the teenager.

"Let's do it like this. First, I'll leave French here and walk to you and let Nimitz smell me. Then you do the same. If that goes well, we can let them smell each other. What do you think?"

"Let's do it." A few minutes later, the dogs were smelling each other. It appeared like a well-choreographed dance as the canines circled each other.

Tom Swift suggested, "Let's take both dogs into my backyard so they can be off leash." Jamal followed to the side gate and removed the leash from Nimitz harness. It took little time before the dogs were romping together, sharing a stick as they ran. "Ms. French does not get enough opportunity to just be a dog and enjoy life."

"Does your family help out with Ms. French, a lot?"

"I have no family," answered Swift. "My wife died three years ago from breast cancer. We never had children."

"I'm sorry."

"You don't need to be sorry. You didn't know. It's just me and my best girl, Ms. French. I have a question for you? Has Nimitz been trained with live fire?"

"Weapons? Yes. Not a lot but I was there when he was trained with live gun fire. By the second time the breeder fired the shotgun, Nimitz didn't even flinch. Then the breeder gave me the empty shotgun shells to work with Nimitz to recognize the smell of gun powder."

"Is he supposed to give you a special signal?" Jamal nodded his head. "Stay here for a minute. I want to give you something." Swift unlocked the garage door and stepped inside. He returned carrying a rag and a plastic bag. "This is a rag I use to clean my weapon. It has the smell of gun oil. Many times, I found, the dog will pick up this smell since perps don't necessarily have gun powder residue on themselves. But they clean the weapon and the weapon has this oil on it. The dog picks up the smell and reacts like this. Ms. French, come."

Both dogs came and sat near the Sheriff. Immediately, Ms. French went down and whined one time. "That's her sign to me. For gun powder she yips."

"Sounds like the same training Nimitz got."

"It's pretty standard training for K-9 dogs."

"Sheriff, thanks but I need to get to practice."

***

"Why in the world was Butcher talking to Adams?" asked Director Leon of Agent Wilkins.

"Butcher told me Adams left him a message asking for a meeting. What Butcher told me was the Maguire family has given up all its illegal activity, but you already know that. He asked if the government could somehow get word to the leadership of the Tijuana Cartel. They hope the Cartel will call off their killers if they figure out there is nothing for them to gain."

Leon sat back in his seat. "How do we know they are out of the business? I can't just take their word for it. How do we verify it?"

"Director, we do have enough information on the Maguire family operation. We could start back checking with informants to see who is giving the orders. Shouldn't take long to point back to Power if it's true. Then, maybe some forensic accounting on the financial records of the Maguires."

"The problem is, how do we get a court order to get into their financial records? Investigating criminal behavior is grounds for a court to issue an order, but I wouldn't want to be the government lawyer who goes before a judge asking to investigate a legal enterprise. We'd get laughed out of court."

Neither man spoke as they tried to find a solution. Leon spoke, "and, what do they think we are, a sign board company? Go down to Mexico with a damned sign that says, *Maguire has gone legit. Call off the dogs*. Let me think about this for a while. There has got to be something which makes sense, 'cause the rest of this is just messed up. Wilkins, did you have anything to do with this Butcher/Adams meeting?"

"You told me to back off. I'm just the messenger."

***

The Pasco High School Football Team coaching staff met to discuss their early impressions following the conditioning practices. The players were now gone. Next Monday would start full pad practice. So far only three players had quit the team. One of those was definitely from the heat on the field. Coach Stoddard started the conversation. "Let's start with the seniors. Who is making an impression so far?"

Coach Allison said, "We are fortunate to have eight senior starters back from last year. Johnson has a lock on quarterback. Wiley, Mohammed, and Crocus look good on the line. Nunn and Gunn on the defensive side seem to be in good shape and ready. I'm worried about Shelley. That shoulder injury from last year seems to have him tentative. Not sure how good his physical condition is at this point. Wills is good to go at end. Two other seniors seem to be ready to go, Nunez and James. My opinion on the rest of the seniors, no one stood out. We'll have to see what happens when they start to hit each other. One good thing, Udell has been working on his kicking skills and he might be our guy." There was some discussion on various players before Coach Sieman spoke about the juniors.

"First, if Nelson can run with the ball as well as he runs without it, we may have a tailback. Miller, Amundsen, Troost, Lopez, and Swensen look good to me. I like the work ethic of Gutierrez and Vector. Overall, the juniors look good. Everyone is working hard. There are two kids who didn't play last year who have promise. Belcher has the size and strength to be a lineman and Fellows has a nose for the ball. Fellows is on the basketball team.

Coach Aldrich began, "The sophomores are the usual mix of potential and possibilities. But, one new kid, Wilson, really impressed me. He's tall, good build, and fast. When we did the receiver route drills, the kid has great instincts and understands how to concentrate on the ball without being distracted by the defense. When he was covering on pass plays, he was all over the receivers. He's a kid to watch. Says he wants to be a linebacker. If he can hit, look out!"

Stoddard asked, "How are we coming with assigning equipment for Monday?"

Sieman said, "The equipment managers told me everyone is ready. We might need a few more sets of the light weight hip pads. And maybe some additional cage style face masks for linemen."

Stoddard asked, "Where do you see possible holes in our team at this point?"

Allison answered, "We are not blessed with fast players. That could impact defensive backs. If someone gets free with the ball, our guys won't be able to catch 'em. We don't have a long snapper nor a punter, yet. But I think we have kids who are taking the weight room seriously."

Stoddard said, "We only have one more week before classes start. Make sure we drill it in their heads they have to take their classes, seriously. See you Monday."

***

"Hey mom, I'm making a couple turkey sandwiches for lunch. Do you want me to make you one?"

"That sounds good. How did practice go this morning? I want a picture of you in your practice uniform."

"It was different. There was some serious hitting going on. There was one drill where there were two linemen across from each other with a ball carrier behind one and a defensive back behind the other lineman. Coach says go, and the linemen beat up each other trying to make a way for the ball. After the linemen fired out, the defensive back flew through the hole and planted the ball carrier like a tomato plant. Bang! Coach said that's how we all need to do it."

"So, when it was your turn, how did you do?"

"Not that good, but I got the ball carrier on the ground. Coach Aldrich said I need to keep my head up or I could miss a good ball carrier."

"Sounds pretty intense."

"It was. I need to be back at school at two for the weight room."

"Seems to me, you're enjoying football."

"Mom, how was your first day at the post office?"

"It was fine. For a little town, you won't believe how much mail goes through the post office in one day. Most of it comes in pre-sorted from Tampa to go right to the carriers, but somethings need to be sorted and added to the carrier's routes. That's what we do plus we have to meet the trucks that bring mail and take it back to Tampa. It will take me a few days to learn all the stuff and then a couple weeks to get up to speed. I'll get there."

"Who are you working with?"

"There is a woman named Margie. She's been working at the post office for twenty years. She's very nice and helpful. She told me she used to be a route carrier but likes this job better. She told me her two boys used to play football for Pasco High but they're grown now and moved out of state. The other worker was Willie. He is really quiet and works hard. He told me he one time lived near Orlando but likes Dade City a lot better."

"What is your schedule each day?"

"I start at ten. First thing we have to do is sort the mail that comes back from the carriers and get it ready to go out to Tampa. The truck comes in at one-thirty and we push the bins out of the truck and replace them with the one's we got sorted. That took us maybe a half hour. Then we all take our lunch break at two-fifteen. Then we organize the mail for the carriers who come in at seven. There are two other clerks who come in when we are ready to leave at six. They work the counter and put the mail in the rental boxes. I just met them in passing today, but they were friendly. Told me, they are football fans and look forward to seeing you on the field for the Pirates."

"When are you going to sleep?"

"I thought I'd go to bed when you leave for practice and get up around eight tonight. When school starts next week, I'll have to reconsider when to sleep."

"Mom, can we make this work?"

Ashley nodded her head, "But we have to keep our guard up."

"Speaking of guard, I'm taking Nimitz out for a walk."

***

Chapter Sixteen

The longer Marcus Leon thought about his discussion with Agent Wilkins, the more upset he became. He felt like Adams was trying to "play" the Department of Justice for their own gain. *No one plays Justice*, he thought. *Justice plays criminals or puts them away in little rooms with no key!* He made up his mind, we will not pass along the message.

In Atlantic City, Maguire was meeting with Adams and Tiny in the secure room. "Mr. Maguire, now that you've had time to reflect on my plan, what are your thoughts?"

"I shared your plan with Teddy Power. We believe it can work and we agree Justice is not going to get in the middle of our plan. They wouldn't know a good plan if it walked up and kissed them on the lips. Idiots!"

Maguire continued, "Power thinks his people will figure out who the assassin is. Then, they will take action. Adams, pitting the Sinaloa Cartel against the Tijuana Cartel is brilliant. It will be ten million dollars well spent. I am a bit concerned about you making yourself "bait" to bring the assassin out.

In Baltimore, members of Power's family were busy collecting intelligence on the Tijuana Cartel. Through paid informers and spies, they had accumulated the names and locations of over one hundred sixty members of the cartel. They discovered only four known female associates with killing on their resume. Three were occupied in Mexico or Central America, leaving only Selena Patel unaccounted for at the current time. Power's family was confident they would have a photo of the woman within forty-eight hours.

What they still had to figure out was who was the local handler. But they had a plan to get that information, too.

Agent Don Ward was still on the trail in DC. It was a long shot, but he decided to ask Homeland Security to monitor cell phone conversations for key words, Maguire and Adams. The bigger problem was he wanted the words only if they were heard in Spanish context. Ward received a .wav file from his contact at Homeland. He listened and confirmed both names were used. He sent the file through a Spanish to English translator.

Male: *It is time to move forward with the plan.*

Female: *Is there a way I'm supposed to proceed?*

Male: *Olf first, Adams second, Maguire last.*

Female: *Method?*

Male: *Up close. Make it personal. Need to scare away other possible suitors. Make blood flow.*

Ward dropped all the information into a computer file and sent it to Marcus Leon. Ward had no way of knowing who the two persons were but he would continue to search. He had the conversation and the general area where the conversations started and ended, Atlantic City. He would find them. He was confident. When Leon listened to the conversation, he had a big decision to make.

***

Jamal couldn't believe how brutal the late afternoon practice was on his body. He would be sixteen in a month and yet his body was so tired and sore. Every hit felt like a car crash. He tried to spit between plays only to find he had no moisture in his mouth.

"Coach, I need a water break." Jogging to the water tent, Jamal noticed Smitty was there sitting on the ground in the shade.

"Hey Smitty, this ninety-two-degree weather is a bitch."

"Yea, takes your energy. You'll get used to it. Takes time. How do you think you're doing with the coaches?"

"I'm not sure. I feel like I'm hitting and learning the linebacker responsibilities. But the upperclassmen seem more relaxed. I see them throwing their bodies around with less worry."

"What are you worried about?"

"I don't know. Maybe getting hurt."

"Man, if you keep thinking about getting hurt, you won't make it as a football player. Everybody gets hurt. Everybody! Do you know how many NFL players get hurt each year? Almost all of them. It's part of the game. That's why we have trainers and medical people hanging around."

"I guess you're right."

"Hey, my dad says Coach Stoddard has already decided four sophomores are going to dress for the first varsity game. He didn't tell me who but you could be one of them."

"Are you serious?"

"Yea. I got to get back. Later."

Jamal took another drink before he headed back to practice. Before he could get in the scrimmage, Coach Sieman grabbed his jersey, pulling him away from the group. "Wilson, you could be a great linebacker, but you need to learn a couple things. Are you listening?"

"Yes sir."

"Blocking is all about leverage." Sieman placed his hands on the shoulder pads of the kid and pushed. "When hands are up this high, how do you avoid them?"

"Go low."

"Right. So, a good blocker is going to go at you low, lower than you can go. If the blocker does that, he wins and you lose. Do you understand that?"

"So, what do I do to counter that?"

"Use your hands and arms to keep the blocker away from your body. It's up to the defensive player to control the blocker. This is the reason for the weight room training. Strong arms. Let me demonstrate. I'll be the blocker; you be the linebacker." In slow motion Sieman went low and blocked Jamal in his midsection with his shoulder. Then he slowly pushed the kid back. And stood up. "This time as I go low, put your hands out and don't let me get to your body." Again, in slow motion, the coach started to block low but Jamal used his hands to keep the coach away. "Feel the difference?" He nodded. "The lower you keep yourself, the better leverage you have against the blocker. Understand?"

"Yes sir."

"Leverage and hands. Now go in for Dahl at right linebacker." Coach Sieman blew his whistle and Jamal went back to his position. Sieman joined the offensive huddle to call the practice play. "I want to run the fullback blast, left. Center, you go after the right-side linebacker and get him out of the hole the fullback will run through. Got it? On one."

As the play unfolded, Jamal read a run coming right toward his spot. From his left he saw the center coming to block. He turned and put his hands out and steered the blocker past him in time to step into the fullback and take him down for a two-yard gain. As the offense regrouped, Sieman went straight to Wilson. "Perfect. Great reaction."

For the final quarter hour of practice, pass drills were done with one receiver and one defender. Each time the tight end came up, Coach Aldrich assigned Jamal as defender. Out of six targets, only one attempt was a completion as Jamal covered like a seasoned defensive back. He had the speed, the agility, and the instincts to deny the ball over and over. It was not lost on the coaches.

Coach Stoddard blew his whistle ending the practice but called the players to gather around him. "Take a knee gentlemen. I know this is not on the schedule, but how many of you could come back to school at seven-thirty tonight for a session of watching tape?" Only four hands did not go up. "This is not mandatory, but will be a chance for you to watch the best ways to play your position. Hit the showers."

That evening, the team including the freshmen, divided into three groups. Linemen were with Coach Aldrich in classroom 107. Coaches Stoddard and Allison had the offensive backs and receivers in classroom 109, while the defensive backs and linebackers met with Coach Sieman in classroom 110. Jamal got the lesson quickly. *Learn to read the offense and take appropriate action.* As he watched, he compared the images on the screen to his own practice actions in his memory. He could do this. He knew in the moment. He could be a good football player.

When Jamal entered the house, it was almost dark. He knew Nimitz needed time to run, so he took him into the back yard with a ball. Nimitz loved to chase a tennis ball. After a half hour, they reentered through the back door. Ashley was packing her supper for work. "Mom, remember I said, I'd get a job to pay for Nimitz care? I need to put it off until football season is done."

"I already figured that out. I'll pay for what the dog needs. You can pay me back. Deal?"

"Deal. Mom, you're the best. I love you," as he threw his long arms around her and squeezed really tight."

"Hey, not so hard. I'm not a tackling dummy! I want you to go into the bathroom right now and step on the scale. You're getting bigger and I want to know how much."

He shouted from the bathroom, "two twelve, mom. And when they measured my height at school this morning, six three and a half!"

Ashley stood in the kitchen remembering a football player she once loved in Ohio. Now she had another one in Florida.

*****

Selena Patel was getting tired of just sitting on her hands. The message to move ahead with the plan was welcome. She went out the door of her rental unit and headed for the neighborhood bus stop. The crosstown bus took her within six blocks of the building owned by Benjamin Maguire. It was late and she figured security would be slightly relaxed. Walking toward the address, she took photos of the surrounding buildings for later study. By the time she completed her walk, sixteen square blocks had been circled and photographed.

She noticed the Maguire building was not quiet. There were several lights on, both in the entryway but also on the second floor. She noticed the security cameras. She learned previously Maguire was no longer spending his nights at his home compound which meant he must be sleeping in the office. There had been no sightings of Tiny Olf or Malik Adams which meant they, too, must be hiding at the office building.

Several years earlier, Tiny convinced Maguire to purchase access to Atlantic City's surveillance camera system. Well-placed political donations to several elected officials allowed access to the entire municipal network. It seemed like a purchase never providing benefit to the Maguire business enterprise, until today. From his office, Tiny was monitoring a curious sight. A woman was walking the area around the Maguire building taking pictures of the area at half past ten on a Tuesday evening. Actually, it was Jason Stark, the twenty-three-year-old computer genius who worked for Teddy Powers who first saw the suspicious behavior on his oversized monitor in Baltimore. Those years studying computer science at MIT were paying results. Jason alerted Tiny and Venessa White who was staying in Atlantic City as part of the mutual defense agreement between the families.

As Patel returned to the crosstown bus stop, she noticed the homeless woman waiting for the same bus which rolled to a stop. Patel took a seat half way back on the left as the old woman shuffled past pulling her rolling basket. The odor that accompanied the old woman was one of musty clothing. By the time the short encounter was done, four photos of the face of Selena Patel were being sent to Baltimore. Before stepping off the bus, she was positively identified from the photo previously obtained through other efforts. Patel went to her room as both the city cameras and

Venessa White monitored her route and final destination. Now the assassin was exposed; it would only be a matter of time before they found her handler.

Even though the hour was late, Tiny walked into the sleeping quarters of Benjamin Maguire who was reading a book. "Sir, sorry to bother you. We found the assassin. We know where she is staying."

Fire came to the old man's eyes immediately. "I want her to suffer."

"She will. They'll all suffer." Tiny closed the door and went back to his office.

***

Ashley was sitting quietly eating the salad she brought from home. The clock said two forty-five. They had the dock door open to let in some of the cooler night time air. Even with the air conditioning, it got stuffy in the back room as the three workers handled overnight duties in the Dade City Post Office. Margie and Willie had joined at the table with five empty chairs. Ashley asked her co-workers, "What are those little packages? They're not really envelopes and too small to be a package."

Willie said, "You're talking about 'SPRS.' Carriers call em spurs cause they're a pain in the ass. They get dropped in the truck, and are hard to find."

Margie asked, "So Ashley, tell us about your life in Michigan. I've never been to Michigan. Farthest north I've ever gone was Kentucky."

For an instant, Ashley's mind went blank so she just kept eating until her practice at Vincennes kicked in. "After I got out of the Navy, I just wanted to go home. Guess you could say I was homesick. It's pretty funny because I never got seasick on board the aircraft carrier. I knew I couldn't move in with my parents so I stayed with a girlfriend until I got done with college and went to work for Dr. Blessing, the dentist. He was a great man. He treated me like a daughter. Can't say enough good things about the man."

Margie asked, "Why couldn't you go home? If you were my girl, I'd want you to come live with me. At least until you got on your feet."

"I was pregnant. My parents were not supportive and when they learned the father was an African American, that was the end."

"Racist?" asked Willie.

"I'm ashamed of them, but yes. Back around the time I was born, there were race riots across the bigger cities in Michigan. I know they were happening in other places, too, but my mother got caught in the middle of a riot and she was really scared. She didn't get hurt, but a friend took a brick to the face. It really changed my parents. Dad had a hard time at the car factory because there were lots of blacks working on the line with him. He became suspicious of his co-workers even though he worked next to them for years. So, my beautiful son became a victim of the riots many years after they ended."

"Some folks can't forget," said Willie. "It's too bad for you. My Pastor is always preaching about how lack of forgiveness is the great sin of our day. I think he's right."

"I'm sorry you had to live through that. Very sad," remarked Margie.

Almost at the same time, Nimitz head came up off Jamal's bed. His hearing caught an unfamiliar sound outside the house. He began to whimper and then he nuzzled his human's hand until he woke up. "What's going on?"

Nimitz jumped down and went to the bedroom scratching at the door. Jamal swung his long legs off the bed and he stood. Then he heard the noise. It was sort of a scratching sound below his window. Jamal went to the window looking down for the source of the sound. Nothing. Nimitz was at the front door of the house ready to take action. The boy was uncertain, but finally turned on the front porch light before opening the door for the dog. The dog immediately turned to the left along the front of the house where he stopped, head down, low growl.

Jamal carefully walked behind the dog. There on the ground was the biggest turtle Jamal had ever seen, pulled totally inside the shell to stay away from the dog who was now sniffing all over the turtle shell. Jamal would find out later it was a gopher tortoise out wandering at night. Nimitz lost interest and was ready to go in following the nocturnal adventure. By the time Wilson got back in bed, the dog was in the middle of the mattress with his head on the pillow. "Move over."

✳✳✳

"Mr. Maguire, Teddy Power calling with the question of the day. Now that you know the location of Selena Patel, do you want to eliminate her, redirect her toward me, or wait to identify her handler?"

Maguire sat back in his chair and thought for a moment. "My gut tells me to go kill her, but that might not be the smart play. If we take her down, someone else will probably show up to take her place. Then we would have to try and track the new killer, if we can. My man Adams is suggesting we wait and find the handler first. He believes killing both of them sends the message we are strong; Tijuana Cartel has no chance of getting to us. At least not without sending a whole army."

"That's an interesting theory. But what if we can't locate the handler, or what if there are multiple killers in play in Atlantic City? Just 'cause we tracked the Patel woman doesn't guarantee she is alone."

"The more we talk about redirecting her toward Baltimore, the more we don't see that as a viable option." He stopped and said nothing for several seconds.

"Mr. Maguire, are you okay?"

"I had a thought. If one of us, or even one of the east coast syndicates tried to communicate with the cartel, would they believe it?"

"Probably not."

"Exactly, but who would they believe?"

"We tried the feds but they didn't want to get involved."

"What about using the Sinaloa Cartel? We talked about starting a war between the two cartels. Maybe we help move that idea along. Adams proposed that from the beginning."

"What do you have in mind?"

"First, who stands to gain the most keeping those cartels away from the east coast, Midwest, or even the southeast?

"The east coast syndicate families."

"I agree. If all the families benefit, possibly all the families would be willing to finance a strengthened Sinaloa Cartel. They could potentially put Tijuana out of business or at least limit their ability to move east."

"What would stop Sinaloa from doing the same thing, come east?"

"If a large enough incentive was provided by all the families, they would understand how powerful the families could be against keeping them out, too."

"You are making a lot of sense and your analysis is dead on, in my opinion. How much money would it take to send the right message?"

"If each family agreed to participate, twenty-five million from each family. Any family choosing not to participate, doesn't become part of the mutual aid group we would establish for future problems. Just think, North Atlantic Treaty Organization."

"A quarter of a billion dollars. The Sinaloa Cartel could supply a lot of fire power for that amount of money."

"For that amount, they could buy the whole Mexican Army."

Power agreed to start contacting the other syndicate heads to explain the plan. When the two men got off the phone, Maguire turned to Malik Adams and Tiny Olf with a smile. "I think he bought your plan." Twenty minutes later, Marcus Leon was reading a transcript of the phone call. He picked up his phone to get a meeting with the Attorney General of the United States.

***

Jamal left for practice and Ashley thought it would be a good time to plant a hibiscus bush in the front yard which she picked up from a local nursery. She fell in love with the big five petal flowers. She chose one with yellow flowers thinking maybe in the future of getting a variety of colors. She went to the garage to get the shovel and rake which had never been used. Nimitz was complaining in the house because she would not allow him to accompany her in the front yard. But she just ignored the whiny canine.

She picked a spot about three feet in front of the house and another three feet from the front step on the side opposite the walk to the driveway. She was confident the bush would look good against the backdrop of the light gray color of the house with the white trim. There was something about flowers and plants that spoke peace to Ashley's soul. She had transformed the front of her house in Ohio with tulips and Hosta's along the front. She smiled picturing the scene in her mind. She did appreciate the fact this house had a decent sized yard with some type of grass that could withstand the brutal Florida sunshine without dying. And, like every other house in the development, it boasted an underground irrigation system that kept the yard well-watered two nights every week.

Digging the hole was not difficult with the sandy soil. She dug it just larger than the pot containing the hibiscus. As she wiped the sweat forming on her brow, she noticed a man walking a dog coming down the opposite side of the block. The dog was a Shepherd. She thought, *could this be the Sheriff Jamal had met?* As he passed, he greeted her with "Good morning," and then crossed the street. She put the tools down and walked to the front sidewalk.

"Hi, I'm Ashley Wilson."

"You're Jamal's mom, right?" She nodded. "I'm Tom Swift." They shook hands. "You should be extremely proud of your son. He is such a polite young man. Sit Ms. French. I have enjoyed speaking with him and he has a great dog. Does that make you Nimitz human mom?"

"I suppose it does. I understand Nimitz has met your dog, and your dog is a trained K-9?"

"She's a working dog. I was very pleased with how well the dogs got along when they were off leash in my back yard. Ms. French does not necessarily get along with every other dog. Has to do with her breed and training. She is trained but she still has her instincts about people and other dogs."

"Admiral Nimitz really is Jamal's dog. He has been working with the dog for a couple months before we moved in here."

"In Kentucky, right?"

"That's right. Got the dog from a breeder we learned about."

"And you used to live in Lansing, Michigan?"

"Sounds like Jamal has been telling you our whole story."

"How does he like football? He told me he was trying out for the Pirates team."

"He tells me he is really enjoying it," said the proud momma. "But it takes a lot of his time. At least he's meeting other students so he won't feel alone when classes start. I'm kind of worried about him."

"I think he'll be fine. He is a quality young man. You've done a great job as a single parent. "Well, we should let you get that hibiscus in the ground. Nice meeting you."

"You too. Maybe sometime Ms. French and Nimitz can run around in our backyard."

"I'm sure they would both enjoy that," answered the sheriff.

***

Chapter Seventeen

Mandan Hillman had a couple problems, maybe many problems. He knew who he was supposed to kill to collect the money promised by Montgomery Maguire. He received the twenty-five thousand for agreeing to the open contract but it meant there was two-hundred-seventy-five-thousand dollars waiting for the completed job. And, he needed everyone of those dollars. James owed an acquaintance for the cocaine he lost while fleeing from a New Jersey undercover cop. It was thirty-five thousand dollars of product but the interest was adding up ten thousand dollars per week.

He was still two years behind in child support to his former girlfriend totaling eighteen thousand. His lawyer who took his case while he sat in Leavenworth prison had placed a lien on his truck for five grand. Delivering pizza was not helping him even make a dent. He had names of the targets but the locations were old and not helpful. The only thing he knew with any certainty, Juan Malik Adams used to work for the Maguire family in Atlantic City before he went to lockup and testified before the grand jury against Maguire.

Hillman did a computer search for the LeMay duo with the final information a news article about the arson fire that destroyed their house in Dublin, Ohio. After that, nothing. He was puzzled. *What happened to these people? Did the earth open and swallow them?* He was able to uncover a small item about Adams. He pleaded guilty to a DUI in Philadelphia and paid a fine.

Hillman's desire for beer sent him to a small bar in a suburb of Atlantic City, Vineland, New Jersey. Murphy's Bar was little more than a watering hole. There was a single pool table and a beat-up bar with ripped stools along the front. There were only four tables. The overhead lights were already dim with three lights burned out, but the music was blaring, mostly Springsteen. He sat on the stool near the far end of the bar. A gray-haired woman was nursing some type of soft drink on the last seat. She was closer to sixty than thirty, he decided. "Coors, please."

"Ya want a lite?" asked the bartender.

"No, I want the real deal. I deserve it."

The woman looked at him. "Bad day?"

"Bad life."

"Sorry. Anything I can do to help?"

He wondered if she was coming on to him but when he looked at her, he knew her question was genuine. "Know anything about finding lost people?"

"Little bit."

"Are you serious."

She took a sip and nodded her head.

Hillman lost interest in his beer. "Seriously, how do you know about finding lost people?"

"I volunteer at the library in the family history section. Lots of people come in looking for relatives."

"You mean like dead relatives?"

"Yes and no. The process to locate lost people is the same for the living and the dead."

"How do you go about it; I mean finding these people?"

"I help people search the internet or newspapers, government records. There are all kinds of information available if you know where to look."

Mandan Hillman was trying to come up with a reasonable story to get her help. He took a long drink of his beer as he thought of a reasonable lie. "See, I know the names of these three people and I'm pretty sure they're all alive. I have somethings I need to get to them. Not legal papers but stuff they will find interesting. How would I start if I came into the library?"

"I'd start by asking questions to start the search. Things like names, birthdates, address, known relatives, locations, stuff like that."

"My name is Mattawan James," he lied. If I showed up at the library, would you help me?"

"Sure, that's why I volunteer."

"Which library and when are you there?"

"I'm at the Main Library in Atlantic City, corner of Tennessee and Atlantic, downtown. Know where it is?"

"Been by a hundred times."

"I'll be there from ten to two on Tuesday and Thursday next week. When you come in the library, go to the help desk, and ask for the Heritage Collections. I'll be there. And my name is Helen."

"Bartender, will you bring Helen here another of whatever she's drinking. On me." Turning back, "You are a God send, lady. See you Tuesday." Hillman drained his beer and headed toward the door. He could not believe his good fortune.

***

Agent Don Ward was able to get some help from other agents until he narrowed down to the identity of Selena Patel. Once he ran the name against the crime syndicate data base, he got a hit as a known member of the Tijuana Cartel in northern Mexico. Intelligence suggested this was not her first involvement as an assassin and it appeared, she had killed a man who was high up in the Maguire syndicate already under indictment for Federal crimes. But there was a definite lack of physical evidence tying her to the murder. He did not know exactly where she was, but he would keep digging. The other question that Agent Wilkins asked was, "Who is she working with, locally?" The crosstown bus route was the key. He would check anything associated with that route until he found her. But he also had the recorded audio file. There were clues. He had to find the answer.

One of Ward's favorite possibilities was voice recognition software used by the Justice Department and CIA for investigations of overseas terrorists. He didn't know if this case would meet the internal criteria to use the software since there was no clear terrorism link. But he knew it would be worth the risk to seek approval. He sent an email to his supervisor with all the rational for the request. When he hit the send button, he could only hope.

He started watching hours of surveillance videos along the crosstown bus route. He programmed his computer to look for any woman fitting the general description which he took from the video on the day of Montgomery Maguire's death. Two days later, he had seen twenty-seven possibilities but nothing definitive.

He was getting anxious when he saw an incoming email from his supervisor. It was an answer forwarded from Marcus Leon giving approval for limited use of the voice identification software with the links to agents who could assist him in the investigation. Now, Ward was pumped!

Two hours later, Ward wheeled himself into the basement level of the FBI building to an area he had never been before. He rolled to room A1-23 and knocked.

"Come in and close the door."

The agent in the room had no desk name plate. The room was filled with equipment and walls were covered in sound cancelling tiles. The place was as silent as a tomb. "Are you the agent from the Maguire case? I'm Mitchell, just Mitchell. Don't ask! No offense, but you're the first agent I've seen in a chair. You must be good at what you do."

"I'm Don Ward. Been here for about six months now. I do computer investigations."

"Give me the overview of your investigation and how I can help."

"Syndicate murder in Atlantic City. High ranking member of the local crime family is the vic. Surveillance points to a woman, Selena Patel, a member of the Tijuana Cartel as the trigger. I got a .wav file from Homeland with the key words in Spanish I was looking for. Two people on the .wav file a woman and a man. We think the woman is Patel. Upstairs wants to know the identity of the male."

"Got it. Is the .wav file on the agency server?"

It's titled "Maguire espanol 7 19."

Mitchell tapped on his keyboard. "Got it. Downloaded. If you watch the screen, you'll see the analysis the computer makes as it's converted to digital. Done. Now, I'll run it against the entire Spanish language file to see if there are digital matches. You can head back to your office. If I get any matches, I'll send them up."

"How long?"

"You have a pretty small file. Probably before the end of the day. If it's going to be longer, I'll let you know by four o'clock."

"Awesome. Thanks."

Just prior to the four o'clock deadline, Ward received an email from Mitchell.

The file comparison is complete. However, I would like to run the file against two other data bases. It will happen overnight. Contact you in the morning.

***

The morning football practice was mostly conditioning since the weather forecast was for cloudy skies in the afternoon. When the players stepped on the field in the late afternoon, there was a coolness to the breeze coming from the north. Coach Stoddard blew his whistle and the players gathered. "This afternoon, we need to work on a couple things. Speed is one, and the other is open field tackling. We'll divide into four group for the speed drill. First, all the upperclassmen who are running backs and receivers, circle up on my right. On the left, I want all the underclassmen and freshmen who are running backs and receivers. Then defenders, go to the same side where your classmates are waiting. All linemen, head for the weight room. You'll be there the rest of this practice. Let's go!"

Once everyone was in their spot, Coach Aldrich explained the drill. "This will be a one-on-one drill; one offensive player versus one defensive player. The offensive player will have a ball at the forty-seven-yard line heading toward the goal line. The defensive player will be on the fifty facing the opposite goal line. When the whistle sounds, the offensive player runs toward the goal line. The defensive player turns and attempts to run down and tackle the ball carrier before they reach the goal line. Questions?" Nothing. "One more thing, as incentive, any player who scores a touchdown and any defender that makes the tackle before the thirty-yard line, moves to make a fifth group. Understand? This is about running down a player who breaks free. No one should work twice against the same player. We're going to do this with six ball carriers at a time, so spread out."

In the first two groups, only Gus Johnson, the quarterback, outran Vector to move to group five. Jamal was in the third group and was pitted against a small kid who was a freshman. The kid, Unruh, looked terrified when he looked at the tall sophomore who would be chasing him. With the whistle, Jamal turned and was in pursuit. Unruh went down at the thirty-two-yard line. Wilson was sent to the fifth group along with the Nelson the tailback. By the end of the first round of the sixty-two players, the fifth group had grown to eight.

The coaches began to pair specific players against each other for round two. When they found they were one short, Coach Stoddard called out, "Wilson, come over here. You be the ball carrier for this drill against Sanchez."

Jamal had noticed Sanchez in the various drills. He was a quick defensive back who knew how to tackle. When the signal was given, Jamal headed at an angle for the corner of the endzone. Sanchez was getting closer by the twenty-five, so Wilson cut right to the center of the field and created a little more room before going down at the five-yard line. He instinctively grabbed the ball with both arms. As the players were getting up, Coach Sieman was running at them at full speed.

He grabbed Wilson's facemask and pulled his head down to his angry face. "Who told you to run at an angle?"

"Sorry coach, I didn't hear we could only run in a straight line."

"Both of you, group five. Now!"

As they jogged back, Sanchez said, "Man, I like the way you think."

After each player had six opportunities, the coaches reversed the defenders with the offensive player. Coach Stoddard shouted, "Every player needs to be able to tackle in the open field."

The second drill was for special teams. Group five finally got back in action as they were the kick-off team. Eleven players were assigned to be the receiving team. Jamal was assigned to be closest to the kicker on the left side of the formation. Before the first drill, Coach Sieman reminded the players, "Remember leverage and use your hands to keep blockers away from your body." Coach Aldrich set up the receiving team and gave some brief instructions.

Once the coaches cleared the field, RJ Udell set the ball on the kicking tee and signaled he was ready. The ball travelled to the fifteen-yard line where it was caught by Maxon who went straight ahead to the twenty-eight. The first defender was Jamal Wilson who managed to evade all blocking attempts. He hit Maxon sending Maxon backward to the ground. The groans from the sidelines were audible and the coaches came on the run. Maxon was not getting up. Wilson was standing over his team mate offering his hand. "Come on, dude. Get up." Slowly he rolled over and made his way to his feet.

Coach Aldrich told the slightly dazed ball carrier to head to the water tent. "Everyone else, back to your place. Do it again. Wilson, you're out for this play." After five repetitions, Coach Stoddard changed player placements to work on the run back. Ahmad Nelson was assigned to be the returner because of his speed and ability to make tackler's miss. Group five players were now split on both ends of the field and Jamal was again on the kick off team. Over the next six kick off exercises, Jamal was involved in three.

After practice, the coaches were sitting in the office discussing the progress of the team. Jamal Wilson had made a positive impression. With only eight days until the first varsity game, positions needed to be assigned. Coach Stoddard said, "There is no way we can afford to leave the Wilson kid on the junior varsity. He keeps making plays. The kid's a player."

***

Hillman walked in the main entrance of the library. He had not been in a library in a very long time. Last time he was looking for information to help him restore a 1949 Ford F pickup truck he bought from a farmer in Pennsylvania. He remembered the library had been no help in finding information. *One hour totally wasted* was all he could think about. He saw the sign for the Heritage Center and headed for the closed doors. As he passed the reference desk, a young woman asked, "Can I help you, sir?"

"I'm looking for Helen."

Pointing, she said, "She's back there helping a woman find the Census records."

Hillman walked in the direction indicated. Helen was helping a woman find something in a very large file cabinet. He stayed back hoping she would be free soon. Helen said, "Here it is. 1920 United States Census for northern Vermont. Let me set this tape up for you on the reader over here and then you can start your search."

He watched as Helen threaded the machine with the broad tape and fed it through catching the end on the take up spool. Then she turned to see Hillman. "Mr. James, glad to see you. You found me," as she stepped away from the family researcher. "Did you bring the information about the people you want to locate?"

Looking around the large library room, he said, "There is a lot of stuff in here. How do you keep it all straight?"

"I've volunteered here for a year and a half and I don't know where everything is located. And it gets frustrating when some book or document is supposed to be here and I can't find it. But, that's a story for another day."

Hillman produced a single sheet of typewriter paper containing a few lines of information he had about Malik Adams, Janet and Cooper LeMay.

Helen said, "Let's start at the computer. Are you computer savvy?"

"Not really. Never saw the need."

"Okay. It's the future and when I'm looking for information about the past, it's invaluable. You sit here and I'll sit at the work station."

Helen tapped the keys and began the search for Juan Malik Adams. "Tell me again why you're looking for these three folks?"

"I like to go to flea markets. I found a family picture album with each of their names in it. I thought I would try to get the album to them. Might be theirs, might not. Maybe one of them will know someone who would like to have it." Hillman had rehearsed this story and thought it sounded plausible.

Helen said, "Look at this, a bunch of hits for Juan Malik Adams. Don't know if this is your guy or which one is your guy but it's a place to start. Maybe I could narrow down the search with more information. Any idea of a place this man lived?"

"Atlantic City." Helen tapped away and the search became more specific.

"Says here there is a person by that name who works for an import/export business in New Jersey. There is phone number here."

"Let me write that down. Is there a photo of the guy?"

Helen tapped again and found Adams listed with a business social media network. "Nice looking guy. Early forties."

"Can you print that for me?"

"It'll cost you a dollar."

Helen hit the print screen button and a printer across the room came to life. Then she said, "Hey, look at this. This guy used to be a college football player. Here's his picture from 1997 at Ohio State."

"I'll take that one, too."

When Helen began the search for the two LeMay family members she found no leads except the article about the arson fire in Dublin. She tried every combination even putting in possible birth locations and years. Nothing. "Are you sure this is the proper spelling?"

"It's exactly the way it was spelled in the album."

"I'm not finding anything on either name. This is really unusual. But let me try one last thing. Last week a woman came in looking for information about her mother in high school. I found this website which has tons of high school yearbooks from across the country. I found her mother in the year book for Salina, Kansas. Did not even know the site existed." She tapped away. "Here's a possibility. Janet LeMay, Pickerington High School. In Ohio, 1993." She hit the enter key and the page from the yearbook filled the screen. On the second line, second photo was a smiling teen ager named Janet LeMay. Do you want me to print this, too?"

"Yea. Where is Pickerington, Ohio and please don't say in Ohio." A few more keyboard strokes and a map of Ohio came up and zeroed in on the suburb of Columbus. "But you find nothing else?"

"No, nothing. Very strange."

"Helen, you've been a big help. Let me pay for the copies."

"If you give me a phone number, I could keep looking. If I find anything, I can let you know."

Hillman thought for a moment. He seemed torn. "No, it's fine. Thanks for your help."

After Hillman left, Helen sat at the computer terminal thinking about the conversation she had with James. Something was not right; it was a feeling. She made a note, Mattawan James, Juan Malik Adams, Janet LeMay, Cooper LeMay, Atlantic City, Pickerington, Ohio State. Maybe she would follow up when she got home. Or, should she make a call to her son? She wasn't sure.

***

Chapter Eighteen

Don Ward wheeled himself to the basement to find out what Mitchell discovered about the voice file he left for analysis. The door was closed and locked. He rolled back to the elevator and went to his own office. When his computer powered up, he had a priority email waiting from Marcus Leon. Ward knew who Leon was but had never interacted. Too many people between them in the structure of the FBI. The communication announced the formation of a task force on organized crime. Ward looked at the email a second time to make sure he was a primary receiver and had not been copied. It was real and he was supposed to be at the first meeting on the fourth floor in two minutes. "Son of a gun!" He rolled back to the elevator with some urgency.

Six agents were sitting at the table with Director Leon as Ward entered the room – one minute late. Leon began, "You have each been chosen as a member of this task force and approved by the Attorney General in DC. We are tasked with stopping a major mob war between the Tijuana Cartel and the Maguire family of Atlantic City. All the intel collected to this point, says the cartel is plotting to overthrow the Maguire leadership to take over the territory on the east coast. Our job is to find a way to stop the war from happening. Our usual plan of operation will not be followed. There's not enough time. The AG wants us to find a new approach."

"Let's review what we know," Leon continued. For the next ten minutes Leon did a recap of information gathered by Agents Ward, Wilkins, and Mitchell. Ward learned Mitchell made a positive identification of the male voice on the .wav file; Miguel Riveria. And, Mitchell was able to trace his conversations with

Angel Felix, head of the cartel. The screen in the room showed photos of Patel, Riveria and Felix. Ward made a mental note. "I have asked Agent Sally McWorth from the forensic accounting office to join us. She will be heading a deep dive into the finances of the cartel and the Maguire family. Agent Orossco is with our Mexico intelligence office. He is our internal expert on organized crime in Mexico. And, Agent Cindy Bronski will be our in-office coordinator. Questions?"

"The AG suggested we do everything possible to keep the Maguire leadership in place. Here is what we will do. I have ordered total protection of the Maguire buildings and operations starting today. Second, he wants us to arrange a face to face with Benjamin Maguire. We need to determine if they are really going legit. Wilkins, you and Ward will meet with Maguire as soon as possible in Atlantic City."

Ward's hand shot into the air. "Director, I am not a field agent."

"I am fully aware of that fact. However, you being in a wheelchair should help put Maguire at ease. Frankly, he won't see you as a threat because of your appearance." Leon looked around the room seeing agreement with his statement about Ward. "Let's get to it."

Ward followed Mitchell to the elevator and on to the basement. "Anything else you want me to know?"

"Sorry man, when the analysis was done, there was so much important information, I couldn't wait for you." By lunch Agent Wilkins had an appointment with Benjamin Maguire for the following morning. He and Ward would take an agency van for the three-hour drive to Atlantic City.

At Maguire's end, he called for a meeting with Adams and Tiny in the private bunker. "FBI is coming in the morning for a meeting about the threat from the cartel. They seem to know all about it. Two agents will be showing up from the DC office."

Adams asked, "Have you notified Power?"

"Not yet."

"They'll want proof you got rid of the illegal portions of the business. I think there is a way for you to prove your position." Maguire's eyebrows rose at the statement. "Allow the FBI to do two things. A forensic accounting exam of the financial records and have the business go public."

"You mean investors?"

"Exactly. No family can go public because the investors would expose themselves to criminal investigation. So, use that to show you are a legitimate business enterprise."

Maguire asked, "Have you researched how to do it?"

"I have. You'll need to make some decisions first. The big one, what will you do with the investment cash? How do you want to grow?"

***

Sheriff Deputy Tom Swift enjoyed his job in law enforcement for Pasco County. Following high school in Brandon, Tom felt no desire to go off to school, but neither did he want to stay home with his younger sisters. The United States Army looked attractive and the recruiter was helpful in setting up tests showing Tom a possible future in military law enforcement. So, at age nineteen he was off to basic training at Fort Leonard Wood in Missouri. He would go on to the United States Army Military Police School also at Fort Leonard Wood. From there it was on to only two other locations as an MP-Fort Hood in Texas and Fort Drum in New York. Of all the aspects of being military police, Swift found himself drawn to patrol. He didn't know why, but he enjoyed the time behind the wheel answering calls for his presence.

It was during his final months before returning to Florida, he met Cheryl Mims, the vivacious brunette with the smile going from one horizon to the other. He fell for the woman with his whole heart. She was working in a café near the base. They were married on his final weekend before his separation from the Army. Tom and Cheryl moved to Zephyrhills so Tom could begin his transition to the Sheriff's department. After a year in Florida, they decided to relocate to Dade City to be near Tom's office. Cheryl got a job as a waitress at the IHOP in Dade City.

When Cheryl got sick with pancreatic cancer, Tom was glad he had his job to keep his mind busy. As the cancer persisted and worsened, Tom became torn between spending time with the love of his life and his position. When the oncologist said, "Stage four. Just a matter of time." Tom took Cheryl home so she could die at their home. At her funeral, Tom understood how short seven years together really was. The Sheriff made Tom take six weeks off. But by week four, Swift was ready to return to his post. It was then he was suggested for the K-9 corps of the department. He was willing and when he finally brought Ms. French home, Tom believed she somehow channeled some part of Cheryl. He realized the dog could smile. It was a comfort as Tom went back to patrol with his new best friend.

One thing Tom Swift learned in law enforcement was to trust his instincts. He could tell the difference between truth and lies without knowing how it happened, but it did. So, when Jamal Wilson talked about obtaining his dog and it slightly differed from the story told by his mother, the deputy could not let it go.

He went to the office an hour early to do some informal investigative work. All the deputies did it from time to time. No one questioned his early presence at his desk. He tapped the keys of his desk computer and checked out Ashley and Jamal Wilson. He found nothing suspicious. Everything seems right. Navy veteran from Michigan. Job with the United States Postal Service. He found her birthdate and other information from her driver's license. There was their previous address in Holt, Michigan. They were the same age, he noticed.

What really bothered Swift was the amount of training Nimitz, the dog had. It was obvious to the dog handler the kid had spent more than a few hours learning how to handle such a dog. Swift decided to look at breeders of Belgian Malinois in Kentucky. He knew there would be a limited number of breeders who would also have the skills necessary to train such an animal. He checked the American Kennel Club records. There were three breeders. He examined Google maps for the locations and found one breeder in Bighill, Kentucky. The location was very close to the route the Wilson family would have used moving to Dade City.

He picked up his desk phone and dialed. "I'm trying to reach Jim Allen."

"You found him."

"My name is Tom Swift, from Florida. I am looking at the AKC website and it says you breed and train Belgian Shepherds. Is that correct?"

"Yes, that is true. I work closely with the US military to raise dogs for their law enforcement and combat personnel."

"Do you ever train a dog for private individuals?"

"I've had a few "washouts" who have gone to private individuals."

"Did you ever have a dog named Nimitz?" The line went dead.

"Lisa, there is a problem. Maybe a big problem," shouted Jim. Then he dialed his contact at the US Marshall's service. Vincennes was currently without extra guests. Jim gave the contact a quick rundown of the phone call and gave the phone number showing on his cell phone screen. The Marshall's service would get back to him in a bit and again the line was dead.

Within five minutes, the call was traced to a desk phone at the Pasco County Sheriff's office in Dade City, Florida and a call was made to the Sheriff to apprise him of the situation. It was "need to know." When the Sheriff was done speaking to the Marshall's office, he was on the phone to the shift commander in the Dade City office.

Tom Swift was preparing to head to his cruiser when Lt Dresden stepped out of his office and said, "Swift, can I see you in my office?"

After the office door was closed, Dresden asked, "Did you make an inquiry of a dog breeder in Kentucky a few moments ago?"

"I did. What's up?"

"I need to ask what is the purpose of your inquiry?"

For the next few minutes, Swift related his discoveries and suspicions concerning Ashley and Jamal Wilson. He told his boss everything, leaving out no detail or suspicion.

"Okay. The Sheriff just called me because he got a call from the US Marshall Service about your call to one of their operatives. Seems the Wilsons are in United States Department of Justice Witness Protection."

"Now I understand," said Swift. "The dog came from a military breeder's program who just happens to also be at a safe house. It answers my question."

"You know this conversation never happened."

Swift nodded. "But since they are my neighbors, I can keep my eyes open."

"Good plan. Now get out there and be safe."

"I will, Lieutenant."

Phone calls went all the way back to Jim Allen who assured Lisa everything was fine.

***

Agent Wilkins found a parking spot near the headquarters of the Maguire family offices. Ward rolled his chair into the lobby as the door was held open. The meeting took place in a first-floor room. Benjamin Maguire and Malik Adams sat across from the federal investigators.

Wilkins began, "Mr. Maguire, Mr. Adams, thank you for seeing us. I hope you can appreciate the unusual nature of the events which have led to our request to meet with you? We are not here to threaten you or seek information to use against you in any legal fashion."

Adams broke into the opening statement. "Agent Wilkins, we know you are a field agent for the FBI, but who is your partner, Agent Ward?"

"This is Agent Don Ward. He is an information technologist in the DC office. He has been monitoring the Tijuana Cartel. Our director appointed the two of us to meet with you."

Adams continued, "I will assume the two of you know the background of what has been happening in regards to the Maguire family and the cartel. Is that accurate?" Both agents nodded. "Why are you here?"

Wilkins responded, "The FBI would like to close our files on the Maguire family and its illegal activities, but to do that, we need proof. Do I make myself clear?"

Maguire said, "You mean my word as a US citizen is not good enough?" The old man laughed at his own joke. "Here is what we are doing to answer your inquiry. Tomorrow, we will be filing papers with the Securities and Exchange Commission to go public as a company. We anticipate our Initial Public Offering will raise about two hundred million dollars. When that sum is added to our current equity value, it should place Maguire Enterprises just past one billion dollars. As you know, it will include vigorous financial reports which will expose our assets and liabilities. Our legal team believes it will give the federal government and the State of New Jersey all the information showing we are only involved in legal business."

"A couple questions. Who is your legal counsel?"

"Broward."

"And do you anticipate restricting who may invest in your company?"

"No, it will be a general stock offering. However, as you can see, I will retain the majority owner. I don't believe that should be a problem for anyone. My track record for running a profitable operation is well documented in the import export business. Mr. Adams heads that part of the company and does a fine job."

Wilkins asked, "Mr. Adams, just a few months ago, you were ready to testify against Montgomery Maguire. I find that very interesting. Do you want to comment about it?"

"My problem was with Montie, not his father or this business. I was and remain loyal to Maguire Enterprises."

Don Ward asked one question. "Mr. Maguire, if and when you identify and catch your son's killer, what do you plan to do?"

"Let me ask you a question. If it was you, what would you do?"

As the agency van left the neighborhood, all participants realized they got everything they wanted from the meeting.

Back on the top floor, Adams sat across from the elder Maguire. "Mr. Maguire, how do you intend to handle the killer and her accomplice?"

"I have an idea, and it will probably shock you. I'm planning to offer each of them a position with the company in our security section. That way, we turn them away from their current loyalties and we should be able to use their knowledge for our benefit. And, if no dead corpses show up, the feds won't have any question about our motives. What do you think of my plan?"

"Brilliant, sir! There is one other thing. Montie took out a contract on me, my son, and his mother before he was murdered. I would like to find a way to tie that up. If he comes after me, that's one thing, but for the killer to go after my family, that is not acceptable."

"Adams, how can I help you?"

"I'm not sure, sir. If I come up with anything, I'll let you know. I don't even know where they are since they went into witness protection."

Benjamin Maguire sat back in his chair and starred at the ceiling with his hands folded in his lap. "I might be able to locate them. All you need to do is give me the go ahead."

"I would like to know where they are. And I want them to be safe, too."

***

Sheriff Swift was not scheduled to work on Monday or Tuesday at the start of the school year. He enjoyed the opportunity to lounge around the house in the morning at least until Ms. French decided it was time for a walk in the neighborhood. As they rounded the corner heading toward the house of his newest neighbors, he noticed Ashley cutting the grass in the front yard. He crossed the street to be on the same side of the street. She saw him and the dog coming. She shut off the mower and waited for them to approach. "Good morning, Sheriff Tom."

"Good morning, Ashley. Why are you cutting the grass and not Jamal?"

"One word – football! He is totally focused on football. I've never seen him so focused on anything. It's coach said this, coach said that; this drill, that practice. Geez, I'm ready for the season to be over. The first game is on Friday. I don't know if I'll survive."

"I suppose I was the same way when I was in high school. Sports have a way of taking over a young man's imagination."

"Would you like a glass of lemonade? I'm hot from pushing the mower. This Florida heat is nuts."

"I guess Ms. French wouldn't mind a break for me to get a drink." Tom took a seat on the front step and waited. He could hear Nimitz whining inside the front door. When Ashley emerged, Tom suggested, "What if I take my dog into the back yard and you can let Nimitz out. They're good together."

"Okay," and she returned inside while Tom let himself into the backyard by the gate. When the backdoor opened Nimitz came running for his friend and the two dogs began to run about the backyard while the humans sat on the steps.

"How is the job at the Post Office?"

"I think it's going okay. I like the people I'm working with. That makes it lots easier. One thing I've learned is Amazon sends lots of packages through the post office. You can't believe the number that show up every single day. I swear, everybody in Dade City orders from them."

"Have you ever seen their new warehouse down by Davenport on US 27? It is huge. Their parking lot isn't big enough for all the employees. They end up parking out by the road. It's crazy. When their shifts end, it's a huge traffic mess. I've been called to go there for traffic control. It's a long way to drive from Dade City"

"Why would you be called. It's a different county."

"We have an agreement with Polk County. Sometimes they need a few extra cars. That's when I get called. Are you working tonight?"

"No, I'm off today. I was supposed to be off tomorrow but I traded shifts so I could go to the first game on Friday."

"That's probably a good decision. Kids like parents to attend their games. I feel for kids whose parents don't attend. It has to be tough being a single mom, at least some times."

"Yea, sometimes, but since I've never been part of a team of parents with Jamal, it's all I know."

"I know you don't know me very well, but would you be interested in going to lunch with me. I'm off today and tomorrow and I don't know your sleep schedule, but I'd like to take you to a little café downtown. Any interest?"

"Hey, that sounds like fun. I don't have too many friends, yet. I'd like that. How about today?"

"I'll swing by at 12:30 pm, work for you?"

"It will give me time to finish the yard and jump in the shower."

***

Helen picked up the phone to call her son. "Tommy, it's mom."

"Hi mom, is everything all right?"

"I was volunteering at the library and a guy came in with a strange request. He wanted me to help him find a couple living people. He was kind of vague about the reason, so I thought I would run the whole thing past you, since you have pretty good senses."

"Tell me what's going on."

"It all started when I was over at Murphy's bar having my usual soda. I was sitting alone at the bar and this guy comes up and starts talking. He was kind of talking to himself and I over heard him say he did not know how to find someone. So, I told him about my work at the Heritage Center. He got real interested saying he wanted to locate three living people. Then he asked if I would help him if he came into the library. I told him when I would be there. He showed up today."

"Who was he looking for?"

"The names were Janet LeMay, Cooper LeMay and Juan Malik Adams. He said his name was Mattawan James and he wouldn't give me a phone number."

"I'm writing this down, mom. Tell me about the James guy?"

"Caucasian, early forties, maybe five ten, a hundred seventy pounds. Dark hair, no facial hair. Don't believe he was much of a library fan since he was never in the library before today but he seems to be local."

"Okay, that's good. How about information you located on the three people?"

"I found several things on the Adams guy. He works for a

company in Atlantic City; import export firm. He was a big-time college football player years ago at Ohio State. James made copies of what I found. I even found a phone number for the place Adams works. He didn't tell me much about the other two but I suspect they are related. Maybe mother and son. But it was strange. When I searched for them by name, nothing. Almost like they disappeared. I found a high school picture of the woman from Kansas, but nothing more."

"I got the information jotted down. I'm scheduled back in the office on Wednesday. I'll run background on the four and see what I can learn. Then I'll get back to you."

"Do you think this guy is dangerous? He said something about finding a photo album at a flea market he wants to return."

"Mom. I don't think you need to worry about this guy being a danger to you. Does the library have a security system with cameras?"

"Yes, they are everywhere."

"I might want to request a tape. I'll talk to my supervisor about it. Listen, mom, I got to go. I'm taking a new neighbor to lunch."

"Oh Tommy, that makes me happy. You need to move on with your life. Cheryl would want you to move on, too."

"Love you, mom."

***

Chapter Nineteen

Jamal looked around the classroom to see if any team members were in Mrs. Benders geometry class. Whippy Monroe, a third string running back, was sitting two rows ahead and two aisles toward the window. Jamal smiled inward as he remembered planting Whippy on the turf during one of the tackling drills. Coach said it was a picture-perfect tackle. So far six teammates were in his classes. Three were in Spanish class.

Mrs. Benders started the hour with introductions. She instructed each student to give their name and one fact about themselves. But she made one clarification. Any student new to Dade City would have to tell three things. At first Jamal thought the exercise was lame, but after a couple students gave their facts, it got interesting. It would be done alphabetically, so Jamal knew he would be near the end.

"Ayisha Adams. I like rap music."

"Babbi Bowers. I enjoy building computers and rebuilding computers."

"Will Connor. I'm planning to be a Navy pilot."

"Raphael Custo. I play tennis. I like to cook enchiladas. My father is a doctor."

"Andrea Donald. I have a brown belt in judo." Jamal made a mental note not to mess with her.

"Erica Emmons. I want to get out of this class as soon as possible." Lotta laughs.

"Erica, that doesn't count. Try again," said the teacher.

"Okay, no laughing. I want to be an actress."

Mrs. Bender said, "That is a great goal. Make sure you try out for the school play. That is how all the great ones start. Next."

"Felix Faundez. I want to start a band."

"What kind of music?"

"Salsa. Not enough salsa bands around here."

"What instrument do you play?"

"Drums and some keyboard."

"Great, anybody want to join Felix band?" No takers. "Next."

"Danielle Franks. I love to play Mortal Combat." Jamal thought, my kind of woman.

"Gissy Guyette. My goal is to be an architect."

Mrs. Bender said, "Gissy, you are in the right class! Next."

"Jacob Hancock. I am a descendant of John Hancock who signed the Declaration of Independence."

"Willie Henry. Last year I was living in Germany. My mom is in the US Army as a translator. I'm a trekkie." Jamal sat up straight listening to those three sentences. Something about this girl called to him. Wow! I want to meet her."

"Wendy Irish. My mom has cancer and it sucks."

"What type of cancer?" asked the teacher.

"Lymphoma."

"I think we all agree with you, Wendy, cancer sucks. Right class?" Every head nodded. "Next."

"Ron Jansen. I moved here to live with my grandma. My mom died from cancer. And I agree with Wendy about cancer."

"Patti Johnsson. I plan to be a nurse and live in North Dakota."

"Why North Dakota?"

"I learned there is a great need for medical personnel in North Dakota and I want to be someplace where I can help out."

"Buzz Lambert. I want to be a cartoonist for Disney."

"Maryann Manferd. I want to be an elementary school teacher here in Dade City."

"Wayne Monroe. I want to build houses, mansions." Jamal thought, *Wayne, really? Why not be a landscaper so I can plant your ass, again?*

"Alexis Noonan. I want to be rich. I don't care how, just rich."

Mrs. Bender asked, "How much money will make you rich?"

"Twenty-five million dollars."

"How did you pick that number?"

"It has a nice sound to it." Chuckles are around the class.

"Sig Opalzewski. I want to change my name."

The teacher asked, "I have to ask, what will you change your name to?"

"Sipowitz."

"Like the character on NYPD Blue?"

"Yep. Sipowitz Opalzewski. That way you can find me in the phone book."

"Kurt Reed. I want to drive for NASCAR."

"Suri Russell. I want to be a professional golfer."

"You are on the school golf team, right?"

"I am."

"Amy Trottel. I want to be a writer. I want to write kid's books."

"Jamal Wilson. Last year I was in Michigan. I joined the football team. I own a Belgian Malinois."

"Tell us what a Belgian Malinois is."

"A Belgian Malinois is also known as a Belgian Shepherd. They are used by the US military to accompany troops in combat. They are beautiful, intelligent, and fearless."

"Chi Wong. I want to visit China."

Mrs. Bender stood, "Thank you, everyone. I appreciate learning about each of you. Now, place your books under your desk and take out a piece of paper and a pen. Put your name on the top of the paper. This will be the first test of the semester. Look up when you're ready."

"There are eleven guys and thirteen ladies in this class. I want you to write every name of the students in the class. They don't have to be in order or be spelled correctly. If you don't remember the name, write the fact the person stated. One point for each correct name and one-half point for each correct fact. Go. You have ten minutes."

The new students were at a disadvantage but Mrs. Bender was making a point with the exercise. When time was up, only two students were not done. "There is one more question. On the bottom line of your paper, how many in this class are new to Dade City this year. Write down the number. Okay, everyone pass your paper to the person behind you, and the last person in the row, send your paper to the front. Place a check mark next to each correct answer.

"Here are the names." She proceeded to read every name as the papers were corrected. Then, from memory, the teacher told a fact about each student. "There are four new students. Count up the check marks and circle the number at the top of the page. Then pass them back to the author."

"Who got twenty to twenty-five correct?" Three hands went up. "Who got ten or less correct?" No one. "Who got ten to fifteen correct?" Eight hands were raised. "Finally, who got fifteen to twenty?" Fourteen hands. Mrs. Bender went to the board and wrote down the numbers – three, zero, eight, fourteen. She totaled the numbers and got a total of twenty-five. Then she said, there are twenty-four students. How is it possible to have twenty-five hands raised?

Patti's hand went up. "Someone raised their hand twice."

"Correct. Why?"

Alexis had an answer. "It was how you asked the question."

"That is right. Alexis, come to the board and explain your answer."

"I know it is the right answer because Wayne put his hand up, twice. I saw him."

"Wayne, is that correct?"

"Yes."

"If you had not seen him raise his hand, how would you express that with math and numbers? Remember you are in a math class. Who can show us on the board?"

Willie raised her hand and went to the board. She drew a line from left to right, marking off twenty-five sections, placing a numeral under five, ten, fifteen, twenty and twenty-five. She turned to the class. "If you plot the correct answer totals along this line, they will all fall between ten and twenty-five." She turned and marked lines through those numbers. "Mrs. Bender, the way you asked the question, if someone had a score of fifteen or twenty, they would have held up their hand twice."

Mrs. Bender asked, "Wayne, which was it, fifteen or twenty?"

"Twenty."

"Class, give Willie a hand."

Mrs. Bender continued. "Today, this lesson was about three things. First, it was designed to get you comfortable with each other. Second, it was a lesson in listening. It did not matter how intelligent you are, if you listened, you could pass the test. And it was a lesson to show math is not only about numbers. She pointed at Willie's drawing and said, that is a line. And a line is part of mathematics called geometry. Questions?"

The bell rang. "No homework today. See you tomorrow."

Jamal said to Wayne, "Hey Whippy, see you on the field after school."

"See you then. And just wait. I'm going to get you back and plant your butt on the field next time!"

Willie pushed through the football players, "Move it, jocks."

As she walked away, Whippy said, "She is fine." Jamal just nodded his head as she walked away.

***

Mandan Hillman sat watching the local news but his mind was elsewhere. He reviewed what he knew of the three targets, LeMays and Adams. Hillman was troubled the information about the LeMay's was so sparce. *How can that be possible*, he wondered? At least he had some information about Adams, Juan Malik Adams. But Hillman knew that pursuing only Adams would not get him the payday he needed.

He picked up the telephone book for Atlantic City which was only three months old. He turned to the Adams listings to find seventy-seven names but no Juan, Malik, Juan Malik or even J. M. He threw the book across the room in frustration. He muttered a few words as the yellow book came to rest on the floor. He remembered Adams worked for Benjamin Maguire, or at least used to work for the man. He retrieved the phone book and thumbed through the book a second time looking for the Maguire business. He found a listing for Maguire Enterprises. 609-555-1212.

He had nothing to lose, he dialed the company number. "Maguire Enterprises, how may I direct your call?"

"I'm trying to reach Mr. Juan Adams."

"Do you mean Mr. Malik Adams?"

"Yes. Thank you."

"I will connect you."

Hillman hung up. Confirmation Adams was back working for Montie's father, again. That was the piece of information he was waiting for.

At the Maguire offices, Adams intercom spoke, "Mr. Adams, phone call, line three." When he pushed the line button, Adams heard the dial tone. He called the switchboard.

"Julie, this is Malik. When I answered the call you announced, no one was on the line. Run the back trace on the call and get me the number."

"Right away, sir."

"Can you tell me anything about the caller?"

"Male. Very businesslike. Caller ID was not blocked."

"Thanks."

Twenty minutes passed before Adams was tapping on the door of Mr. Maguire. "Sir, I believe we have a hard lead on the hit man."

"What do you have?"

"Switchboard got a call from a male asking for me. He hung up before I answered. Julie traced it back to an apartment on the west side. A man named Mandan Hillman. Tiny is running a background check on him right now."

"Address?"

"Right here, sir." He handed his boss the address.

"I'll contact Powers and have him put a tail on the guy once Tiny finishes the background check." Tiny walked in to join the conversation.

"My instincts tell me this is the guy Montie worked with. He is a former military sniper, dishonorable discharge. Single, no steady source of income. Owes a fair amount of money to bookies."

Maguire said, "Let's hope the man is not some dumb-ass. He's got to know he has to kill all three of you to collect."

Tiny asked, "Boss, why not just take him out? No hitman, no hit."

"Before going legit, I would have called Montie in here to take care of the problem. New day, new ways. There is no way this guy gets close to Adams without our consent."

The following morning, Hillman left his apartment to do surveillance on the Maguire building, and hopefully he could catch a glimpse of Adams. And, if the stars lined up just right, maybe the man would lead Hillman right to the other two. Then, three kills, one payday. Hillman never thought he would be watched by two of Powers people.

Back in the Maguire building, the call came from Powers guy. "Mr. Maguire, he is sitting down the block with binoculars. We will keep watching."

* * *

Tom Swift reflected on his lunch with Ashley Wilson the previous day. The shrimp stew was as good as always, but the company was even better. *What a nice woman.* He found her to be a great conversationalist. She was easy to talk to and she listened to what he shared. Their lunch at the diner lasted two hours. They laughed; Tom knew since Cheryl's death, he missed having intimate conversations more than anything else. And he seldom laughed. *What was there to laugh about, anyway?*

So much of his world was dark. As a sheriff's deputy, he saw things, things fine citizens seldom had to deal with, crime, death, attitude and making split second decisions were all part of the job. They were not things he could tell his mother or others outside the department. He used to tell Cheryl but now, she was gone.

Tom's mind reviewed the things his mother had told him the previous day. He had zero proof, but somehow the information she had shared seemed connected to the Wilson family. *Could it be?* Tomorrow he would start checking the information at his desk before he went on patrol.

Swift thought, *will there come a time when I can share any of this with Ashley?* He did not know.

Ashley Wilson could not remember the last time she enjoyed time with a man like yesterday. She found herself on the edge of admitting to Tom the whole story of the past six months. It was wearing her down. She felt they were living a lie. It did not feel right, even if it was protecting their lives. As she was starting the laundry for her boy, she daydreamed about laundry for a bigger family. Living in a house crowded with people and sound and love. It had always been her dream before she went off to college. Then Ashley heard her father's voice in the back of her mind-a memory. "Janet, reality can be a bitch!" She was ready for a new reality.

When they parted after lunch, there was no talk of another meeting. Maybe she would have to take Nimitz on a walk past Tom's house. Why wait for him? That's the old way. She looked over by the backdoor to where Jamal hung the leash. Now is as good as any. "Nimitz, go for a walk?"

At the sound of his name, the Belgian was sitting at her feet, ready. They rounded the corner and started down the street where she knew Tom lived with Ms. French. But she did not see his cruiser and was not sure which house was his. So, she walked slowly holding back the dog who was used to going much faster with Jamal. Ashley heard the sound; a dog was whining in one of the houses up ahead and as she got closer the sound increased in volume until she was standing at the driveway. The front curtains were fluttering as Ms. French was pacing back and forth near the window.

Hesitating, she approached the front door to ring the bell. Tom opened the front door, upon seeing his neighbor his face broke into a big smile. "Tom, I wanted to tell you how much I enjoyed our lunch yesterday. I don't think I told you."

"Would you like to come in?"

The dogs ran in the backyard as the two sat at the kitchen table.

Ashley started the conversation. "It has been so long since I've had such a nice time with a man."

"I don't know what to say. I have spent little time with a woman since Cheryl died two years ago."

"Tell me about her. I would like to know who she was, what she was like."

For the next forty minutes, Tom opened his heart to share his memories of his late wife. He went to the photo album and sat next to Ashley explaining the settings of the pictures. He became tearful showing the photos and sharing the memories of her battle with cancer. This was a first for the sheriff's deputy; letting down the emotional walls he held up to protect his heart from the pain never far away. And Ashley listened, actively listened. She asked questions and offered verbal comfort by her manner.

The conversation was mostly one sided but Ashley felt strange feelings for this man as the story poured forth. She heard of the good times, the vacations they shared and even some of their common dreams. Dreams he now carried, alone. She asked about his parents, and his time in the military. Then she asked about their move to Dade City. They had some common troubles with the Florida weather and especially the high humidity.

Swift finally stopped and turned to Ashley and asked the perfect question. "Ashley, what are you hiding?" Suddenly, she was very self-conscious. She wanted to open up but there was doubt she could not get past. Not at the moment, maybe never. She kissed Tom on the cheek and made an excuse about needing to get home to sleep before going to work later in the evening. She never addressed the question he asked. Tom said as she was going to the back door to put the leash on Nimitz. "Ashley, we should do this again. I have enjoyed being with you."

"We should." She went out and left via the yard gate and headed home.

In the block walk, she thought, *I almost told him everything. What's wrong with me?*

***

Coach Stoddard announced in the locker room. "When you are dressed and ready for the field, just sit down and wait for me. I want to speak to you."

When he returned, there was anticipation in the air as each player wondered what was coming. "Okay men. Our first game is in three days and today, I want to announce the starting lineups. Some of you will not dress with the varsity, this week. You will be playing in the Junior varsity game on Saturday afternoon. And some of you who dress for Friday will also be playing on Saturday. The coaches have met and decided who we believe gives Pasco High the best chance of beating Cypress Creek. If anyone has an issue with our decision, see me after practice today. I will be handing out this paper which will list each player, position, varsity, Junior varsity, and uniform number. The number will be your number for the entire season. Oh, one more thing, the list is final subject to injuries and replacements. Let's go Pirates!" Jamal's eyes went to the bottom of the sheet to find he was listed as a linebacker for both the Junior Varsity and Varsity. He would wear number fifty-seven. He knew tonight he would be looking on the internet to see which pro players wore the same number.

He headed out the door for the practice field. A couple important pieces of information were shared with him by the coaching staff during the practice. Jamal would be on the kick-off team and he would not be starting as a linebacker. But he would replace Jones as outside linebacker on obvious passing downs because of his speed in coverage. He also learned he would start Saturday as middle linebacker. He would be calling the defensive plays. He understood, it was an important responsibility. There was still much for the youngster to learn about football, but he had made a great impression on the coaching staff. What he did not know, he made an even bigger impression on his teammates.

For the final thirty minutes of practice, the Junior Varsity players went to the west end of the field to work on their plays for Saturday. Jamal found the middle linebacker position gave him a great look at the offense formation. He started picking up clues from the offense about the coming play and he was pretty accurate in his assessment of what was coming. By the end of the practice, he was directing the defensive players to be in the best possible location and angle for stopping the offense. Coach Sieman, the JV coach, did not miss the fact his middle linebacker was something special. He had a good feeling about their first game, at least on defense.

When Jamal got on his computer, he discovered two Football Hall of Fame linebackers wore number fifty-seven, Tom Jackson with the Denver Broncos and Randy Jackson with the New Orleans Saints. *Pretty impressive company.*

***

Chapter Twenty

Following the meeting with the FBI, Maguire Enterprises understood the time arrived to cut their ties with the other crime families. But how to do it was the question posed by Benjamin Maguire to Malik Adams. Maguire was adamant, "There is unfinished business with Montie's murder. I just can't let that go."

"Sir, I understand your feelings. Is there a different way to approach the problem so you can still get the closure you need?"

"I'm guessing you have some plan? Adams, you always have a plan! Tiny, what do you think?"

"Mr. Maguire, if you want the company to go legit, we cannot have law enforcement watching every move we make. That will be a disaster. I think Malik has a solid plan."

Maguire sat and looked at his assistant with a scowl on his face.

"First, let's turn over our information on the killers to local law enforcement. We know where the two are holed up. We have information about their involvement with the murder. I can speak to the local district attorney. It's a murder. Every DA wants to prosecute a murder case. It's good for their future aspirations. I'm sure this one will feel the same. Especially if the case is as tight as this one."

"Then, either Tiny or I will make the trip to Baltimore to meet with Teddy Power. He has the money to establish the training center for the Sinaloa Cartel. Together the families finance the training center to keep the Tijuana Cartel bottled up in Mexico. They won't have the resources to fight Sinaloa and expand east at the same time. You and Power have the plan in place. It will work. Your hands stay clean. The IPO should be ready for release within sixty days according to the legal team."

Maguire asked, "Are you certain the killers are still in the places we located? And don't you think the feds are watching the two of you?"

"Sir, we have been watching them since the day we located their hiding places. The feds will be watching us. We know that. But as long as you aren't seen with Power, there is nothing to use against you."

"Do you think the FBI are still monitoring our offices?"

"Yes, I do. That's why we're meeting in the safe room. You want them to hear what You are doing. Most of what you're doing. Feed the feds information you want them to hear. Nothing more, nothing less."

***

Tom Swift's opportunity to check out the information received from his mother was not priority but he got to the office on Friday morning and went straight to his desk to check the names on the law enforcement data base. He started by checking out the name of Mattawan James. It was an alias for Mandan Hillman, former military sniper, gambler, all around sleaze ball.

After making a few notes, he saved the information to an investigative file on the desk top computer. The next search was for Juan Malik Adams who was employed by Maguire Enterprises of Atlantic City. The information noted Maguire Enterprises was owned by Benjamin Maguire, a crime boss in the Atlantic City area. Swift was starting to smell a foul odor about the information from his mother. He looked a little deeper to find the college football career of Adams at Ohio State University. There was a high-resolution picture of Adams from his college days. Something about the face, but Swift could not place where he had seen the face.

Again, Swift saved the information to the file. Then he tapped in the name of Janet LeMay and he waited while the search ran. The hourglass on the screen continued to spin with no results. When he finally gave up, he did the same with Cooper LeMay and received the same results. He sat back in his chair and starred at the ceiling. One of the Sheriff's detectives walked by and said, "Swift, are you daydreaming?"

"Connor, you got a minute?" He gave the detective the quick synopsis of his investigation and the results. "Why don't I get results on these two?"

"Hmm. How old are they, the LeMay's?"

"Not sure but from the information I received, she is probably the mom of the kid."

"Is your source of the information good?"

"It's from my mother."

"Have you checked her out, recently? Just kidding. Let's see." Connor thought for a minute. "What about normal ID stuff, driver's license, Social Security number?"

"Nothing."

"Were the LeMay's connected to the Adams character?"

"Somehow."

"Bring him up again. Did you check warrants, arrests?"

"No, let me do that." After a pause, "Here he is in federal custody following a DUI in Philly. That makes no sense. Feds and a DUI. Got to be something more."

"Go to the Federal Court in Philadelphia and put in his name." By now Detective Connor was getting interested in the case. "There's his case. Look at that. The case was dropped with prejudice after six months and sealed by the judge. You said Adams worked for Benjamin Maguire, right?"

Swift nodded.

"Do a Google news search for Benjamin Maguire in New Jersey over the past year and see what comes up."

Swift said with astonishment, "Look at this. There is a front-page article about the murder of Montgomery Maguire, son of Benjamin, in Atlantic City, and the date is two weeks before the judge dropped the case against Adams."

"Without any more facts, I'd say these are all somehow related. Think about it. Guy tries to find three people to give them something supposedly from a flea market and yet I can't find a link between the three. Something is going on here. Conner, thanks for your help."

It would be a long day for Swift as he was working security at the Pasco High Football game later in the day. With a kick off at 7:30 pm, Swift and Ms. French needed to be at the school before 6 pm.

***

Tiny Olm was chosen to make the trip to visit with Teddy Power. As the Lincoln Town car left the garage, Hillman almost fell out the driver's door trying to see who was in the car. He could not let Adams get away. He was relieved to see the passenger was not his target. The men tailing Hillman got a good laugh watching the amateur's observation. They called the information to Maguire's number.

Across town, a group of twelve Atlantic City officers were coordinating arrests for the killers of Montgomery Maguire. When the police breeched the door of Miguel Riveria, there was no resistance. The handcuffs were on the suspect within thirty seconds as he was taking a siesta following a big meal of fajitas and Corona beer. The officers not only arrested the man, but retrieved his weapon, four bags of speed, and three telephones along with a laptop and tablet. It would take the forensic personnel less than sixty minutes to retrieve files and phone calls linking Riveria to Patel and to the cartel leadership in Tijuana. Law enforcement at several levels would be salivating to learn this intelligence.

But the story at the apartment of Selena Patel would not have such a peaceful ending. Patel was careful and observant. She knew something was coming as she had paid a teen-age boy to send her a text if more than one police car pulled into the parking lot of the motel. The additional ninety seconds got Patel out the door, down the steps and over the back fence to her secondary vehicle. As she pulled from the liquor store lot, the apartment door was smashed open finding an empty, recently occupied room. There was enough DNA to keep a technician busy for several hours, but Patel was in the wind. By the time the police put out an all-points bulletin, Patel was in New York City heading north near the Hudson. She had it planned. She was no fool.

Seventy-two hours later, she was crossing the United States and Mexico border at Tecate, California heading for the cartel headquarters in Tijuana. Selena made her report to the head of the cartel. She had spoken with him at least five times since fleeing Atlantic City. He wanted all the information about the operation. When she walked out of the meeting, a new enforcer placed a bullet in her brain. The newest assassin did not realize how short his life would be once he failed on a single mission.

***

The four coaches were meeting in the office of Stoddard. Stoddard said, "Have you seen our pre-season ranking in the state of Florida? Eleven hundred ninety-three. Jesus, what do we have to do to get some respect in Florida High School Football?"

Coach Allison said, "Don't get too excited, Jerry. I think our offense will be solid. We should be able to run the ball down their throats. My question mark is our defense. We need some solid play."

Sieman jumped in the conversation. "I want to try something with our defensive backfield. We know Cypress Springs quarterback, Nickles, had a solid season last year throwing the ball but he had an experienced offensive line. This year he has one returning starter, the center. If we run some upfront crosses and stunts with some blitzing, I think we can shake them up. Mess with their confidence early, run the ball against them, we should be good."

Stoddard said, "But if you send a cornerback to bring pressure, who is going to cover the outside receiver on that side?"

Sieman smiled. "My secret weapon. Jamal Wilson."

"The kid is brand new to football. Can he handle it?"

"Do you remember the speed drills? He is the second fastest guy we have on the field. He is quicker than any of our defensive backs. He is going to surprise you. You'll see. He will be on the field for most passing third downs. I've been working with him on rolling out to cover on blitzes on his side. He's ready."

Coach Allison said, "Jerry is your 'win one for the Gipper' speech ready?"

"I've been ready since the end of last season. I can't believe the butterflies I have. I want to put on pads and go out there with the kids and hit somebody." Stoddard pulled out the traditional Styrofoam cups for the coaches from his desk drawer. Placed in a tight circle, he lifted the bottle of Gatorade and put one good swallow in each cup. "Gentlemen, to our team. Raise your cup to the Pasco Pirates."

The first players started arriving an hour and a quarter before the start of the game. The atmosphere was subdued until Gus Johnson walked in with his sunglasses and sombrero hat. Quarterbacks can get away with silliness as long as they inspire the rest of the team. When the guys saw his hat, they lost their quiet attitudes. Jamal was sitting in front of his locker as the place took on a carnival atmosphere. "Smitty, what's going on?

"Johnson just came in with a goofy hat on. He does this every week with a different hat. My dad told me, last year he wore one of those lodge hats called a fez. He is a goofball!"

Jamal responded, "Glad he's our goofball."

The players helped each other get their jerseys over the pads. The black helmets looked formidable as the sixty players went out the door to warm up for the first game of the season. As they took the east end of the field for pregame, the fans gave a cheer. High School football in Florida was back!

Cypress Springs won the coin flip and chose to receive the opening kick. Kicker Udell carefully set the ball on the tee, measured his steps back, raised his hand awaiting the whistle to start the game. The end over end kick was fielded at the nine-yard line by Tassman who cut to his right, got two great blocks and he was off heading toward the goal line. Jamal closed to the twenty-yard line but got caught in traffic. He turned and pursued down the side line, closing on the ballcarrier. He caught Tassman at the twenty-five and they went down at the twenty-two-yard line. When Tassman broke into the open, Coach Sieman slammed his clipboard into the turf and then started jumping when he saw Wilson catching the return man. Jamal returned to the bench to back slaps from his teammates. Coach Stoddard understood the comments about speed of his sophomore. First down, Cypress Springs.

The fifth play from scrimmage resulted in an eight-yard touchdown run by a wide receiver on a reverse. The point after failed with a score of six to zero for the visitors. Jamal stood helplessly on the sideline watching the first score of the day.

The first offensive series stalled at the forty-yard line with the punt rolling dead at the twenty of the opponents. The next two plays gained only three yards leaving a third and seven. Coach Sieman sent Jamal in with instructions to cover the tight end. With the snap of the ball, Wilson delayed the tight end's release to his receiving pattern. The quarterback looked in Wilson's direction, then overthrew the end on the opposite side of the field. Cypress Springs was forced to punt with Pasco taking possession at their own forty-five-yard line.

On the first play, the offense lined up in a different formation, the wish bone. With the snap, Gus Johnson pivoted and faked left to the fullback, Gonzolos, ran towards the defensive end and at the last instant flipped the ball to Armando Nelson who turned the corner and outran the defense for the first score of the season. A fifty-five-yard run. Udell kicked the extra point giving the home team a one-point lead. The remainder of the first quarter was a back-and-forth struggle with neither team taking control.

On the second play of quarter two, Coach Sieman had a hunch. Up to this point, Cypress Springs had only attempted passes on third down with limited success, so Jamal was sent in with a defensive play. It was an outside linebacker blitz on the weakside, meaning it would be Jamal shooting outside the offensive tackle on the quarterback's blind side. The ball was on the opponent's thirty-two. Jamal's locker mate, Smitty was the weak side defensive end. When the ball was snapped, Smitty went to the inside shoulder of the tackle giving Jamal a free path to quarterback Nickles, who set up to pass to the wide receiver on his right. He never saw Jamal as he was nailed in the middle of the back. The ball popped out in the collision, with Smitty recovering on the twenty-six-yard line for the Pirates. The first turnover of the season led to a second down right-side screen pass to Nelson who took the ball to the two. Gonzolos carried the ball over the goal line with five minutes left in the half.

At half time, Coach Stoddard praised his players for not allowing the opening kickoff to affect their thinking. His most memorable statement was, "We do not need stars on the field, we need every player doing his job and supporting those around him. You do that, you will win this game."

The Pirates opened the third quarter with a sustained drive of seventy-yards on ten plays giving them a lead of twenty-one to six. On the final drive of the third quarter, Cypress Springs was having little success running the ball so opened with a passing formation which brought Jamal back on to the field. The defense was ready when Nickles retreated and threw over the middle of the field towards his running back. Troxel, the Pirates safety saw the play developing and stepped in front of the receiver taking the ball forty-one yards for the final score of the day; an interception for a touchdown.

As the fourth quarter was opening, the Pasco coaching staff decided to let the reserves play the final quarter. They were concerned with giving away too many plays to the other league teams who would watch the game tape in a few hours. This meant Jamal would move to middle linebacker and be surrounded by the same players who would be playing in the Junior Varsity game, the next day. As in practice, Wilson took charge of the defense. Crystal Springs offense managed one solid drive and scored in the final minute of the quarter. Final Score, Pasco twenty-eight, Cypress Springs thirteen.

As the teammates returned to the locker room, excitement was running like water in the shower. Gus Johnson got up on a bench to address the players. "Dudes, you were awesome tonight. Every one of you should be all conference. Next week we go on the road to Auburndale. Celebrate tonight because when Monday practice starts, we need to be all business. There are always ways we can be better. Let's do it!"

When his shower was finished, Gonzolos asked Jamal, "Do you want to come hang out with the guys after the game? We are going downtown to the ice crème shop."

"Thanks for asking, man. I appreciate it, but my mom is waiting for me and she is my ride. How about next time?"

"Yeah man, that would be great. Plan on it. One of us can drive you home. Okay?"

"Sounds like a plan."

Smitty looked over at Jamal and said, "Kid, you were great. I'm glad you decided to play football. Good game." There were many hand slaps before the locker room emptied for the night.

An assortment of students, fans and parents were waiting in the school parking lot for the players. Jamal saw Ashley next to the minivan talking to someone. When he got closer, it was Tom Swift. "Great game, Jamal. The Pirates looked like they could go a long way this season," said Swift.

"Thanks, Deputy. Where's Ms. French?"

"She's in the cruiser over by the field. No one will bother her in my car. I wanted to ask you a question. Would you be interested in bringing Nimitz to a training session with the area K-9 units? It will be Sunday morning at nine. You could show off your work with the dog to others who appreciate canines."

"Mom, what do you think? Sounds interesting and would be good for the dog."

Ashley said, "It's okay with me."

"Deputy, can you pick us up? The JV game is in the morning and I do have an informal practice at seven thirty in the morning, Sunday. Just some of the guys getting together to run. You know, more conditioning."

***

It was two weeks later on a Thursday morning, Malik Adams received an email from his old roommate, Gordon Banks. The message was simple: *Take a look at this link. Reminds me of you. Gordy.* The link was to an article from the most recent issue of *High School Football News*. Linebacker has career day in win over rival. Jamal Wilson, a sophomore at Pasco High School in Dade City, Florida, made twenty-three tackles, eighteen solo with four for loss of yardage in a game with rival, Auburndale. Head coach, Mel Stoddard said, "Wilson is a natural talent and played a great game." Adams gazed intently at the head shot of the player. His eyes opened wide as he recognized his own son. "Cooper!" he whispered.

By the end of the day, Adams learned the schedule of the Pasco Pirates football team for the remainder of the season as well as places to stay along the route to central Florida. In his mind, this was important. He needed to see his own flesh and blood play the game he loved so much.

When he spoke to Mr. Maguire about taking time off to make the trip, he was reminded of the security situation faced by the company and the directors of the business. The threats were still out there, real and potentially dangerous. Maguire said, "You will probably be followed. Hard telling what might happen. Keep your eyes peeled. I don't want you to end up like Monty."

"Thanks for looking out for me. This is about my boy. I've missed his whole life. It needs to stop, now." With that, Adams headed towards the door.

With Adam's exit, Maguire called Tiny. "Call Powers. I need him to put men on Adams for this trip to Florida. Make it happen. I have a bad feeling."

Powers sent the call from Tiny on to his security chief, Ted Ansel. Ansel was a former detective from a large western city who spent time tracking fugitives for a bail bondsman out of Newark. After receiving the general information, including vehicle information, license plate, point of origin and destination, Ansel said, "Tell your boss not to worry. I'll have his boy under surveillance within the hour. Adams won't even know we are watching."

Tiny reminded Ansel of the Mattawan Jones situation. "We're still watching him, too. If we get lucky, Jones will follow Adams all the way to Florida. The key will be to stop any second or third possible threat. I'll stay in touch with you."

Tiny returned to Maguire's office to let the old man know the arrangements. Maguire listened and began to nod his head. Then very softly said, "Be glad you never had kids, Tiny. They not only drive you crazy, they make you blind in certain areas of life. That's what happened with Monty. There were some things I just refused to see."

"Sorry boss," as he retreated to his office.

***

Chapter Twenty One

"Oh mom, I'm so sorry. I forgot to tell you what happened after going to the dog training session with Deputy Swift. There were eight dogs plus Nimitz. They were working on having the dogs recognize gun cleaning chemicals. The dogs can smell the gun oil within thirty feet of either the gun or the hands of someone who has been using the oil."

"What do the dogs do when they smell the oil?"

"That was the really cool part. Each dog responds differently because the oil hurts their nose. One dog actually sneezed. Nimitz shakes his head like he has water in his ears. I've never taught him that or seen him do it any other time. When he shakes his head, I'll know he either has water in his ears or he is smelling gun oil. Deputy Swift says it is a good warning for anyone in law enforcement who works with dogs."

Ashley said, "Let's hope Nimitz never has to use that lesson around us."

***

The final game of the regular season would be against the Bulldogs from Zephyrhills. A home game for the Pirates. Malik Adams found a parking spot on the front side of the high school and followed the other fans around to the stadium. He paid the five dollars for the ticket and decided to sit in the visitor side of the field. He figured he knew no one so it really didn't matter where he sat. He decided on a seat about halfway up on the forty-yard line. He resisted the urge to bring a camera but did bring along a set of inexpensive binoculars. Since he arrived an hour before the scheduled kickoff, he had a chance to look over the other fans and parents as the players were still in the locker rooms. He wondered, "How many times was that me in the locker room waiting to take the field?" He felt a rush of adrenalin course through his body just from the thoughts of football.

Out in the parking lot, Mattawan Jones located Adams vehicle. He waited until most of the parking lot had filled with other cars before he slipped a small GPS tracking device into the wheel well of the vehicle. He did not know Benjamin Maguire had a similar but better-quality device under the rear bumper of the same vehicle. Powers people used the time to place one on Jones car while he was standing by Adam's vehicle. When one moved, many would follow. And two FBI agents were using a small drone flying two hundred feet in the air to watch all of them.

Adams had picked up a program when he walked into the stadium. There it was: Jamal Wilson, Sophomore, Linebacker, 6'3" 215 pounds – Number 57. This is who he came to see. Adams did a quick calculation to compare himself to his son.

Let's see. When I was a sophomore, I was an inch shorter and seven pounds lighter. He should be just the right size to play college football someday. I wonder about his foot speed and his foot work? What's his muscle tone? Does he work out in the weight room? How's his diet? All these thoughts flooded the mind of Malik Adams as he waited for the son, he never had really shown any interest in getting to know. Until now!

Ashley Wilson did not want to arrive too soon for the game. She agreed to help with concessions at half time thanks to being recruited by the mom of two other players. She didn't mind. It helped her get to know the other parents. But she was still being cautious as counselled by the US Marshall's Service. She parked her minivan fifteen minutes prior to kickoff and made her way to the main entrance where she saw her friend Tom Swift with his canine sitting just inside the gate.

Swift said, "Hi Ashley. Are you excited about this game? It is a big deal here in Dade City. If the Pirates beat the Bulldogs, they go to the state playoffs. It would be the first time in many years, and Jamal is a big reason for this opportunity."

"It's all he seems to be focused on in the past week. Gotta win. He's been explaining the whole game plan to Nimitz each night as he goes to bed. It's really funny the way the dog tilts his head every time Jamal talks to him. I wonder how much he really understands?"

"These Malinois are smart dogs. He probably understands more than you think."

"If that's true, that dog knows more about football than I will ever know. I'll see you after the game," said Ashley as she moved towards the parent's section in the stands. Hillman decided he would stay out in the parking lot to monitor the situation and the Power's people stayed in their vehicle too. The FBI was on the opposite side of Stadium Street in a parking lot monitoring it all from their communications van. And unbeknown to everyone, the US Marshalls were keeping tabs on Ashley and Jamal from inside the stadium.

When Ashley got to her seat, the teams were in the final stages of warm up drills and the kickers were practicing across the endzones. It was a warm evening in November but as the sun set, it seemed a perfect night for Florida High School football.

In the parking lot, Mandan Hillman reviewed his plan while he checked his handgun. A rifle would not be of any use in his plan. He needed to get up and get personal before pulling the trigger three times. The last time he had pulled the trigger three times, other than on the gun range, had been in Afghanistan in a small village. He was the point man of a five-man Army team. He walked around a corner of a hut to see three Taliban having smokes with their weapons slung over their shoulders. Jones pulled his service revolver and shot all three in back before they could react. It was the final act leading to his dismissal from the military and time in prison. He had ignored the US military's engagement protocols. But, in Hillman's mind, he would do the same thing again. There was too much money to be gained to grow a conscience, now.

***

The Pirate coaches decided to make a change before the final game of the season. Jamal Wilson would start the game as the middle linebacker and direct the defense on the field. Jose Till, the regular middle linebacker got spiked in the calf during practice two days earlier. He could still play, but his ability to run was hampered by the injury.

The coaches knew something from watching the Zephyrhills team videos. The center for the opponent was a six-foot eight-inch 270 pounder, Marques Walker. When high school coaches talked about Walker, he was compared to the Pouncey brothers who came out of Lakeland and played in the NFL. He was being recruited by every college in the SEC and ACC conferences. With his size, footwork, and athletic ability, Walker would be starting for some big-time college program within two years. And on running plays, the offensive center was responsible for blocking the middle linebacker.

During warm ups, Coach Sieman took Jamal aside to give him some special instructions. Coach said, "You see number fifty out there?" Sieman pointed at the big opponent.

"Walker?"

"That's who I mean. Don't let him get into your body on running plays. He's too big, strong and experienced. Do what you can to stay away from his hands. He is the real thing and the best player you have seen this year."

"I understand, coach."

"He has one weakness. When he fires out on running plays, he puts his head down and signals which side the ball carrier is going to take. So, if you see his head drop and he appears to be ready to use his right shoulder, the ball is going to the left and vice versa. Do you understand?"

"Got it."

"And he is quick. You hesitate, he wins every time. If you can get under his block and take his legs out from under him, your teammates will have a chance to make plays."

"I'll give it my best."

"I know you will, now finish your warm ups."

As the conversation was taking place, Malik Adams was watching through the binoculars. When the coach pointed, Adams swung his vision to the giant on the other team. Instinctively, he knew what the conversation would be. He glanced at the game program to see what information there was on number fifty. Adam's eyes got big as he read the name, class- senior, size and weight. He remembered playing against some of the best in college football. He knew his boy would need to play with his head. He pulled his phone to see what was on the internet about this kid. Adams was impressed, a high school All American.

Zephyrhills kicked the ball to the Pirates. The return brought the ball out to the twenty-nine. The offense stalled at their own forty-one and were forced to punt the ball away. The Bulldogs started from their own twenty-one-yard line. The first play was a blast right up the center of the defense. With the snap of the ball, Jamal watched Walker fire directly at him followed by the blocking back and the ball carrier. Jamal found himself on his back with the center on top of him as the ball went up the field to the forty where a safety made the stop. The next play was a fake up the middle with a pitch to the running back around the left end. Jones fought off the tackle and made a tackle limiting the gain to two yards. The third play from scrimmage was a repeat of the first play. When Walker got up off Jamal, he made a statement. "It's going to be a long day for you, kid. Better get used to it." Six plays later, Zephyrhills quarterback optioned around the right end and walked into the end zone.

As the teams were lining up for the kick off, Coach Sieman was in Jamal's face. "Now, do you understand?"

"I got this, coach." Jamal called his two-defensive tackles to the bench where he knelt in front of them.

"Guys, we need to make an adjustment right now. You see the problem that big dude gives us? Here is what we are going to do. They are using wide stances in their line. Move into the inside shoulder of their guards. If you hear me yell blue, try to hit both the guard and center with each of your shoulders. That should give me some time to react to what's happening in the backfield. If you don't hear me, just play off the guards. Understand?"

They both nodded their understanding.

By halftime, the score was Bulldogs 21 and Pirates 7. But the opponent's offense was having much less success running the ball up the middle as the adjustment took hold. And, the Dade City offense finally started making progress as they took the ball down the field with a combination of speed and passing.

Three minutes before halftime, Ashley made her way out of the stands toward the concession area to help out. She was about fifty feet away from her destination when she heard a voice from behind, "Janet!"

She stopped dead in her tracks and turned to see the man she once loved, Juan Malik Adams. She walked straight to him and said very softly, "Don't use that name, here. Understand?"

He nodded very slowly and asked, "Can we talk?"

"Not right here, and not right now. I'm on my way to help with the concessions. When the second half starts, I can talk to you, briefly. I don't know who is watching right now. The Marshalls told me to be very careful."

"I get it. I'll be over by the stands over there." He pointed and walked there while Ashley went to do her parental duty.

With two minutes remaining in halftime, Sheriff Tom Swift made his way to the concession booth. He made sure Ashley would be his server.

"Hi, Tom, what can I get you?"

"I'll take a popcorn with a root beer and a side of Malik Adams."

She just stared at him in shock. "I'll get that for you right away." She turned and picked up the refreshments. When she returned to her spot, she said, "Yes to that side. That will be four dollars."

As Swift pulled the bills from his pocket, he said, "Don't say anymore. I will be keeping my eye on the situation. Just in case you need me."

"Thank you."

Swift turned and walked to a place where he could see Adams and Ashley.

With two minutes left before the start of the third quarter, the concessions closed the metal window and the volunteers began to move back toward their seats in the stands. Others would come to run the booth following the game.

In the locker room, Coach Stoddard praised the play of his team. He knew they still had a chance to pull this out. The final thing he said was, "Wilson, I want to move you back to the outside. Jose, can you run things from the inside?"

"Yes coach."

"I want the offense to make some adjustments. Their corner backs are not fast and they have not shown the ability to make open field tackles. We are going to use crossing patterns to try to get them isolated on our wide outs. We will still run the ball enough to keep them honest on defense, but this will be a passing game for the rest of the game. Johnson, are you ready to throw the ball?"

"Coach, they won't know what hit 'em." With that declaration, the quarterback waded up a paper towel and threw it across the locker room where it went right in the trash can. That was all it took for the team to rise as one and head for the field with new confidence in their own abilities.

As Adams stood near the stands waiting, a thousand thoughts flooded his mind. Most started with *what if?* But he realized it could never work – him and Janet and Cooper. There was too much time and distance between them, and he noticed immediately, the feelings just were not there. He did not harbor secret thoughts of love toward these two. But he knew in the moment, he wanted more than nothing. Whatever that could or would be he was not sure.

Ashley knew she had no time for games with Adams, but he deserved more than a brush off or cold shoulder. "Malik, why are you here? How did you find us?" Her eyes sparkled with anger as she awaited his reply.

"My college roommate, you remember, Gordon Banks – he sent me an article from a high school football magazine about a kid in Florida who played linebacker. Gordy said the kid reminded him of me. When I saw the photo, I recognized Cooper, right away. With everything that has been going on in my life, I realized I needed to see him play football. That's why I'm here. To watch my boy play. That's all."

Ashley said, "Listen, don't use our old names. Those people are gone. I'm Ashley and he is Jamal Wilson. We had to go through hell to get away from the threats on our lives, and now you are here. Who knows who followed you? We spend a lot of time looking over our shoulders, because of you and your employer."

From the body language of Ashley and Malik, Sheriff Swift thought he should make his presence known, just in case. He approached and asked, "Everything okay?"

"We're fine, Tom." Then Ashley introduced the two men who seemed a bit cautious as they shook hands.

"So, you're Jamal's father?" asked Swift.

"That's right," said Adams.

Swift asked, "And you work for the Maguire Crime family in Atlantic City?"

"The answer is yes, but the family has gone legit. I'm sure you will need to check that out, but it's true. I can provide you with contacts in New Jersey who will back my story," said Adams. "It's a long story, but I'm willing to tell you sometime. But, can this wait until after the second half? I really want to watch my son."

Just then, Swift's communication system announced an incident was taking place in the front parking lot of the school. Ashley said, "I know you need to go. I'll keep Malik with me and we will see you at the gate at the end of the game." Off ran the Sheriff.

When Swift came around the building with Ms. French who he released from his cruiser, he saw three black SUV's with flashing lights surrounding a vehicle in the lot. Swift thought as he ran, *those look like Feds.* As he quickly approached the scene, there was a man spread on the asphalt with an agent on his back, placing handcuffs on the man while another agent trained his service revolver on the scene. The agents turned the man and had him sit as they began the interrogation.

Swift stood six feet from the third agent and asked to see identification. The agent pulled back his jacket to reveal his FBI badge. Swift asked, "What is happening, here?"

"The FBI has had this man under surveillance for the past thirty-six hours. We have a credible tip that he is here to carry out a contract killing on multiple individuals."

"What's his name?" asked Swift.

"Mandan Hillman, but he also goes by the name Mattawan Jones. He is a convicted felon from his days in the military. When my partner checked his vehicle, he found two hand guns and two rifles with at least a hundred rounds of ammunition."

Swift asked, "Do you need me to call for a car to transport Hillman to local lock up?"

"Thanks for the offer but we will be taking him to the Federal lock up in Tampa. His felony was a federal crime, so he will be returning to our hospitality. But thanks for the quick back up. Hey, I like your four-legged partner. You're a K-9 officer?"

"Yea, this is Ms. French. We've been partners almost three years."

***

Coach Sieman looked across the field at the Bulldogs. He thought he saw a certain swagger in their collective demeanor, and then it dawned on him. *Zephyrhills is up two touchdowns and they will go for the kill as soon as they get the kick off. And, I know how I would do it!* Sieman got together with the other coaches and discussed his idea. They came up with a plan.

Coach Stoddard called the kick-off team together and said just two words – "Yellow Rose." They had worked on this in practice the entire season but never used the play. Kicker Udall would do an on-side kick to his right side to start the half. Udall said, "Remember, block their front guys and let me and Sanchez get the ball once it goes ten yards. We can do this!"

When the whistle blew to start the second half, Udall made the kick and his teammates executed their blocks to perfection. Sanchez fell on the ball on the forty-seven-yard line of the Bulldogs and Udall jumped on top of Sanchez for insurance.

The second play from scrimmage was a fake pitch to the running back going left and Gus Johnson, dropped back, looked right to the wide receiver doing an out cut, then threw the ball to the tight end, Bruce "the Moose" Moore, who went straight up the field covered by a much slower linebacker. Touchdown! After the extra point, the Pirates were down by seven points with lots of time on the clock.

Coach Sieman was sure he saw a change on the opponent's bench as they doubted their own abilities in that moment. The following kick-off was brought back to the twenty-six. As Marques Walker settled over the ball for the Bulldogs, he noticed a different player across from him. It did not concern him. He knew he was good, maybe the best in the blocking line. What he did not know: Jamal was back in his familiar spot behind Smitty.

The second half defensive scheme was based upon the actions of the All-American Bulldog center. When he moved forward with the snap of the ball, the defense performed an inward pinching move to stop up the middle of the line while the linebackers shot through the line either outside or inside their defensive ends. Either way, there was no place for the running backs to go except to bounce toward the ends of the line where the safeties and cornerbacks stopped the run. When Walker, the Bulldog center snapped the ball and back pedaled, the linebackers and defensive backs knew a pass was coming. They were ready, either way. Within two sets of offensive plays, the Zephyrhills team was frustrated and barely able to move the ball. The third quarter saw the Bulldogs with only forty yards of offense with three punts and no points, while the Pirates moved the ball with ease and tied the score on a screen pass to Sanchez.

As Ashley and Malik watched the action, Malik began to ask questions about Jamal, and about what the boy was really like? Ashley answered with pride, realizing she had influenced the boy in positive ways for the past sixteen years. Malik was surprised to learn this was Jamal's first year playing football and any level. As he watched, he said, "He's a natural. I think he could be better than me!"

"Maybe," said Ashley. "But I know he wants to meet you. He wants to get to know you and have a relationship with his father."

"Seriously?"

"He has researched your entire college football career on the internet. He is a linebacker because you were a linebacker."

Malik did not know how to answer.

Halfway through the final quarter, Sanchez fielded a punt at his own twenty-yard line, and ran all the way back for a touchdown and the first lead of the game for the Dade City Pirates. The Pasco High School fans were giddy with excitement and joy. Coach Stoddard called a time out. Instead of kicking the extra point, he decided to go for a two point try with a trick play. Gus Johnson lined up in the shotgun and took the snap from center. He handed the ball to the fullback going around the left end, who flipped the ball to the wide receiver on the left side who was going back the opposite direction. A reverse. In the meantime, Johnson went into the right corner of the endzone where he caught the ball thrown by the wide receiver.

The home crowd was standing and cheering as their team took an eight-point lead with under five minutes left in the game. The Pirate's reserves were jumping up and down while they twirled towels over their heads, screaming their support.

Kicker Udall, made a big mistake on the kick-off as the ball went out of bounds. The Bulldogs would begin from their own forty-yard line. The coaching staff for the opponents pulled out all their best plays for what could be the final offensive drive of their season. With only twelve seconds left on the game clock, the Bulldog's quarterback ran around the right end at the ten-yard line and dove into the endzone for a touchdown. The only choice for their team was what play would they attempt for the two-point conversion to tie the game.

The game referee came to the Pirates bench to tell the staff number fifty, Walker, was declaring to be an eligible receiver. Coach Stoddard immediately called his final time out and motioned the defense to the sideline. The team had exactly sixty seconds to design a defensive play to keep the Bulldogs off the scoreboard.

"Guys. This is your season, right now. Either you stop them here or we miss our chance to be in the state playoffs for the first time in many years. No one thought you would come this far, but you believed in yourselves and here we are. Now, this is what we will do." Stoddard then explained the defensive scheme and the players ran back onto the field.

The Bulldogs lined up with the quarterback in the shot gun. Clearly a pass play. Jose called a quick adjustment as he saw three Bulldog receivers including Walker, reset to fifteen yards on the right side of the formation. The remainder of the team stayed in tight to block. Jamal knew immediately what was going to happen. There would be a quick pass to Walker while the other two receivers blocked for him heading for the endzone.

Jamal drifted out to join with the cornerback and safety on that side of the formation. Three on three. This would be the challenge. Jamal glanced over at Walker who was grinning like a child with an ice crème cone on a hot day. With the snap of the ball, the quarterback turned directly to his right and fired the ball to Walker who caught it. One-half second later, before the receiver could take a second step, Jamal split the two blocker/receivers and hit the big man with a picture book tackle dropping Walker short of the endzone.

As Jamal stood up, he said, "Fifty, you are a great player. But my dad was an All-American in college as a linebacker at Ohio State." Then he ran to the bench where he accepted the congratulations of his team.

As the fans left the stadium, no one could remember a more exciting game ever played at Dade City.

***

Chapter Twenty Two

Sheriff Tom Swift was waiting by the stadium gate as Ashley and Malik approached. "We had a little excitement in the school's front parking lot. The FBI took a man into custody. Said they received a credible threat he was in the area to kill some locals."

Malik asked, "Did you hear his name?"

"No. I'll follow up later. But it's unusual to see the FBI here." Swift made the statement in a "matter of fact" manner and watched for reactions. *Could this be connected to these people?*

Ashley said, "Sorry you missed the final plays of the game. It was pretty exciting." She continued, "Tom, I owe you an explanation. Can you come by the house later?"

"It would need to be around ten o'clock."

"That will work. See you then." She turned to Adams, "Follow me," as she walked toward the front entrance of the school where the families and friends of the players would wait for the team.

Adams said, "Janet – oh, sorry. I should get going. I saw what I came here for."

"Your son needs to meet you. There is no better time than right now."

Ten feet away was a woman watching every move of Malik Adams. She was guessing this woman with him was the mother of his son. She had no interest in the mom or the boy but she had her orders to take out Adams. But there were too many witnesses as a large excited crowd waited for the victors to emerge from the school entrance. The woman's confidence was soaring knowing Hillman had been taken into custody. Her little tip to the FBI paid off in a big way and they had moved away from the deputy Sheriff. This was not designed as a suicide mission. She needed to kill him in a manner that allowed her to get away, and timing was crucial. She needed to wait for the signal in her earbud.

***

Tiny Ohm was on his way home from the Maguire building with his long-time driver, Robert. It was Robert who noticed the Jeep which seemed to be changing lanes and direction with their vehicle. They were being followed.

"Mr. Ohm, I think we have a tail. Two back – green Jeep. I make out two males."

"How long have they been back there?"

"I noticed the Jeep about ten blocks ago."

"Take a right on Summit and then pull over and stop. Let's see what happens."

Robert maneuvered the car to the curb and watched as the Jeep slowed momentarily then took off passing the car. Robert looked straight ahead but Tiny got a look at the passenger as they went by. "I don't recognize them," said Tiny. "Let's wait a minute and see if they return."

Robert saw the Jeep reappear coming around the block. "Get down!" As the Jeep passed again, Tiny and Robert dove to their right out of sight just as a semi-automatic weapon fired multiple rounds through the side windows of the Maguire vehicle shattering glass across the car's interior. Robert reached for the gear selector and placed it into reverse and hit the gas. The car went back into the intersection where Robert simultaneously sat up and hit the brake, spinning the steering wheel left, changed the gear selector to drive, and left the area in a hurry.

Robert asked, "You, okay?"

"I think so."

Robert spotted a police patrol car up ahead and decided to enlist some immediate assistance. He rear-ended the squad. After both vehicles stopped, the cruiser's emergency lights came on and the two officers were out of the vehicle heading to check on the Maguire vehicle. While Robert explained the incident to the officers, Tiny pulled his cell phone to call Mr. Maguire.

"Mr. Maguire, we were caught in an ambush on Summit. Get in your safe room. They could be after you."

As Benjamin Maguire was making his way quickly to the safe room, fifty feet from his office, he heard gun fire erupt on the first floor of the building. He realized it was not one or two shooters but maybe five or six as he went into the safe room and shut the door. After securing the door, he flipped the four switches which turned on the lights, the emergency generator, the emergency ventilation system and the closed-circuit video system in and outside his building. As he toggled between camera views, he saw the gravity of the situation. Several cameras were taken offline which meant he would need to switch to the tape backup. There he saw three dark vans pull up around his location. Four men in each van. They breached the front and side doors at the same time as Maguire's security team began a futile attempt to repel the invaders. Maguire knew from the videos and the numbers; his only hope of survival was the strength of his safe room.

The lights in the safe room went out for five seconds. The power had been cut. The generator took over as the lights came back. Maguire heard the whirring sound and knew it was a high-speed industrial drill attempting to cut through the door. It was at that point Benjamin Maguire realized his fatal error. When he entered the safe room, he forgot to hit the alarm button. It had been placed on the outside of the door.

Tiny Ohm sent a two-word text to Malik Adams. It said, "Yellow bird." He prayed his friend would see it in time.

***

Jamal Wilson stood four feet from the man who had to be his father. He was now tall enough to almost look him in the eye. Ashley said, "Jamal, this is your . . ."

"I know who it is, mom. Why is he here?"

"He wanted to see you play football."

"How did he find us?"

Malik said, "I will gladly fill in the details if you give me a chance." Jamal continued to stare into the eyes of the man he had wanted to know for his whole life.

Ashley said, "Why don't you follow us to our house? We can talk there and not be in the middle of all these people."

On the short drive to the house, Jamal had only one question for his mother. "Did you know about this? About his coming here?"

"No. I am as surprised as you."

"I don't know what to say to him, what to call him. He's the reason we had to leave Ohio."

As their minivan pulled into the driveway the remote opened the garage door and Adams parked at the curb. Jamal entered first to be greeted by Nimitz. As Ashley came into the view of the dog, Nimitz began to growl even before he could see the unknown man accompanying her.

"Nimitz, it's okay. Sit." Ashley said to the dog.

Jamal positioned himself between his parents and Nimitz holding up one finger. The dog was immediately quiet. As the garage door descended, Adams stopped in the doorway to the garage. Ashley walked on in. Jamal said, "This is Nimitz. He is a well-trained security dog. Stand still and I will let him meet you. Then he will be fine." With that, the teen waved his arm from left to right and Nimitz arose to sniff the new person.

After a few seconds, Jamal said, "Offer him the back of your hand," which Malik did. "Now, slowly turn your hand around so he can smell and see your palm. Now you can pet him. He has accepted you into our little pack."

The three sat in the living room with Nimitz beside his owner as Adams relayed the story of why they were in witness protection and who wanted to harm them. For fifteen minutes the story unfolded about the Maguire family. There were only a couple interruptions as the tale came forth. When Adams began to tell how the Maguire family was becoming a legitimate company and turning away from its criminal beginnings, suddenly Jamal got to his feet and said, "I'm sorry but I need to take Nimitz out for a walk. I forgot." "Okay, go ahead. I am expecting Deputy Swift here in about fifteen minutes. Be back by then." While Jamal was taking Nimitz around the block, the adults were trying to be cordial. Both were nervous. Ashley finally got up enough courage to ask, "Did you ever find someone to be with?"

"You mean after you? No. When we stopped seeing each other I believed two parts of my life had ended. You and football. Looking back, I'm not sure if I loved you or football the most. I guess my actions said, I loved football the most, because when that died, it took the rest of my life with it." Malik sat forward and looked down at the floor. "I did love you, Janet. I have never loved anyone else. My biggest regret is walking out on the two of you. I had these huge dreams about us being a family while I made money playing in the NFL. Now I have none of it, just regrets."

Adams asked, "What about you, Janet? Surely, you've had men in your life."

"I've only had one and he has a dog named Nimitz. He's been my whole life. I have no other family."

"What about your sister?"

"Since my parents' estate was settled, she moved on. I've never heard from her again. I have no idea where she is and now. It's like she does not exist."

"I'm sorry." After a pause, Malik continued. "I know this won't mean much, but I've had the means to sort of keep track of you and Cooper. About every six months I would call my friend, who is a private investigator in Columbus and have him check out the two of you. He would send me photos. I knew where you lived, what schools Cooper went to, where you worked."

"Why didn't you contact us?"

"At first, I was ashamed of how it ended between us. Later, I was afraid you would reject me. I wanted to reach out; I even talked to Mr. Maguire about it. I messed up your life once, I did not want to do it again." Malik dropped his head into his hands.

Ashley said, "I knew you were working in Atlantic City for an import export business but I never looked any farther. It has not been until recently that Cooper, I mean Jamal had wanted to know about his father. I always tried to be honest with him. I had kept all the articles about your football days in a trunk for him. But when the Marshall Service came for us, the trunk was destroyed with the rest of our house. When he discovered those things were so close to him, but he never got to read them, it hurt him. I think that is what motivated him to play football this year. Malik, promise me one thing. Don't hurt him. He's a good kid and I want him to be a great man. I've done all I can do."

"Looks to me like you have been a fabulous mother. He could not have done any better than to have you here with him."

"That means a lot coming from you. Listen, are you willing to stick around and talk to Deputy Swift? I think he has figured out our situation even though we have been very careful. Nobody except you, him and the Marshalls know who we are."

"Yea, I'll stay. Do you have something going on with him?"

"He lives on the next street over and he has taken an interest in Jamal and Nimitz. He and I have been out on two dates. His wife died of cancer several years ago. He has no kids. Just his K-9 partner, Ms. French. He's a really nice guy."

"Do you like him?"

"I kind of think so. He is the first guy I've dated since you."

"I'm happy for you. I'm happy for all of you, Janet. If I'm right about the FBI arrest at the school, you may be able to return to your old life. The guy they arrested might be the one Montie Maguire contracted to have all of us killed. I'll know for sure when I hear his name. Do you think I could have a glass of water?"

Ashley had just entered the kitchen for the water when the front door bell sounded.

"Expecting someone?" he asked.

"Just Tom. Here's your water," and she went to the front door.

Jamal was in front of the neighbor's house when he saw a woman standing at their front door. She appeared to have some type of gun in her right hand aimed at the door. As the door opened, he heard his mother's voice ask, "Who's there?"

In the same instant several things happened. Jamal pointed. Nimitz covered the space from the neighbor's yard to the door step, Ashley said, "Oh my God!" The gun discharged and Nimitz hit the shoot's arm crushing her wrist in his mighty jaws taking her into the flowers next to the entrance. The shooter began to scream in terrified pain as she dropped the weapon while the dog attempted to rip her arm from its shoulder socket. Ashley turned to see Malik grab his right shoulder where the gunshot had entered and exited his upper chest.

Jamal saw the gun on the door step and picked it up, aiming at the would-be assassin. "Nimitz, sit." He did not have to repeat the command as the dog backed away and sat by his human's leg. "Nimitz, good boy!"

Tom Swift came on the run when he heard the gun discharge. He was already on his way from his house. "Jamal, I'll take the weapon. Is everything all right inside the house?"

"It looks like my dad has been shot."

"Go call 911. Tell them there has been a shooting at your address. Request ambulance and police. Tell them a sheriff deputy is present and has the shooter in custody."

"Should I take Nimitz inside?"

"No. He's my backup."

***

Chapter Twenty Three

In Atlantic City, an evening delivery driver saw the occupants of the vans with assault weapons firing at the Maguire Building and called 911. A city patrol car was just blocks away and arrived on scene as the second set of attackers entered the building. It sounded like a fourth of July celebration with all the gunfire. Within two minutes, every patrol car in the city was either setting up a perimeter or was enroute to help along with the city SWAT team. The local FBI office heard the initial emergency transmission and put their helicopter in the New Jersey sky with two snipers on board. Four minutes passed as eight of the attackers were killed by the combination of SWAT and snipers. The men on the second floor attempting to breach the safe room gave up the effort as they ran for the exits only to be met by a hail of gun fire from outside.

When the weapons were finally silenced, officers began the job of finding and identifying the dead and wounded. They quickly assessed six defenders had been killed attempting to repel the attack. Of the twelve attackers, ten were dead and two were gravely wounded. The incident commander was notified the FBI was heading to the local trauma center to interview the survivors, if possible. And the FBI was taking control of the overall investigation based upon who was the target of the attack. The local fire department swept the building looking for any fires started during the siege. In process, they located the safe room on the second floor. A security specialist was contacted to open the safe room.

An hour later, an older man emerged from the safe room very slowly after being checked out by the paramedics on scene. His name, Benjamin Maguire. Maguire asked the lead FBI agent on scene to make a cellphone call to his partner in Baltimore, Teddy Power. The call was made from the incident command center while everyone stepped outside.

"Power, it happened just like predicted. They came after me and my operation."

"Mr. Maguire, I'm so glad you are alright. We have been monitoring from here."

"Did the action in Tijuana take place?"

"I've been watching on a closed-circuit feed. Our allies in Mexico along with some special ops people from the Mexican military took the war to the cartel. Those handheld missile launchers made short work of the headquarters building. There is no way anyone in the building survived. It's a pile of rubble. Even if their leader survives, his operation is in shambles. Good planning and a great plan execution. Thank your guys."

"I will. No doubt, I will," answered Maguire.

As Marcus Leon listened to the conversation at the Hoover Building in Washington, he commented to a subordinate, "That was as efficient as any military campaign I've ever seen. Just goes to show, sometimes the government needs to stay out of the way."

***

Back in Dade City, the street in front of Wilson's house was crowded with emergency vehicles of every type. The shooter was sitting in an ambulance with two armed sheriffs while a paramedic attended to her broken right wrist and puncture wounds from

Nimitz teeth. She just kept mumbling "perro," over and over.

Juan Malik Adams was laying on the couch with a dish towel pressed against the wound from the bullet just under his right clavicle bone. There was a second dish towel being held against his back where the round had passed through his large frame. Adams was breathing quickly as the paramedics checked his vital signs and spoke with him to make sure he did not go into shock. He had never lost consciousness. A detective from Pasco County was questioning Adams and Ashley Wilson trying to take down all relevant information about the shooting. Tom Swift was speaking with Jamal who was experiencing his own trauma from the events of the evening. Every nightmare he imagined over the past six months had just occurred in front of his eyes. Surreal. The Sheriff rolled up a little later and proceeded straight to his K-9 officer.

"Where is your dog?" he questioned.

"At my house."

"Take my cruiser and go get her. US Marshalls called. They believe a sniper had a nest three houses down on the opposite side of the street."

Swift ran for the vehicle and returned in ninety seconds with Ms. French and his own vehicle. He yelled to Jamal, "get Nimitz on leash. You can help." They headed to the house pointed out by the Sheriff. A Marshall Andrus was taking cover across the street behind an old pickup truck.

The Marshall said, "I saw a rifle barrel over that privacy fence" and pointed.

"How long ago?"

"Couple minutes," answered Andrus.

Swift said to Jamal, "Stay behind me, keep Nimitz quiet. If anything happens, drop on your face and let go of the dog." Swift and the Marshall carefully led the way weapons drawn. When they reached the fence, they paused and listened before the Marshall opened the gate. Swift and his partner entered first and found a sweater on the ground. Sheriff Swift picked up the garment and presented it to his dog to sniff. Without releasing the leash, "Seek." Ms. French's head went down where she found the scent and began to pull her handler across the back yard.

When Jamal entered the yard, he did the same with Nimitz to get the scent, then circled back out to go around the fenced yard via the next-door neighbor's yard which had no fence. By the time they reached the backside of the fence, Jamal could hear French jumping, trying to follow the scent. Jamal said, "Nimitz has the scent over here. Do you want me to follow?"

Swift replied, "No, stay put and wait for us. Too dangerous. We'll play leap frog while we track."

Fifteen seconds later, the three men and two dogs were moving quickly across the yards, then across the street into other yards. The Marshall had an earpiece communicator and stopped as he was getting information. He said, "Their vehicle has been located, parked the other direction. The shooter is going away from it."

One more block and the subdivision ended. Swift said, "The shooter is either headed toward the storm water runoff area – like a swamp, or he will be looking for a hiding place. I'm letting Ms. French off leash, but keep Nimitz with us." With that, he unhooked the dog who shot toward the swamp but at the last second turned left, up the back property line of the subdivision, barking as she ran. The Marshall communicated to his partners their location and direction as the group followed the dog's lead.

As they approached the final three properties, there were two sheds in the backyards. Suddenly a shot rang out and Ms. French went silent. Jamal got Nimitz attention and held up his left hand signaling to the dog, *silence*. They moved carefully towards the image of the dog laying on the ground when another shot rang out and the Marshall went down clutching his right leg. Swift said, "Into the swamp, now."

Jamal and his dog went over the embankment out of site while Swift went the opposite direction to find cover behind a live oak. Another shot rang out. On his belly, Jamal moved slowly up the embankment to get a quick look. In a second, he saw the images of the dog and the Marshall on the ground, while Swift was crawling left toward the far side of the shed. Jamal looked again and noticed the shed had no windows towards the swamp, so he and the dog worked their way to a point where they could not be seen.

Marshall Andrus rolled onto his abdomen with great effort and began to shoot at the shed near the door where the nuzzle flashes were coming from. There was no return fire but everyone remained cautious and waited. Jamal heard more sirens in the distance and decided to head towards the back of the shed opposite the Marshall's position. There was a window about forty inches above the ground and the lower sash was slowly sliding upward.

Jamal saw a head look out the window so he and Nimitz dove for the ground hoping not to be seen. Then a rifle came out the window to be leaned back while the shooter exited. When the leg came out first, Jamal pointed toward the shed and Nimitz covered the thirty feet and flew through the air to snag the shooter by the groin of his pants and dragged him out the window onto the ground. Screaming in agony, the shooter had no choice but to try to beat the dog off with his hands. Jamal saw his opportunity and sprinted toward the struggle where he grabbed the rifle and threw it back through the window, out of reach. Tom Swift limped around to the back of the shed and held his service revolver on the suspect.

Jamal began to call Nimitz from the attack until he saw Swift shake his head. When the back-up finally arrived, the suspect had passed out from the pain and Nimitz was still pulling with all his strength.

Once additional law enforcement arrived at the shed, Swift and Jamal hurried to the front of the shed to check on the Andrus and Ms. French. Marshall lifted his face from the dirt and asked, "Get him?"

Swift answered, "Yep!" and moved to the K-9. As he approached, so did Nimitz. French's tail began to wag while Swift called others for assistance.

Extra ambulances were called in from Polk County to handle the wounded. The assassins were sent to Orlando in separate vehicles with armed escorts to be treated for dog bites and broken bones. Tom Swift and Juan Malik were sent to the Emergency Room in Dade City on King Street. Each was treated for gunshot wounds. Marshall Andrus was taken to Zephyrhills hospital. He was taken to surgery for a bullet in his leg. Ms. French was sent by ambulance to the University of Florida Veterinary School in Gainesville. She needed special surgery to repair her right lung and chest. All would make full recoveries but Ms. French's working life was over.

Jamal Wilson and Nimitz were given a ride home by the Sheriff. The house was empty when he walked in the front door. The minivan was gone. So were all the emergency vehicles. The neighborhood had returned to its quiet state as if nothing had happened that night or any night. Nimitz went to his water bowl in the kitchen and took a long drink, then walked down the hallway to Jamal's room where he jumped on Jamal's bed and passed out in thirty seconds.

Jamal saw the bullet hole in the wall above the couch along with a small blood smatter. Then he felt the hunger pains and headed for the refrigerator to find something, anything to eat. At one in the morning, he was still sitting at the kitchen table when Ashley pulled in to the garage.

Ashley walked in and looked at her son. "Are you okay? I was so worried when you left with Sheriff Tom."

Jamal said, "I'm fine, just tired. Where were you?"

"I followed the ambulance to the hospital. I was there when Tom was brought in, too."

"How are they?"

"Both will survive, and Tom got a call from the Emergency Vet hospital. His dog is in surgery but the vet expects her to pull through."

Jamal said nothing, just nodded his head at the news. Ashley said, "Let's get some sleep and talk more in the morning."

***

Epilogue

The following Wednesday, several things happened to affect the Wilson family.

Pasco High School Pirates received the information on their opponent, Lecanto High, in the Class 4 A playoffs. Second, a meeting was called between the Wilsons and US Marshall Wiest at two in the afternoon. Unknown to the Wilsons, Wiest had previously met with Malik Adams, joined by Benjamin Maguire on the phone. The subject affecting the Wilsons was their continuing in the Witness Protection program.

The meeting took place at an office at the high school. Wiest began, "We discussed your situation based upon the incident over the past weekend. The Marshall service, the FBI, and the Department of Justice believe there is no longer a reason for you to continue in Witness Protection. If you choose to remain in the program, you will need to relocate. If you choose to exit the program, you can stay here in Florida, or return to Dublin, Ohio. You can remain as the Wilsons or return to your lives as the LeMay's. It is entirely up to you. The government will adjust your history, accordingly."

Ashley asked, "What about the threats?"

"Well, as you know, Montgomery Maguire is dead. The contract he placed upon you is no longer a problem as Mandan Hillman was apprehended. He has chosen to work with Federal prosecutors in Tampa to take down the Dark Web site where he got the contract, in exchange for a reduced sentence and a promise of future employment."

"With whom?"

"I am not at liberty to share that but we are confident he is no longer a threat to you."

"And Maguire Enterprises in New Jersey has expressed a desire to oversee your personal safety in the future. I cannot be more specific. They will be reaching out to you about it soon."

Ashley asked, "When do you need our answer?"

"Not today. However, there is one minor problem. If you decide to stay here in Dade City and take back your original identities, there is a slight chance Pasco High School football will have to forfeit all its games this season due to using a player who was playing under a false identity. The federal government would attempt to intervene on Jamal's behalf, but we cannot control that outcome."

Jamal turned to Ashley, "Mom, you know my feelings about the name Cooper. I loved our life in Dublin but we have nothing to go back to without our house. I like my friends here and I really like playing football. I'd like to stay."

Ashley thought for a moment and responded, "I understand what you are saying. To be fair, I need to have conversations with your father, Sheriff Tom, and the Postmaster. And, I don't miss driving in snow."

"Whatever you decide, let me know," said the Marshall as she stood to leave.

As the Wilsons followed out into the hallway, Jamal put his hand on Ashley's shoulder. "Mom, this might make a pretty interesting story!"

***